I0629331

The
Soulburn
Talisman

David McIlroy

Copyright © 2024 David McIlroy
Content compiled for publication by
Richard *Mayers of Burton Mayers Books.*
First published by Burton Mayers Books 2024.
All rights reserved.

*No part of this publication may be reproduced or
transmitted in any form or by any means, electronic or
mechanical, including photocopy, recording, or an
information storage and retrieval system, without
permission in writing from the publisher.*
*The right of David McIlroy to be identified as the author
of this work has been asserted by him in accordance with
the Copyright, Designs and Patent Act 1988*

A CIP catalogue record for this book is
available from the British Library
ISBN: 978-1-917224-00-0

Typeset in **Garamond**

*This book is a work of fiction. Names, characters,
businesses, organizations, places and events are the
product of the author's imagination. Any resemblance to
actual persons, living or dead, events or locales is entirely
coincidental.*

www.BurtonMayersBooks.com

For Christine, who proves magic is real every day.

Prologue

At sunset, they met by the shore.

There were two of them. They wore cloaks and shrouded faces. Salt waves foamed up to their feet, then slid back into the sea, then came again, sucking white sand into the water. They were alone on the beach, and had been since they arrived.

Neither spoke. There was no need.

After some time, a ship came into view on the horizon, a black silhouette against the sinking red sun. They watched in silence as it grew larger, driving into the bay against the outgoing tide, its sails bulging in the breeze. Two dozen oars helped it along, dipping into the water in tandem. The ship made no sound as it drew closer.

Finally, its approach ceased. The sail went up and the anchor dropped. Another smaller boat - a skiff - came around the far side of the ship and started towards shore, driven by a single pair of oars. There were two figures on deck.

The pair on the shore watched and said nothing.

It took just a few minutes for the little boat to reach them. They heard the bottom of the hull scrape over stones, and then its passengers leapt noisily into the water, going in up to their knees. They waded onto the beach, dragging the skiff with them. The sun was almost gone as they stepped onto the loose sand, puffing with exertion.

'You're late,' said one of the cloaked figures coolly.

The sailors didn't respond. Instead, one of them reached back into the boat and, with a grunt, hauled something out. It looked like a bundle of wet rags.

There was a muffled cry from the bundle as it was dumped on the sand.

'*Oomph!*'

The cloaked figure standing nearest said, 'Untie him.'

The sailors obeyed, then stepped back. The other cloaked figure, taller than the one who'd spoken, tossed them a coin purse. After glancing inside, the sailors turned back to the skiff. Within seconds, they had it on the water again, rowing away from the shore. Dying embers of red sunlight burned across the horizon beyond the ship.

The bundle of rags groaned at the feet of the cloaked figures.

'Get up,' said the taller one.

The rags shifted and fell away, revealing a man in filthy, tattered clothing. He was barefoot, curled up on the sand, holding his head. He groaned again.

'Get up,' the tall one repeated.

The man squinted at them from between crusted eyelids. With a gasp, he scrambled to his feet.

'Don't run,' said the shorter one. 'You won't get far.'

Ignoring the warning, the man from the skiff turned and bolted.

A flash of violet lit up the beach. The man shrieked and collapsed to the sand. He clutched at his back, now singed and smoking, moaning pitifully.

The cloaked figures walked the few paces to where he lay and stood over him.

'I did warn you,' said the shorter one.

The man rolled onto his side and stared up at them. His face was deathly white; his grey eyes, now bulging out of their sockets, flooded with rage and fear.

'What is this?' he spluttered. He glared from one to the other, still holding his injured back. 'Why've you brought me here?'

'*Freed* you, you mean,' corrected the tall one.

'Don't feel so free right now.'

'Strictly speaking, you're not,' said the shorter one. 'But you will be, if you do as we say.'

The man looked from one shadowed face to the other, rising slowly to his feet. He winced again at the pain in his back.

'This isn't a trick?' he said warily.

'No.'

'I won't go back there.'

'That's entirely up to you.'

The man swallowed. He ran a hand through his greasy brown hair.

'What d'you want me to do?'

The shorter one reached into his cloak and pulled out a pouch, much like the coin purse given to the sailors. He held it out with a gloved hand. 'Here.'

Cautiously, the man in rags took the pouch. He looked at each of the cloaked figures in turn, but they'd fallen silent again. Loosening the draw string, he peered inside the pouch.

His grey eyes widened. He stared at what was inside, then at them.

'Are these…?'

'Yes.'

'Where did you get them?'

'It doesn't matter.' The shorter one threw a glance towards the horizon, where the skiff had reached the ship again. 'You understand what they are?'

'I do.' There was awe in the ragged man's voice.

'Good. Then your task is simple. One must be delivered to our associate - it must be placed *directly* into his hand. The manner in which you achieve that is up to you. We know of your abilities. You were selected for this task based on the unique… talents… you possess. Think of this as a second chance, to redeem yourself.'

The ragged man grinned, baring teeth the colour of mustard. The pouch trembled in his filthy hands.

'And the other?' he said.

'Keep it for yourself,' answered the tall one. 'The time will come for you to use it. You'll know when.'

'How?'

'*He* will show you.'

His grey eyes were wide again. 'So it's true? Everything they say?'

'You're his servant, are you not?'

The man in tattered clothing gazed into the pouch, then pulled the drawstrings tight again. He stood tall, suddenly oblivious to the burn on his back. 'I am.'

'Good.'

'I do this,' he said, 'and I'm free? You won't send me back there?'

'If you succeed in this,' said the shorter one, 'you may well end up commanding those who imprisoned you.'

The ragged man's eyes flashed with malevolence. 'Now wouldn't that be something?'

'Come,' said the tall one, motioning. 'We'll tell you more on the way.'

They started up the beach. On the horizon, the final glimmers of eventide light faded and the ship disappeared.

Darkness had fallen.

Chapter One: The Mountain

Brooke Woods was lost in the fog.

Really, properly lost.

She wrung her hands anxiously, turning on the spot. *Where am I?* she thought, not for the first time that day.

She couldn't have chosen a worse place to get lost, either (if there ever *was* a good place to get lost). She was fairly sure she was on the side of a mountain, and the fog - thick, white, can't-see-your-own-hand-in-front-of-your-face type stuff that'd dropped around her like a ghostly curtain - obscured her view in every direction.

But that wasn't the worst thing. The worst thing was, she couldn't remember how she'd gotten there. Not at all.

She knew her name was Brooke Woods - that much was easy - and she knew she was thirteen years old, but that was about it. Everything else was going from her head, or had already gone.

'I'm… I'm Brooke Woods,' she told herself for the tenth time since remembering. 'I'm… thirteen… and a bit. And I'm from… uh… I'm from…'

Her boot snagged on a rock and she staggered, just about staying on her feet. If she'd been walking downhill rather than up, she would have tumbled head over heels for sure.

That was too close, she thought. *Where* am *I?*

'My name's Brooke Woods,' she said again, once she'd caught her breath. 'I'm thirteen years old and... and I'm on a class trip.'

Yes, of course! *That's* why she was on the mountain, stumbling around in the fog. *That's* why she was dressed in these clothes and had a rucksack on her back. *That* explained the heavy boots, and the waterproof trousers, and the waterproof coat.

She was on a class trip, and she'd gotten lost in the fog.

But it didn't explain why she couldn't remember much else. It didn't explain why she'd forgotten her own *name*, did it?

Did I hit my head or something? she thought, touching her scalp gingerly.

No, there were no bumps or cuts. She hadn't fallen.

And suddenly, as she clumped her way over rocky, uneven ground, other stuff started coming back - memories, vague at first, dripped into her mind one tiny drop at a time.

'The bus,' she said.

<<>>

She remembered being on the bus - the *Farmont High School* bus - and Mr Green gripping the steering wheel hard with sweaty hands, apprehensively repeating, 'It's starting to ease off, you know,' as April rain hammered against the windscreen.

Tonya Miller, who'd been sitting next to her, had muttered, 'This is going to suck. It's tipping down, and we're going camping. This is going to *suck*.'

Brooke hadn't heard her at first - she was reading a book at the time and, as always, everything beyond the words on the page became white noise. Tonya elbowed her and she looked up with a start, as though she'd woken from a deep sleep.

'Look out there, Brookles,' said Tonya. 'What do you see?'

Brooke brushed a dangle of blonde hair from her face and squinted through the window. Her eyes, bright and blue, reflected in the rain-soaked glass.

'Umm... fields? And cows.'

'Really wet cows. Because it's still raining, Brookles.'

She hated "Brookles" and Tonya knew it.

'It doesn't look so bad now.' Brooke kept her thumb lodged firmly between the pages of her book. 'And at least we're not on the motorway anymore. Are those mountains in the distance?'

'Yes. Big ugly mountains.'

'Then we're nearly there, right?'

'Yes, we're nearly at the campsite. In the rain.'

Tonya scowled and went back to her phone, but Brooke kept her eyes on the green English countryside blurring by outside. The mountains loomed in the distance, irregular dark shapes in a grey haze, growing larger by the minute.

We're nearly there.

She was looking forward to the weekend ahead almost as much as Tonya wasn't. She loved the outdoors, and when Mr Green announced the class trip a few weeks back, her hand was the first up. The idea of spending a couple of days hiking in the mountains, of getting a break from home life for even a short while, felt like a dream come true.

Freedom, she thought, breathing in the word.

Of course, that had been then.

Now, here she was, lost and alone on the mountain they'd come to climb. All the fun stuff that came before - collapsing tents, smores by the campfire, Molly Sharp screaming about badgers in the dark - all that seemed like a lifetime ago. More memories came to her with each passing step, but none of them made her feel any better.

She pushed a matted tangle of hair out of her eyes and sniffed. It was cold and damp inside the fog.

'I'm Brooke Woods…'

She was scared now, wasn't she? Properly lost, and properly scared.

What if they never find me? she thought, and as the questions came her heart rate began to quicken: *What if they've all gone back and haven't realised I'm not with them? Would Tonya tell Mr Green, or Miss Harington? Would she even notice I'm not there?*

A new sensation started at the back of her throat and she swallowed it down before it reached her eyes. No, she wouldn't let herself cry. Crying was for little kids and wouldn't solve anything. Not right now.

She needed to be smart. She needed to get *out* of the fog.

'Why am I still climbing?' she said aloud, and stopped. The white nothingness swirled around her, threatening to numb her brain, to make her forget again.

She gritted her teeth. 'I'm Brooke Woods. I'm thirteen. I go to Farmont High. I'm here on a class trip. I'm… I'm…'

I'm lost!

'Hello?' she called abruptly, panic rising inside her. Then, louder: 'HELLO?'

I need to find the others…

She was just about to shout a third time when, out of nowhere, a figure began to materialise in the fog up ahead. She couldn't quite see who it was, but right then, she honestly didn't care very much. Relief flooded through her and she started forward again, trying to make out who it was.

The person was tall, too tall to be a student. Was it a teacher?

'Hello?' Brooke called again, drawing closer. 'Mr Green? Miss Harington?'

She saw the figure move, turning in her direction. Whoever it was, they were *very* tall.

And they were wide. Too wide.

'Who's there?' she said, uncertain now. 'Who are you?'

The figure began to darken, becoming more distinct. Then Brooke saw two small circles of scarlet, glowing in the gloom like rear lights on a car.

Red eyes, staring back at her. Unblinking.

A low growl rumbled through the fog, permeating the air with a horrible stench.

The stench of death.

Brooke's heart leapt inside her. She was about to scream when a cold hand closed around her wrist and yanked her sideways.

Chapter Two: The Fog Monster

The owner of the hand tugged her to the right, and then she was running behind someone. Her heart hammered in her chest and her breathing came in short, hard bursts. On she ran, stumbling across the mountainside, disoriented by the fog and the abrupt change in direction.

Somewhere far behind them the beast's snarls grew faint, and the person leading her slowed to a stop. He was also breathing heavily, sweat running down from his dark hair, slicking his forehead.

'You ok?' he panted.

'Yes,' Brooke replied, out of breath. 'What was that?'

'I have no idea,' said Charlie Flint, wiping his brow. 'I saw it just before you did. Don't know where it came from.'

Charlie. She remembered him, didn't she? The memories were coming thick and fast now.

Charlie Flint sitting at the back of the bus between Noah Hastings and Zak Marshall, sniggering as they flicked rolled-up sweet wrappers at Alex Johnson and Dale Reed across the aisle. Charlie, cool and popular, who rarely talked to her in school.

Why'd it have to be him?

'We have to find the others, Charlie.' Brooke looked back the way they'd come, sure the beast was following them through the fog. 'We have to get out of here.'

'We will,' Charlie said, also looking around. 'If we can just find – '

He was cut off as something big and black darted past them, just a few feet away. Brooke caught the death scent again, that stench of rotting meat. Her stomach churned. There was another snarl – deep and monstrous – and suddenly they were running again, downhill this time.

'Charlie,' Brooke managed, grabbing lungfuls of air. 'Do you know where you're going?'

'No,' Charlie panted, 'do you?' Brooke heard the fear in his voice and it dialled hers up to eleven.

'What if it got the others?'

'It didn't, they'll be ok.'

'But what – '

Charlie wheeled back to face her. 'They'll be fine! We're the ones who got lost. I wasn't watching where I was going. They're looking for us *right now*.'

As Charlie stepped off the bus, he thought, *I don't want to be here.*

Unlike most of the other dozen students (bar Tonya, maybe), he hadn't chosen to come on the trip at all. That decision had been made *for* him by his parents. They'd agreed, along with the principal, that a weekend hiking in the mountains with classmates would "do him a world of good" after recent goings-on at school.

Charlie strongly disagreed - he recognised thinly-veiled punishment when he saw it - but he knew better than to resist. No-one really listened to thirteen-year-olds anyway, did they? No, he'd pick his battles. And until they came along, he'd have some fun of his own.

Their campsite was little more than a patch of grass on the edge of a forest. Tonya had started muttering about it as soon as they began pitching their tents; when she asked where the toilets were and Mr Green pointed towards the trees, her muttering became full-blown outrage.

Charlie didn't especially mind the whole sleeping in tents thing. He was bunking with Noah and Zak and knew they'd undoubtedly be up all night, gorging on their secret stash of sweets and fizzy drinks. He also knew Molly Sharp was afraid of woodland animals and had perfected his badger mating call ahead of the trip.

And everything had pretty much gone to plan.

Their midnight growls had sent Molly into hysterics, much to the chagrin of Miss Harington, and they'd even managed to get a good-sized spider into Dale, Alex and Henry's tent the next morning before breakfast. Alex, despite being the biggest thirteen-year-old in school, was petrified of bugs and almost tore the tent down in his bid to escape.

The actual hike was easy, too. Mr Green led them cross-country from the woods to the lower slopes of the mountain, first passing alongside fields of cows and sheep before later zigzagging between huge boulders and over fast-flowing streams. The mountain peak shifted in and out of view up ahead, sometimes obscured for periods of time by a rise in the trail, other times appearing closer than ever.

Some members of the group grumbled most of the way, complaining variously that they were tired, hungry or bored. Charlie was weary too, but the further they hiked, the more he actually began to look *forward* to reaching the summit, if that was even possible. Normally he'd spend his weekends staring at a screen with a video game controller in his hands, or kicking a football around the park. He'd never climbed a mountain before and, up until the moment the fog descended, he was starting to think it wasn't half bad.

He'd been walking with his head down as the white shroud dropped, and when he looked up, everyone else was gone. He'd stopped where he was on the steep slope, breathing hard from the exertion, puzzling. Like Brooke, he couldn't remember his own name at first, or where he was, or how he'd gotten there. It'd taken several minutes of aimless wandering for those basic facts to return to him.

Then he'd heard the fog monster, snarling somewhere nearby in the white, and he'd started running. He'd run until his chest burned and his knees ached from constant jarring on the loose ground of the mountainside, hoping he'd stumble into one of his classmates, or even one of the teachers. Anything but that thing in the fog. He'd been afraid by then, more than he'd ever been in his life, and he hadn't stopped running until he heard Brooke calling for help.

Fortunately, he saw the fog monster before she did. She'd been about to scream when he grabbed her hand - if she had, he imagined that would've been the end of her. Of both of them.

Now, he saw the fear in her bright blue eyes, mirroring his own. Brooke Woods, the girl who always had her nose stuck in a book, who rarely paid attention to him.

'D'you think they're really looking for us?' she asked. 'Have you seen anyone else?'

'No,' he replied, casting a nervous glance about them. *This is the thickest fog I've ever seen.*

'We should go down,' Brooke said. 'You know, make our way back to the campsite. That's where the others will be.'

'Yeah.'

'They're probably on their way down, too.'

'Yeah, you're right. Let's - '

Something crashed across the mountainside nearby. They heard the snarl, unmistakable.

'Charlie!' Brooke cried.

'Let's go!'

They started downhill as fast as their tired legs would allow, stumbling over protruding rocks and through heathery thickets. Charlie didn't offer his hand this time, though he honestly wouldn't have minded if Brooke had grabbed it. Heck, he might even hold Miss Harington's hand right now.

'We'll be out of the fog soon,' Brooke gasped breathlessly from just ahead of him, 'once we're lower down. Then we should be able to see the trail again.'

'Straight back to camp,' Charlie said, dodging a jutting rock.

'Exactly,' Brooke said. 'Straight back to… whoa - '

Charlie saw her go down, tumbling over something in her path. It was too small to be the fog monster.

'Ow!' it cried.

'Who's that?' Charlie said.

'It's me!'

Dale Reed's voice came to him, trembling with fear. Charlie saw him on the ground, clutching at his ankle. Brooke had tripped over Dale's outstretched leg and was scrambling back to her feet, rubbing her elbow.

'Brooke! Is that you?'

'Dale!' She threw herself on him and Charlie saw tears welling in her eyes. Both she and Dale were shaking.

'What happened?' Dale said. He sounded confused. 'I was with Alex, and then I fell. I… couldn't remember anything for a while. Geez, my ankle hurts.'

'Did you see it?' Brooke said, blinking away her tears.

'See what?' said Dale. Then, as the realisation hit him: 'That thing was *real*? I thought I was hallucinating when it ran past me.'

'It's real, all right,' said Charlie.

'Dale, let's go,' Brooke said, clutching his arm.

'Brooke…'

'We have to get out of here, Dale! Charlie - '

'Brooke,' Dale repeated in a flat voice. 'Behind you.'

<<>>

A shiver travelled down Brooke's spine. She and Charlie turned, following Dale's gaze.

The fog monster was just a few feet away, close enough for them to see it clearly. Brooke's breath caught in her chest. She thought it was like nothing she'd ever laid eyes on before, standing about as tall as Mr Green but twice as wide, covered from head to toe in thick, black hair. Its limbs were long – much too long – and ended in three-fingered hands and feet capped with talon-like nails. It wore clothing of sorts, colourless rags. Glowing red eyes bulged from the ugliest face Brooke had ever seen – it vaguely resembled something human, but its nose was almost non-existent and its jaw looked as though it'd been pulled down by some invisible weight. Pointed white teeth protruded from its mouth. She could smell rotting meat again.

Dale was breathing fast next to her. All three of them were frozen on the spot, unwilling, or unable, to run.

There was a movement to their right and Brooke's breath stopped altogether as a second beast drifted into view. It looked like the first, except it was skinnier and had longer hair trailing over its wrinkled forehead. She saw its mouth curve up into what must have been a grin. It circled them slowly.

The first beast growled, breath steaming round its face. Then Brooke saw it raise one of its gnarled fingers and, to her amazement and horror, press it to its lips. It smiled, baring more teeth, and emitted a 'shhh' sound.

Brooke whispered, 'What are they?'

The second fog monster briefly looked away, as though it'd heard something, but at the sound of Brooke's voice it began to move towards them, its grin extending into a fearsome and hideous snarl. Brooke squeezed her eyes shut, bracing herself.

This is it, she thought. *It's scarier than I thought it'd be.*

Abruptly, the beast's hungry snarl turned into a howl of surprise.

'Who is *that?*' she heard Dale exclaim.

Brooke opened her eyes in time to catch a flash of electric blue, like lightning, and saw the approaching beast fly backwards and explode in a plume of dazzlingly-bright sparks.

Suddenly, someone was standing there with their back to them, someone dressed in a hooded brown cloak, their face concealed. The first beast roared in anger and lunged at the figure, but was thrown backwards by a second burst of light, neon green this time. Brooke heard it shriek as it tumbled away into the fog.

'Who - ' Charlie started.

Brooke screamed. She saw the third beast appear in the fog behind Charlie, half a second before his body jerked backwards. He let out an 'oomph' of surprise and then he was gone, vanishing into the whiteness.

'Charlie!' Dale cried weakly.

Brooke simply stared in shock at the spot Charlie had occupied just a few seconds before, her scream still echoing across the mountain around them. Not a trace of him remained.

The figure spun to face them, whipping fog with her cloak. Brooke caught a glimpse of reddish hair, a feminine face, and eyes that glowed golden beneath her hood.

'You have to come with me,' she said, 'right now.'

Brooke hesitated, but Dale was already staggering to his feet. He winced in pain.

'Dale, your ankle,' Brooke said, also rising.

The hooded figure's golden eyes shifted to Dale's feet. She pulled something from her pocket and said, 'Quick, eat this,' and shoved what looked like a purple sweet into Dale's mouth before he could protest. His eyes took on a glazed appearance, and for a moment Brooke thought he was going to collapse. Then he seemed to come-to and looked down at his ankle.

'The pain… it's gone.'

'It's temporary,' said the hooded figure. Brooke noted her voice also sounded female. 'Now come with me. Hurry up!'

There was no other option. Already, Brooke could hear the low growl of the beasts somewhere in the fog. They were coming back.

The hooded girl took off at a run and they followed, almost losing sight of her straight away. She was fast, racing across the mountainside on nimble feet, her cloak flapping in the wind. Brooke clutched Dale's hand as they stumbled after her. His skin was clammy and cold; she imagined hers felt the same.

Is this a dream? she wondered. *Maybe I did hit my head after all.*

For a couple of seconds, the girl disappeared and they lost their bearings, squinting into the breeze and the fog for a sight of her. When she reappeared, she was to their right, waving them on.

'This way!' she called urgently.

They followed her for what felt like an age, staggering over the rocky mountainside, the rising breeze stinging their eyes, stitches digging into their sides. Each time the cloaked girl disappeared, she would reappear at another angle and urge them on. Brooke thought she could hear the fog monsters pursuing them, but she dared not look back.

Then, without warning, the girl stopped dead and they very nearly ran into her. She pointed at a cluster of large boulders nearby, in the centre of which was a dark, narrow opening.

'In there.'

'We can't fit,' Dale replied, letting go of Brooke's hand. 'It's too small.'

'It isn't,' said the girl.

'Our friend,' said Brooke, trying in vain to catch her breath. 'They... they took him. We have to help him.'

She saw something flicker in the girl's expression and her golden eyes flared, but all she said was, 'It's too late for him.'

'What?' Dale cried. 'It can't be!'

'It is, but not for you. Follow me or die here, too. Your choice.'

And without another word, she dived headlong into the hole and was gone.

'Brooke, we can't!' Dale exclaimed, panic-stricken. 'I don't like narrow spaces, I'm claustro – '

There was a bloodcurdling roar somewhere behind them.

Brooke decided. 'No choice!' she yelled. She grabbed on to the slippery boulders and swung her legs into the dark hole. It was going to be a tight fit with her backpack on, but there was no time to unclip it.

'Brooke!' Dale cried, reaching for her.

She just managed to grab hold of his hand before her momentum carried her through the gap. Dale came flying headfirst after her, and together they tumbled down into the darkness.

For a few seconds, Brooke had the sensation of being inside one of those big curved slides at a playpark as they hurtled downwards at speed, swinging every which way. She had no sense of what was up or down, left or right. There was nothing but pure blackness and the feeling of travelling very, very fast. She was also vaguely aware they were both screaming, all the way down.

And then she saw it, just up ahead and moving rapidly towards them - a pool of white light. As they rocketed towards it, she began to discern colours shimmering through the white – pinks and greens and blues and yellows – every colour imaginable, and more.

Just before they slammed through it and the light enveloped them completely, Brooke closed her eyes and pictured the sun setting over the mountain. A sunset she'd never see.

It was peaceful and calm.

Freedom, she thought.

Then she *was* in the dream.

A staircase extended ahead of her and she began climbing. Her footfalls reverberated along the walls and off the steps themselves, all smooth stone, neatly carved. Higher and higher they went, spiralling upwards. Something was up there, where the stairs ended, and she wasn't sure if it was a something she wanted to see.

Her fingers trailed on the wall, brushing across undulations in the stone. It was cold to the touch and seemed to shudder.

She became aware the staircase was ending. Darkness was ahead, just above, cloaked in shadow. Her heart pounded, thumping blood towards her brain, making her feel faint.

Was it fear she felt? Or anticipation?

You are wise. You've chosen well.

The voice came from within, but it wasn't hers. It made her heart race faster, until it felt like it would burst from her chest.

You are wise. Come.

She reached the top of the staircase. There, in shadow, was a closed wooden door. It had an iron ring handle and iron hinges; there was a symbol set into it, something she didn't recognise.

The voice had spoken in her mind, but it had also come from the other side of the door. She knew it. That fearful, familiar, wonderful voice.

Brooke reached for the handle and the door swung open.

Chapter Three: Through the Portal

When Dale opened his eyes, he found he was flat on his stomach and his face was pressed to cold, smooth stone. With a groan, he pushed himself onto all fours. Stars danced and popped in his vision for a few seconds, then faded.

Brooke was a few feet away, lying on her back. He crawled over to her, dimly aware he could no longer feel the breeze beating at his face. They weren't in the fog anymore.

'Hey,' he muttered. 'Brooke, wake up.'

She was breathing softly; he shook her shoulder.

'Brooke - '

She sat up with a small cry and clunked him on the chin with her forehead.

'Ouch!'

Brooke pushed blonde hair from her face and looked around, dazed. Dale wondered if she was seeing stars, too.

'Where are we?' Brooke said.

'I'm not sure – '

'Oh no! No, no, NO!'

Dale looked up. The hooded girl was standing nearby, her back to them. She waved her arms frantically, yelling into the gloom.

'What have they done? What have they DONE?'

For the first time, Dale properly took in his surroundings. The room they were now in was dark and cold, and there was an odd smell in the air, like scented candles at Christmas. Rubbing his chin where Brooke had head-butted him, he looked up to the ceiling but could see only darkness. The hooded girl's voice echoed around them.

'This can't be happening,' the girl said to herself, as though they weren't there. ' Oh no, no no…'

Brooke staggered to her feet. 'Is everything ok?'

The girl ignored them, her head bowed low; Dale noticed her shoulders were heaving.

'Excuse me,' said Brooke, taking a step towards her. 'Are you alright? Do you know where we – '

Suddenly, the girl threw back her head, spilling a tangle of dark red hair down her back. She rounded on them, fists clenched.

'Of course I'm not alright, stupid!' she spat. 'Can't you see what's happened here?'

Dale stared at the girl's face, which even in the dim light appeared not entirely human. Her eyes were large and puffy with tears, and her irises were now hazel, flecked with golden shimmers. She was perhaps an inch taller than Brooke, who was herself slightly taller than Dale.

'Well, actually we can't see very much at all,' replied Brooke. Dale heard the coolness in her voice. 'It's dark in here, you know.'

The girl met her gaze and held it; for a moment, neither said anything. Dale, horribly uncomfortable, opened his mouth to speak, but the girl beat him to it.

'Fine.'

She spun on her heel and marched across the room, disappearing into the darkness. Dale glanced at Brooke, saw her jaw was set, and decided to say nothing.

Somewhere in the shadows, the girl said '*Eydrom*' and a flare of green briefly illuminated where she was standing. Then with a *whoosh*, multiple balls of purple light fizzed through the air and zipped away in different directions above their heads, each leaving a hazy trail in its wake; after shooting around for a few seconds, they erupted into blazing purple flame at intervals high above them, driving the darkness further upwards and casting a violet glow down the walls, all the way to the floor.

And now Dale could see the sheer size of the space. It was an immense room of sorts, larger than any he'd ever seen; the walls extended up from a circular floor, rising in a cone shape towards the still-shrouded darkness of the uppermost ceiling. Everything was smooth stone that glinted in light thrown out from pyres ringing the walls (at least a hundred feet up, Dale estimated), which the purple orbs had ignited; the walls themselves were etched with words and symbols he didn't understand, and in places the likenesses of people and strange creatures were carved into the stone. A single set of narrow stairs opposite them wound their way from the floor to the level of the burning pyres, ending at a doorway cut into the stone. It felt like they were inside a massive cathedral, one that could comfortably contain a football pitch.

The girl was in the middle of the room, standing next to a huge stone pedestal. It rose almost to her eye level, and from it branched seven raised sections in the floor, each with a groove carved along its centre; these sections ended at seven enormous stone archways spaced at equal distances around the walls. Each archway, reached by three wide steps from the floor, bordered nothing but smooth, blank stone with a single rune carved in the centre. Dale and Brooke were standing at the foot of one of the archways.

And as the girl crouched next to the central pedestal, her mutters echoing across to them, Dale began to understand why she had been hysterical a few moments ago - the entire room had been decimated. Chunks of stone lay scattered all over the place; there were scorches and deep cracks in the walls and archways, all of which looked fresh, and debris (from ornaments, maybe) was littered everywhere. In places, it looked like a wrecking ball had smashed into the walls.

'Dale, what is this place?' Brooke breathed next to him, awe-struck. 'Are we... *inside* the mountain?'

'I don't think so,' he replied, bending his neck back to stare at the ceiling. 'This doesn't look like it was made... by people.'

The red-headed girl stood up with a despondent sigh. 'It's called the Great Cavern.' She walked back over to them, some object wrapped in her arms. 'Though I'm not sure why you don't know that. Did you hit your head when you came through the portal?'

'Portal?' said Dale and Brooke in unison.

The girl sighed again, exasperated this time. 'Of course, the portal – what do you think *that* is?' She nodded at the archway behind them. 'It's closed now, obviously. But the ghouls will come through soon. We don't have long.'

'Ghouls?'

She narrowed her golden-brown eyes at them.

'Who exactly are you?' she asked, her tone hardening. 'You look... wrong. Where's your armour? What've you got on your backs? And where are your weapons?'

Dale looked at Brooke, who gave a small shrug. The girl started to say something else, but Brooke interrupted.

'Our friend, from school. Is he ok?'

'Ss-kool? What's ss-kool?'

'We go to Farmont High. He's called Charlie, he's in my Geography class. One of those... ghouls... grabbed him on the mountain, just as you showed up. Is he ok? And the others, what about them?'

The girl looked slowly from Brooke to Dale, and a flicker of realisation began to creep into her expression.

'Wait,' she said, unsure now. 'Aren't you – '

Suddenly, there was a muffled clunk from behind them. Dale turned and saw that the rune in the archway had begun to glow blue, brightening rapidly, and blue geometric patterns were spreading out from it.

'Oh no, not now! Not already!' the girl cried. She spun wildly and ran to the stone pedestal. Not knowing what else to do, Dale and Brooke followed.

The girl reached up and placed a large, ornate-looking hourglass on the centre of the pedestal. Shimmering blue crystalline sand started to tumble down from its top half.

She faced them again. 'We have to leave, right away.'

'But Charlie, and the others…' Brooke began.

'Forget them,' the girl snapped. 'If we're still here when the ghouls come through that portal, we won't stand a chance. Let's go.'

She made for the stairs and they followed, dodging pieces of debris on the floor. As they started up the steps, Dale felt the room begin to vibrate around them. A humming noise filled the air, growing louder. He scrambled up the steps behind Brooke, using his hands to keep his balance – the stairs were narrow and twisting, and he didn't dare look down while they ascended.

The girl reached the top first and disappeared through the doorway. Brooke followed with just a fractional hesitation. Dale paused at the top of the stairs, breathless, and stole a glance back.

They were dizzyingly high up, further than he'd thought, and he had to lean back against the cold stone of the wall to fight the tug of vertigo. The pyres around the walls, now level with him, blazed with violet light; far below, he could see the devastation of the room clearly. The "portal" they'd apparently come through now glowed blue all over, no longer a stone wall at all. The humming sound in the room rose in pitch and the floor beneath his feet trembled.

If we're still here when the ghouls come through that portal, we won't stand a chance.

Dale Reed hurried through the doorway.

<<>>

They followed the girl along a dim passageway, descending gradually towards some brightness up ahead. Their footsteps echoed off the walls. The further they went from the Great Cavern room, the fainter the humming sound became.

After several minutes they emerged into open air, which was unexpectedly fresh after being inside the narrow passageway. Dale in particular was relieved to be outside again, and gulped it in.

'Hang on,' said Brooke, 'why's it almost night?'

Indeed, the sky was now a deep navy streaked with purple, as it had been the previous evening as they sat around the campfire while Mr Green told ghost stories. But when the fog descended on them during their hike, it had been no later than midday.

The girl either didn't hear or chose to ignore the question. 'We should leave, they'll be right behind us.'

She pulled her hood up and started along a path ahead of them leading down the mountainside – they had no option but to follow. Except, as Brooke scanned their surroundings, she saw that they couldn't possibly still be on the same mountain. They were now descending a stony trail hewn into the side of a *different* mountain, a much smaller one, with no fields, sheep or cows in sight.

The trail sloped down to the edge of a luscious green forest and then ran parallel to it, eventually disappearing over a hill. Somewhere in the distance (presumably where the path led), thin columns of black smoke rose into the air. The hooded girl paused only once on the way down the mountainside to stare at the smoke, clenching and unclenching her fists, before continuing on.

Brooke had been sure she was dreaming all this – the fog monsters, the tunnel portal, the big cavernous room, even the girl with strange eyes – but as they made their way down this new path, doubt began to creep into her mind. She could feel a warm breeze on her face, one that brought the scent of flowers and trees to her nostrils, as well as the faint smell of smoke; the path beneath her feet was uneven, made from stones carved into rough square shapes that frequently caught the toes of her boots as they hurried along. It definitely *felt* like she was outside, in a real place. If she was asleep and dreaming everything, it was incredibly vivid – if she was awake, then she had no idea what was going on. And it seemed like Dale didn't, either.

She glanced at him. His face was strained and dirty from having lain on the floor of the cavern, and he was beginning to limp a little on his injured ankle. His green backpack was muddied along the bottom, as were his trousers and boots. She imagined she looked the same. The straps of her red backpack (borrowed from a friend) had loosened since that morning, and she could hear its contents clinking inside.

'What is *that*?'

The hooded girl paused, looked to where Dale was pointing, then carried on, calling back, 'Never mind that now.' It was a statue, Brooke thought, but what it depicted couldn't have been human. Standing just to the left of the path, it was about eight feet tall with bulging muscles under rune-engraved armour, all made from stone. A huge axe was strapped to its back. Its face was humanoid, but instead of a nose there was a snout, and its ears hung down well below the chin, punctuated with many rings. And it had four arms.

More statues appeared on the path the further down they went, usually upright, though a few had toppled over. Some were people, others were definitely not. Brooke saw one that looked like an enormous wolf walking on its hind legs, and shivered. All the statues had two things in common: they all seemed to be made from the same dark grey stone, and the people or creatures they depicted were all running up the mountain path towards the Great Cavern.

Why are they all in such a panic to get there?

The path had begun to level out when the hooded girl hissed 'Wait!' and ducked down behind one of the toppled statues. 'Quick, get out of sight!'

Brooke and Dale crouched down next to her. Close up in the daylight, Brooke could see her brown cloak was weaved from some strange material and smelled like earth. It wasn't an unpleasant smell - it reminded Brooke of trees after heavy rain.

'What is it?' asked Dale, rising to peek over the statue. The girl grabbed him by the shoulder and pulled him back down.

'Enemies,' she said in a low voice.

Brooke leaned around the broken base of the statue and squinted down the path. The sun was low in the sky and it was now difficult to make out what was ahead. But she could indeed see figures coming in their direction, still some distance away.

'What should we do?' she whispered.

The girl looked her way for a moment. Brooke noticed for the first time that her skin, which had appeared alabaster white back in the Great Cavern, was actually tinged with green. Her lips, now pursed, were a darker shade of green. She was pretty, though perhaps not beautiful; Brooke wondered what age she was. There was indecision in her golden-brown eyes.

She's frightened.

'The forest,' whispered Dale as the figures drew closer. 'Let's go into the forest. They won't see us there.'

Brooke and the girl both looked past him. The path had started curving along the edge of the forest several minutes ago and the trees were now close, densely packed together. They could hide in there easily, if they could make it.

The hooded girl deliberated for a few more seconds. 'Alright,' she whispered at last. 'Suppose we'll have to. We can – '

She stopped, frowning. Brooke thought she looked like she'd either heard or smelt something. Then, peering over the top of the statue, her eyes widened in fury.

'It's *him*!' she seethed from between gritted teeth. 'He's actually here! *I'll kill him!*'

She started to stand. Brooke and Dale each grabbed a shoulder and forced her back down. They had to strain every muscle to do so – she was stronger than she looked.

'What's *he* doing here?' she snarled under her breath.

'Who?' said Brooke, trying to keep her voice low. Faint conversations drifted towards them.

'It doesn't matter,' said Dale. 'We have to go, right now. Brooke?'

'I'm coming.' Without thinking, she grabbed the girl's green-tinged hand and squeezed it. The girl turned her golden-brown eyes on her, startled by the touch. 'We have to go,' Brooke said. 'You saved us - now it's our turn to save you. If we go now we can reach the trees before they see us.'

The girl stared at her, clearly torn between the desire to attack whoever was coming up the path and the logic of escape.

Finally, she whispered: 'Yes, you're right. But the forest is – '

'Let's go!' said Dale, grabbing her other hand.

As one, the three of them scrambled off the stony trail and into the undergrowth near the edge of the forest. Crouched low, they quickly crossed through tall grass and heathery shrubs to the trees. They stumbled breathlessly over exposed roots and rocks until they'd gone some distance into the forest and the mountain path was no longer easily visible. Once there, they ducked behind separate trees, pausing to catch their breath. Brooke could feel her heartbeat in her ears.

The girl sat with her back to her tree, hands covering her face. Her shoulders were shaking as though she was crying again, but when she took them away, Brooke saw no tears. Only rage.

'I would have killed him,' the girl said in a trembling voice. 'I would have, you know. I… I *could* have.'

'I know,' said Brooke gently, though of course she didn't.

'Who were those guys?' asked Dale, looking back towards where the path was. Dusk settled quietly around them; it was dark in the forest.

'Enemies,' the girl repeated, her voice steadying. 'Evil, monstrous enemies. And he's with them now. That liar… that coward. That *betrayer*.' Brooke looked across at Dale, who shrugged.

The girl sniffed and rose to her feet. 'Let's keep going.'

'Shouldn't we go back to the path once they've gone?' said Brooke, also standing.

'Of course not, they'll be looking for us soon. And the ghouls will come. But they don't know the forest, and I do. So come on.'

With a final glance back the way they'd come, where the rapidly-fading evening light silhouetted the trees, Brooke and Dale followed.

Chapter Four: Charlie and the Ghouls

Charlie remembered little after he was grabbed in the fog. His memories of the mountainside were fragmented and sporadic.

He recalled being dragged backwards, away from Brooke and Dale, and then there was nothing but mountainous terrain sweeping below him and the nauseating stench of rotting meat. The creature had him pinned to its side, carrying him like a sack of potatoes across the mountain. And then for a time, there was only darkness.

When he awoke, he was lying on the cold stone floor of some huge space illuminated by purple fire. His backpack was gone. There were shards of debris all round him. Not far away in the centre of the room, blue sand cascaded through a large hourglass.

The monsters from the fog stood nearby, talking in a weird garbled language Charlie couldn't understand, interspersed with snarls and grunts. He could see their legs, sinewy and covered in black hair, and the three toes of their feet splayed out on the stone floor. He kept his eyes half closed and didn't move, clenching his jaw in an effort to stop himself from trembling.

One of the creatures barked something and approached the hourglass on the stone pedestal. Charlie watched through eyelid slits as it reached out and grabbed it. There was an instantaneous explosion of green sparks and the creature was thrown backwards with a shriek of pain, crashing to the floor. It writhed and howled, clutching its severely-burned hand.

The other three creatures burst into deep, throaty laughter that made Charlie's skin crawl. The one with the long hair slapped its knees and guffawed, spraying spittle.

After a solid minute of obnoxious cackling had passed, one of them made to grab him again. Charlie swung his boot and kicked it hard in the ankle. It roared in anger and hoisted him roughly to his feet, yanking him by the collar to within an inch of its hideous face. The smell of meat-gone-bad was almost overwhelming.

'*Geero rappa ja?*'

Its voice was harsh and abrasive, cutting through him.

'*Geero skan rappa ja.*'

'I don't know what you're saying, ugly!' Charlie spat back.

He was unable to hide the waver in his voice, though, and the creature grinned, baring pointed white teeth. Then, without another unintelligible word, it threw him over its shoulder, knocked the wind out of him, and headed across the enormous room towards a set of stairs snaking up the far wall. The other creatures followed, the injured one still nursing its burned hand, moaning pitifully.

They quickly ascended the stairs and left the room through a small doorway, travelling along a narrow passage. Charlie could see nothing but the dusty stone floor and the heels of the creature that carried him, its claws digging painfully into his side.

Emerging into daylight, they started down a path composed of square-shaped stones set into the ground. The stones were all Charlie saw as they blurred past beneath him, and the longer his midriff bounced up and down on the bony shoulder of the creature, the more he wanted to throw up.

Abruptly, they came to a halt. He heard new voices now and found he could understand them, though the accents were strange.

'Where were you lot?'

'Been waitin' days for you to show up.'

'What's happened his hand?'

Then, another voice, smooth as silk: 'What have you brought me?'

Charlie was swung off the creature's shoulder and dropped unceremoniously on the ground with a *thump*. Wincing, he stared at five pairs of boots, dusty in the late evening light. One pair stepped closer; Charlie twisted his neck to look up at their owner.

A man stood over him. He was dressed in jet black armour from head to toe (like a knight, Charlie thought); the armour was engraved in various places with strange shapes and symbols. One black-gloved hand rested on the pommel of a fierce-looking sword sheathed at his side. His light brown hair was cut short and his face was clean-shaven and handsome, except for an ugly purple scar that ran along his lower jaw and down his throat. He regarded Charlie with eyes that were cold and intensely blue.

'What is it?' he asked.

'*Greer stoobah rappa ja*,' rumbled the creature who'd carried Charlie. Its three comrades huddled behind it, suddenly not so menacing. The black-armoured knight's eyes flicked to the creature's face and back to Charlie, studying him.

'Can you speak?'

Charlie kept his mouth shut, glancing at the three similarly-dressed men standing behind the knight.

'No, then.' The knight waved his hand dismissively. 'You may eat him.'

The creatures all came forward, growling hungrily.

'No wait!' cried Charlie.

The knight's smile was sly. 'I expected so. Tell me, what's your name, and what exactly are you?'

'My name's… Charlie Flint. I'm… from Farmont High.'

'I didn't ask what backwater village you're from,' said the knight, 'I asked *what you are*. You appear to be an Ulander, but you could just as easily be some magical creature in disguise.'

Abruptly, he crouched down on his haunches. Charlie heard the clink of his armour.

'You see these things?' the knight said conspiratorially, gesturing at the creatures salivating just a few feet away. 'They're ghouls. They want to eat you, and I don't really care if they do. They're bound to be famished, after all, and who am I to deny them their supper? I'm not cruel. So let's have a little honesty, Charlie Flint – what *exactly* are you?'

Before Charlie could reply, the creature with the long hair said something in its gravely voice, and the knight looked up sharply. 'What do you mean, he came through the portal?'

'He couldn't have survived,' said one of the other soldiers.

'Ulanders can't travel by magic,' added another.

'I'm not an Oo-lander,' said Charlie. 'I'm… I'm a boy. I'm *human*.'

A hush fell over them all. Charlie felt his blood run cold. Had he just given up a vital secret? The knight stared at him and slowly rose to his feet.

'Fascinating,' he breathed. 'I never expected to see one in the flesh. And yet, here it is.'

The long-haired creature spoke again.

'*Two* more? With one of the Woodspeople?' He stroked his chin thoughtfully. 'Remarkable. The Druyads are gone from Aibal and things are already changing.' He addressed the creatures. 'They can't have gotten far, they must be in the forest. Find them, before something else does.'

The four creatures bounded off towards the trees nearby. The setting sun cast a blood-red glow over the face of the knight as he smiled down at Charlie.

'It appears you're bound for Doomgaard, Master Flint.'

<<>>

Skinny tree branches whipped at Dale's face. He was already out of breath and his ankle hurt again. Up ahead, the hooded girl darted nimbly between trunks and over logs, passing through bushes without disturbing their leaves while he and Brooke crashed noisily after her.

'Hey, slow down!' Brooke gasped.

They'd been running for what felt like an hour, moving deeper and deeper into the forest. The further they went, the darker and more dense it became. Shafts of evening light still knifed through the tree canopy above them in places, but dusk was fading fast.

'Hey!' Brooke called again. 'We can't keep up! Stop!'

And suddenly, as she'd been in the fog, the girl was right there. She perched on a fallen tree, perfectly still. Her eyes glowed golden beneath her hood; a curl of red hair dangled down her cheek.

Dale leaned against a tree to catch his breath. Brooke bent double, pressing at a stitch in her side. The girl watched them in silence until they'd recovered enough to talk.

'Who are you?' she said at last.

Dale looked at Brooke, who flopped at the foot of a tree, then back at the girl. 'We'll tell you. But first, tell us who you are.'

She considered this for a moment, then pushed her hood back. Dale watched as red hair tumbled down to her shoulders.

'My name is Willow,' she said. 'What's yours?'

'Willow,' he replied. 'My name's Dale Reed. And she's Brooke Woods.'

Brooke gave a half-hearted wave and started unzipping her backpack. The girl – Willow – looked them both up and down.

'You each have… two names?'

'Yes.'

'Dale… of Reed.' She pronounced his name carefully, like someone tasting a strange dish for the first time. 'And Brooke… of Woods.'

Brooke nodded as she rummaged in her pack. 'Close enough.'

Willow seemed to turn their names over in her head, analysing them, before announcing: 'I like her name more.'

'Ha!' Brooke said triumphantly, uncapping her water bottle. 'I win.'

'Shut up, Brookles.'

Brooke stuck her tongue out, then took a swig. Willow watched their exchange curiously.

'You two are... friends?'

Brooke blushed in the dim light; Dale dropped his gaze.

'We're classmates,' he said.

'Class… mates?' said Willow, her brow furrowed. 'You're married?'

'What? No!'

'Eeuww!'

'What, then?' Willow said. 'What's your – '

'Wait, that's your go over,' said Dale, as Brooke struggled back to her feet. 'It's our turn for a question: where are we?'

Willow looked around her, a little incredulous. 'What do you mean, "where are we?" – surely you know where? This is the Forest of Lost Souls.'

'The forest of *what?*' exclaimed Brooke.

'It's also known as the Wraithwood, of course,' said Willow. 'Maybe it was called something else when you were last here. I don't know how old you are.'

Dale thought about delving deeper into that one, then changed tact. 'Those things back there, with the red eyes. What were they?'

'Ghouls,' Willow said. 'Creatures of the night. Servants of darkness.'

'Oh,' said Dale. He rubbed his ankle again and winced. Willow, observing, asked, 'You're still in pain?'

'Yeah. I remember hurting it, but I don't remember hitting my head.'

'You hit your head?' said Brooke.

'I must have - I couldn't remember my own name at one point.'

'Me neither! I thought I was going crazy back there.'

'It's the fog,' Willow explained. 'It comes with the ghouls. It disrupts the thinking of the... weak-minded.'

Brooke snorted. Dale said hurriedly, 'Just one more question, please... back there, in the big room – '

'The *Great Cavern* Room.'

' – yeah, that. Why'd you turn over the big hourglass before we left?'

'The Time Keeper, you mean? It's for protection. And it marks how long you have before you need to go back. The sand stops flowing after three days. Give or take.'

'So it's like a countdown?' said Brooke.

'What happens when time runs out?' asked Dale. Willow held up a finger.

'You've asked more than one,' she said. 'My turn: you say you're not friends and you're not married' – Dale and Brooke averted their gaze from one another – 'so you must be comrades in arms, yes? Warriors?'

'Umm, no...' Dale said.

Willow frowned. 'But if you're not warriors, then you must have magic of some sort. How else could you have come through the portal? Are you mages? Witches? Changelings?'

Brooke shook her head.

'Have you been in Uland before?' Willow said uncertainly.

When they didn't respond, her eyes widened and her voice rose in pitch. 'So you *haven't* been here before, ever? And if you're none of those things – if you can't fight or work magic or do anything useful – then, then… then I've made a huge mistake!'

She leapt from the log, scattering dead leaves at their feet.

'You shouldn't be here,' she said. Her tone was a mix of anger and panic. 'I shouldn't have brought you. And now the Time Keeper's been turned. Oh no… I thought you were someone else.'

'Who?' Brooke urged, stepping towards her. 'Who did you think we were?'

But Willow was already edging away from them, her large eyes suddenly brimming with tears.

'This is all my fault,' she blurted, shaking her head. 'He saved me, and I've failed him. It's all my fault. Again.'

She turned away and Brooke grabbed at her cloak. Dale suddenly understood she was about to abandon them.

'Go to the Seer,' she said, pulling her hood up. 'She'll help you.'

'But we don't know where we are,' Brooke insisted. 'We need your help.'

'No you don't,' said Willow. 'No-one does. I can't help anyone.'

'Hang on,' Dale said. 'You can't…'

It was too late. With a whirl of her cloak, she spun away from them and darted into the trees.

'Willow!" Brooke cried.

But she was already gone.

They were alone in the forest.

<<>>

The scar-faced knight crossed the floor of the Great Cavern Room, his footfalls echoing off the walls and up to the ceiling. Far above his head, the huge stone pyres still burned with Willow's violet light, though the flames had already begun to die.

The knight was alone - he'd ordered the other black-armoured soldiers to remain outside. They'd already accomplished what they needed to in this place, there was no reason to scour the cavern again. The ghouls had done the bulk of the work for them, anyway.

He looked across the vast, debris-littered space towards the archway the beasts had brought the Other-worlder through. It had long-since turned back to stone, useless to them now.

There were two more, though, weren't there?

The knight walked towards the pedestal in the centre of the room, his boots crunching on fragments of broken things. He thought the Great Cavern Room was eerie at the best of times. And now, silent and darkening as magical flames dwindled in the pyres, he disliked it more than ever.

He stopped next to the hourglass, watching the luminescent blue crystals tumble. Each one glowed brighter as it settled onto the pile in the lower half of the glass.

'You probably shouldn't touch that.'

He didn't flinch as the voice drifted from the shadows.

'I wasn't going to,' he said, still watching the Time Keeper.

The figure materialised from the darkness to his right, moving soundlessly towards him.

'Why are you back here, Commander?'

The scar-faced knight didn't answer right away. 'I had to see it for myself,' he said finally, 'to know she'd really turned it. Ghouls lie - I had to be sure.' He turned his head to look at the figure, just a few feet away, bathed in the cold blue glow from the hourglass. 'Why are *you* here? You're supposed to be at Hammerfall.'

'All in good time.'

He couldn't see the figure's face clearly under the shadow of his hood, but the white hands clasped by his chest were confirmation enough. And he was still a little hunched over under his cloak.

'I've been told to delay, you see.' The words came in a rasp. 'Plans have changed. I've been directed to take a new route.'

'Directed?'

When the other didn't respond, the knight turned his gaze back to the hourglass. It wasn't a question that required an answer. Not anymore.

'The portal's been opened.'

'Yes,' replied the knight. 'The same one. She returned, as did the ghouls. And there were three others.'

'Others?'

He nodded. 'We've captured one - it's being taken to Doomgaard as we speak. We'll retrieve the others soon.'

'Hmmm.' The one in the cloak stroked his chin. 'Perhaps that's what necessitated my being delayed. I'll await further guidance.'

'We each have our parts to play,' said the knight, turning away from the hourglass. 'I'll return to mine now - you should do likewise.'

The cloaked one spoke quickly: 'Do you still have it?'

'Of course.'

'On your person?'

The knight sighed and said, 'It's always close to my heart.'

The other chuckled - the ugly sound of it went around the room. The pyres had almost burned out.

'Keep it that way,' he croaked, 'and you'll have no trouble fulfilling your goal.'

'And you?' said the knight. 'You have its twin, I assume?'

There was no response.

He looked, and found he was alone in the cavern once again.

Chapter Five: The Forest of Lost Souls

Trees swayed and creaked in the breeze, their green leaves made black by the night. Somewhere far off, a bird cawed morosely.

'Dale, what do we do?'

Dale had only gotten lost to the point of being terrified once before. He'd wandered from his parents in a busy shopping centre one Saturday afternoon and had to be tracked down by security guards. He was six years old when it happened. And now, seven years later, he felt the same panic from that day bubbling up from the pit of his stomach.

What he said was, 'We need to stay calm.'

'Calm?' Brooke exclaimed in the near-darkness. 'We're somewhere called the Forest of Lost Souls. A girl who's probably not human brought us here, through a *portal*. We were chased by monsters with red eyes. And we have – what was it – three days before… before…'

'Before we turn into statues,' Dale finished.

Brooke moaned. 'Ohhh, I hoped that wasn't it, but now you've said it.'

'We won't be here that long.'

'But what do we *do*, Dale? Why did she leave us?'

Dale tried to focus, pushing his rising panic to one side.

'Find the Seer,' he said, echoing Willow's parting words. 'We have to find her, whoever she is. She'll help us and – '

He broke off as something crashed through the trees behind them, back the way they'd come. They heard a familiar snarl and caught a glimpse of red in the shadows.

Ghouls.

'Run!' Brooke cried.

They ran.

It was almost impossible to see where they were going. Every few steps, one of them tripped and stumbled, or blundered into a tree. Dale felt his clothes snag on branches; he held one arm up to shield his face as he ran. Brooke was somewhere nearby, but he couldn't see her. Behind, he could hear the ghouls giving chase. His heart pounded in his chest; the panic in his stomach surged to his throat, desperate to become a scream.

Suddenly, Brooke grabbed his arm. 'Do you hear that?'

He listened, slowing down. For a moment, all he heard was the crunching of leaves beneath their feet and the whisper of branches moving just above their heads. Then, he heard it too.

Music.

'This way,' said Brooke. Still holding on to his arm, she moved off at an angle, heading towards the sound. He staggered after her, trying to keep one ear on the music and the other on their pursuers, who seemed to be getting closer. The forest drew in around them as though it was purposefully trying to slow them down.

Maybe it is, he thought.

As they closed in on the source of the music, Dale began to pick out different instruments in the melody. He could hear fiddles, or violins. Drums, flutes. It was a merry, upbeat tune, some sort of jig. They continued towards it through the undergrowth, groping into the darkness. The music was loud now; they heard laughter and singing, dozens of voices belting out a song. The sound of the instruments swelled, the voices reaching a crescendo. Brooke pushed through a thick tangle of snaking vines and, dragging Dale behind her, tumbled into a clearing.

Instantly, the music stopped and the voices became silent.

Dale gazed around the clearing. Based on the noise, he'd expected to see a large crowd of people gathered around musicians, laughing and singing while they skipped arm-in-arm to the music. But he saw none of that. There was only an empty grassy space, almost perfectly circular, with a small, gnarled tree in the centre. The area was bathed in bright moonlight pouring through a gap in the forest canopy above them, glistening on the damp grass.

'Dale, what's going on?' Brooke whispered.

Getting to their feet, they walked cautiously into the centre of the clearing towards the little old tree. Its bark was pale and flaking off the trunk; its branches, devoid of almost all leaves, stretched up towards the sky. Stones the size of footballs lay around its base, intersecting exposed roots. The silence in the clearing was unsettling in the wake of the joyful music that came before.

They reached the tree. It was just a few feet taller than them. Dale imagined he could still hear the music, very soft now, still ringing in his ears. And as he leaned towards the tree and reached out a hand to touch it, the music seemed to rise in volume again…

With a crash of breaking branches and foliage, the ghouls burst through the vine barrier into the clearing behind them. Dale and Brooke spun round to face them with a cry, their backs towards the tree.

The four beasts eyed them hungrily, fanning out in a semicircle. The one with the long hair grinned, teeth glinting in the moonlight, saliva dripping from its elongated jaw. Dale could smell rotting meat again. He and

Brooke backed away, moving around the tree. The sound of fiddles still lingered faintly in the air.

What do we do? Dale thought. *How do we get away this time?*

But his mind was blank, numbed with fear. White tendrils of fog had already begun to seep into the clearing, tracing the ghoulish footprints in the grass.

One of them, bigger than the others, said something in its gravelly, incomprehensible language and pointed; another moved their way, flexing the clawed fingers of a burned hand. Its red eyes swept over them, settling on Dale, and it uttered a deep, rumbling growl of hungry anticipation.

'Stop it!'

Both Dale and the ghouls looked at Brooke in surprise. She'd taken a defiant step forward. Her hands were balled into fists.

'Just… go away! Leave us alone!'

For a second or two, Dale actually thought the ghouls were going to obey. They looked at one another, a little taken aback by the teenager glaring at them, strands of blonde hair falling across her face. She had the same look in her eyes as when they first spoke to Willow in the Great Cavern.

Then the largest ghoul threw back its head and emitted a series of barking noises that must have been laughter. The others immediately joined in, guffawing loudly, thumping their chests. Brooke gritted her teeth in anger.

Finally, when they'd laughed themselves hoarse and drool ran down their chins, the biggest ghoul motioned their way again, and as one, the four beasts stomped towards them. Dale saw the look in their eyes - they were moving in for the kill this time. He and Brooke stumbled backwards, past the tree, backing quickly to the other side of the clearing. The ghouls closed in, narrowing the semicircle, cutting off any chance of escape.

This is it, Dale thought, *we're done.* He wondered crazily what his parents would say when they heard he'd been dismembered by a pack of red-eyed monsters. *What did you expect, son, wandering round in the woods at night? You won't do that again.*

The ghouls passed the little tree in the centre of the clearing. One pushed a withered branch aside and it broke off with a sharp *crack.*

The effect was instantaneous. The ghouls suddenly began swiping at the air around them and kicking at the ground, roaring furiously. Dale saw the one with the long hair topple over sideways, its greasy locks tugged by some invisible force. One of the others had its legs knocked out from under it and thumped face down on the grass. The biggest ghoul was staggering in circles, howling as it clawed its own face.

'What's happening?' Brooke cried, watching as the first of them fled through the vine barrier and disappeared into the forest.

'I have no idea,' Dale replied, then added hopefully, 'Maybe it's Willow?'

One by one, the set-upon ghouls abandoned the chase and retreated into the trees, howling and shrieking as they went, until Dale and Brooke once again found themselves alone in the clearing. The fog dissipated as soon as the creatures were gone. There was no sign of Willow.

'Dale,' Brooke said, 'the music…'

He could hear it again too, floating across to them from the tree - strings and drums and wind instruments. The melody tugged at them, drawing them towards the tree. Dale felt a sort of drowsiness seeping into his brain, making him sluggish. It was like being in a dream, like sinking into a subconscious fantasy after falling asleep. A little like the ghoulish fog, but different. He thought the music was wonderful, and the closer they came to the tree, the more he wanted to hear it. To be *consumed* by it.

Nothing else mattered now, not really – the ghouls were gone, they were safe, and all he wanted to know was where the music came from, and who was playing it.

As he and Brooke reached out to touch the tree, Dale was sure all their problems were about to vanish forever.

Everything's going to be ok…

'I wouldn't do that if I were you.'

The voice came to them from outside the dream. They barely heard it.

'Don't touch the tree.'

Dale stretched out his hand; the music swelled, drowning all other sounds.

Suddenly, he was jerked backwards and fell to the ground, landing on his backpack. Its contents dug into his spine and the abrupt pain snapped him out of the hypnotic haze. Brooke lay nearby, also wincing after falling on her pack.

'Sorry about that,' said a woman standing over them. Dale saw her upside-down, looking at them with some concern. 'Are you both ok?'

They scrambled to their feet. The woman was draped in a red cloak that reached to her feet, with a hood pulled up over her head like Willow. But her eyes were brown and she wore round gold-rimmed spectacles, which flashed in the moonlight. Dark chestnut curls protruded from inside the hood.

'Did you touch the tree? Even just a graze?' Dale and Brooke shook their heads. The woman breathed a sigh of relief. 'Good. That was close.'

There was a movement behind them. They turned quickly, half expecting to see the ghouls again. But instead of four black-haired monsters, a group of very short people stood in the clearing, watching them curiously. They were dressed in what Dale could only have described as "olden-time" clothes: loose shirts with sleeves rolled to the elbows, baggy trousers hitched up with suspenders, and tweed caps (some flat, some pointed). All of the men had bushy beards, and the women, who wore dresses, had their hair in elaborate buns or pigtails. A couple of them also wore spectacles and one puffed on an enormous wooden pipe, sticking out of his beard as though there was no mouth at the end of it.

He spoke first: 'Alright, Miss Butterfield?'

'Alright, Peter,' the woman replied, with a nod. 'Up to more tricks, I see?'

'We was just 'avin a laugh, is all,' said Peter. 'Bloody ghouls ought to know better than t'lay a finger on our tree, let alone damage it.'

'I think we can all agree that ghouls don't know much of anything.' The little people chortled in response.

'Right you are, indeed.' Peter's eyes shifted to Dale and Brooke, who were taking in this exchange with open mouths. 'This pair near had their paws on it as well, so they did.'

'We're sorry,' Brooke said quickly. 'We heard music, and… well…'

'Music, you say?' Peter's eyes sparkled with something Dale didn't quite like. 'And did you think it was nice?'

'Yes, it was.'

The little people erupted into gales of laughter at this, clapping their hands and slapping one another's shoulders. Two of them did a mock jig on the grass. Brooke, whose bravery had now been met with laughter twice in quick succession, went redder than the woman's cloak.

'Yes, it's *always* very nice, isn't it?' said the woman. 'And if you'd touched that tree, you may have found yourself dancing merrily for all eternity.'

Peter chuckled and puffed on his pipe.

'All's fair'n the forest,' he said. 'They know how it is, same as everyone else round these parts. They disturbed our dance, so we've the right to do as we please.'

'We were being chased,' interjected Dale, unsettled now. 'It wasn't our fault.'

Peter shrugged. 'Can't say that'd be our problem, young sir. This here's our circle and that there's our tree.'

The woman – Miss Butterfield – cleared her throat. 'And if they give you something to compensate you for your trouble?'

A hush fell over the little people. Peter puffed on his pipe for a moment, turning the suggestion over in his head.

'Depends what it is, I 'spose.'

Miss Butterfield turned to Dale and Brooke expectantly. Dale looked at Brooke, who shrugged.

Just then, he had an idea. 'One sec.'

Slipping off his backpack, he unzipped the front pouch and rummaged through it. The little people crowded forward, craning their necks to see what he was doing.

'How about this?'

Dale held up his head torch, the one he'd worn last night at camp. Peter stared at it from beneath heavy eyebrows, unimpressed. One of the others spoke up in a high-pitched voice: 'What's that?'

'It's a torch, for your head,' said Dale. He pulled it on, tugging the straps into place. 'See?'

'You couldn't have used that before now?' Brooke muttered.

Peter snorted. 'Nought but a silly trinket. What're we to do w'that? Sell it to the goblins at the market for – ' Dale flicked the torch on and its three LED bulbs bloomed white, illuminating the whole clearing. Several of the little people screamed and vanished. Peter shielded his eyes from the light but stayed where he was. He no longer puffed his pipe.

'Squirrel's beard,' he murmured, 'that be a *magic* lantern. I've heard of those, so I have.' Dale turned it off;

several of the little people reappeared, drifting towards them from the tree. Peter stared greedily at the head torch.

'Have we got ourselves a deal?' said Miss Butterfield.

Peter nodded. 'Aye, we have. You give us that and we'll call it square, and you can be on your way. How's about that?'

'It's a deal,' said Dale. He took off the torch and handed it to Peter, marvelling at his chubby little fingers as he took it. Peter's eyes gleamed in the moonlight.

'Alright then.' He tossed the torch to one of the others, who immediately disappeared. 'All's square. Now be off with you both, and don't be touchin' our tree again unless you're wanting another chinwag, which we'll be more'n happy to oblige you for.' To Miss Butterfield, he added, 'Wouldn't be out here much longer, Jayne. Night's full up. Puca'll be about.'

'Good to see you, Peter,' she replied. 'We'll be off.'

Peter winked, and the little people vanished.

'Now,' said Jayne Butterfield, producing a glowing lantern from absolutely nowhere. 'I imagine from the look on your faces that you're rather confused, tired and hungry, yes? Then let's get going.'

<<>>

While Dale bargained with Peter and the little people, Charlie Flint trudged down the mountainside trail between two black-armoured soldiers, his wrists bound with rough rope. One of the soldiers held the end of it and occasionally gave an unnecessary tug, causing Charlie to stumble. The other soldier chuckled every time.

The blue-eyed, scar-faced knight hadn't accompanied them, instead heading inside the mountain while Charlie was escorted in the other direction. The sun had dipped below the tree line by the time the trail levelled out; as darkness fell, they followed a new, wider path (also set with stones) along the edge of the forest, towards the distant smoke columns. Neither the soldiers nor Charlie said anything along the way.

As the last slivers of daylight gave way to stars, eerie sounds began emanating from the forest to their right. Trees rustled when there was no wind; unseen creatures swooped through the air, wings flapping noisily. Somewhere in the distance, a mournful howl rose briefly and fell away. Charlie noticed the soldiers now kept to the left of the trail, as far from the trees as possible. Had it not been for the moonlight, it would have been impossible to see where they were going.

Finally, they came to a rise and the source of the smoke columns appeared. A small village – or what remained of it – lay smouldering in ruins about half a mile away. Several pockets of flame burned on in blackened buildings. Even at distance, Charlie could see figures moving through the wreckage.

Where on earth are we? he wondered.

They drew near the village and the choking smell of smoke intensified. Charlie could feel his eyes watering. One of the soldiers coughed a number of times then gave the rope a sharp tug, as though Charlie had caused it. Two more men in black armour stood sentry on either side of the road as they entered the settlement. They barely glanced at Charlie as he passed between them.

Then they were in the village itself, and it was like navigating a nightmare.

Every way Charlie looked there was death and destruction: little stone cottages with thatched roofs were now smoking husks spewing orange embers into the night air; carts and wagons were smashed to pieces and strewn over the dirt road; in the middle of the village, what had once been a pleasant green bordered by colourful flowers was now just a muddy square with a smashed statue in the centre. Muddied, Charlie saw, by enormous hoof prints.

Just beyond the green, they came to a small group of terrified-looking people guarded by more soldiers. Their faces were tear-stained and haggard in the flickering light cast by still-burning buildings.

'Got another for the wagon,' said the one holding the rope. The biggest and ugliest of the guards looked Charlie up and down.

'He can walk. No room in the wagon.'

'Has to be. Orders.'

The ugly guard grunted and spat at Charlie's feet.

'Fine,' he said. 'It's over there. Get them in.'

Charlie joined the surviving villagers as they were herded towards a large wooden wagon stationed nearby. Two huge horses, clad in their own black armour, were hitched to the front of it. They snorted angrily as the rear doors swung open and the villagers were shoved inside. Charlie found himself wedged between a shivering old woman and a skinny young man who blubbered non-stop until the doors were closed and bolted, and they were plunged into almost total darkness. Everyone inside the wagon reeked of smoke.

One of the soldiers thumped the outside of it and they moved off, lurching terribly from side to side as they rolled over bumps and dips in the road. The passengers (*prisoners*, Charlie thought), jostled uncomfortably inside. Their wrists were all bound with rough rope, which dug painfully into their skin.

The wagon rolled on, leaving the village and the heavy stench of burning behind, until the only sounds were the rumble of wheels and the *clip-clop* of horse hooves. If there were soldiers on or around the wagon, none of them spoke. It was impossible to tell where exactly they were or what awaited them at the end of their journey.

And yet, as the skinny man continued to sniff and sob, Charlie discovered he wasn't afraid. Or at least, his fear didn't *feel* real, because none of it was real. How could it be? Just a few hours ago, he'd been hiking in the mountains with friends, and a day before that he'd been at home with a video game controller in his hands, ignoring his parents as they shouted up the stairs about homework. He'd be back there soon enough.

Right now, Charlie was sure of only two things. One: he was tired and hungry, which probably accounted for his willingness to get into the wagon without kicking the soldier who pushed him there. And two: none of this would have happened if that little squirt Dale Reed hadn't ratted him out last week and forced his inclusion on the school trip as punishment.

All your fault, Dale, he thought, his head dropping.

And in spite of the wagon's lurching and the skinny man's weeping, Charlie found himself drifting to sleep, with thoughts of campfire hotdogs and fizzy cola in mind. He could practically smell the sausages.

He wouldn't be asleep for long.

Chapter Six: The Seer's Supper

They made their way through the forest by the light of Jayne's lantern. It cast a warm, orangey glow on the trunks of passing trees, creating a pool of comfort around them in the blackness of the Wraithwood. Like Willow, Jayne moved through the woods with incredible ease, as though the trees parted to form a path for her. Brooke noticed her red cloak didn't catch on a single twig as she walked – she and Dale weren't so lucky.

Her classmate stumbled for what seemed like the hundredth time since they'd left the moonlit clearing. 'Where are we going?' he asked, regaining his footing.

'Somewhere safe,' said Jayne. 'My house.'

'Is it far?' asked Brooke, glancing around nervously. She was sure something followed them in the darkness, some unseen presence, coming steadily closer the deeper they went into the forest. She did her best to stay within Jayne's lantern light.

'It'll be around here somewhere.'

She doesn't know where her own house is?

Dale cleared his throat. 'What's that Poo-ka thing? The little man said something about it.'

Jayne carried on in silence for a few moments before answering.

'The Puca's a creature living in this forest. Maybe in other forests, too. It roams around at night, taking different forms. It's not something we want to run into. Trust me.'

Dale didn't ask any more questions after that.

They carried on walking, Jayne's lantern swaying gently. Brooke had the sense the forest was coming to life around them. She could now hear movement in every direction as animals (she hoped) scurried away from their approach. Somewhere far off, a creature howled. She thought it sounded like a wolf, but bigger.

'Ah, there it is,' said Jayne.

Up ahead, just visible in the orange lantern light, was a very small wooden hut, overhung precariously by the branches of ancient trees. Its single window was cracked and grimy, and the front door clung desperately to its frame on rusted hinges. A stone chimney on the roof teetered on the brink of collapse. The hut was covered in creeping vines and dull green lichen. It was dark inside.

'This is… your house?' said Brooke.

Jayne, fumbling in some hidden pocket, produced a key and slotted it into the door, which shuddered. 'Yes,' she said, 'it is. You're welcome to come in, unless you'd rather stay out here tonight with the Puca, and who knows what else.'

She opened the door and stepped inside. They followed. Jayne closed the door behind them, and Brooke gasped.

From the outside, Jayne's ramshackle hut looked like a strong wind could blow it over. Inside, however, it was bright, toasty warm, and lavishly decorated. Large, comfortable armchairs were positioned next to the hearth; chopped logs crackled merrily in a roaring fire. The wooden floor was swept clean and embellished with thick sheepskin rugs. An enormous bookcase next to a reading chair and standing oil lamp was chock full of old tomes; an overturned hardback and a flower-patterned mug still half-full of tea rested on an end table, as though it had just recently been set down. A heavy wooden dining table displayed a crystal bowl laden with all kinds of fruit, and four chairs were neatly tucked in around it. A narrow spiral staircase in the corner wound up through the ceiling to a second floor.

Impossible, Brooke thought. *There* was *no second floor.*

The kitchen, set along the wall to their right, showed evidence of recent use: chopping boards with discarded vegetable pieces on top, unwashed dishware in the bulky ceramic sink, a teapot on the hob with a trickle of steam rising from its spout. The whole room smelled of freshly-baked bread and cinnamon.

'How…?' Dale began.

'How what?' replied Jayne, setting her lantern down.

'It's… bigger on the inside,' said Brooke, gazing longingly at a golden-crusted pie on the kitchen counter.

'Only to those who're invited in.' Jayne removed her red cloak and hung it on a rack next to the door. Underneath, she wore a floor-length cream dress and brown leather bodice, laced in the front. A red belt was tied around her waist, from which a sackcloth pouch hung on one side. Her curly brown hair dropped well below her shoulders.

She's pretty, Brooke thought. She got the distinct impression that Dale, who was blushing for no good reason, agreed.

'If you hadn't been invited in,' Jayne continued, 'you'd have found the interior to be just as unappealing as the outside, and would have left without a second thought.'

'That's clever,' said Dale. Jayne flashed him a smile and his flush deepened.

Brooke rolled her eyes. *Boys.*

'Now then,' said Jayne, gesturing towards the fireplace, 'have a seat. Actually, kick those muddy boots off first, if you don't mind – that rug came all the way from Strobor. Are you hungry?'

'Yes!' Brooke and Dale replied simultaneously.

Jayne smiled again. 'I'll see what I can do.'

With her boots and backpack removed, Brooke sank into one of the armchairs. It was so soft and the fire so warm that her eyelids became heavy right away. Likewise, Dale's head flopped to the side and he had to prop himself up on one elbow to stay awake. For the first time since their meal back at camp, Brooke felt herself begin to relax.

A minute later, Jayne appeared between them bearing a tray laden with food – thick slices of hot buttered toast with tangerine marmalade and strawberry jam on the side, just-baked chocolate chip cookies, and two steaming mugs of hot chocolate topped with whipped cream and marshmallows. Brooke and Dale fell upon it, suddenly ravenous, while Jayne waited patiently in the reading chair with a freshly-brewed cup of tea.

Five minutes later and the tray was picked bare. Brooke and Dale, pleasantly full and still cradling their almost-empty mugs, sank back into the armchairs. Their eyelids had grown even heavier.

'Done?' said Jayne. They nodded happily. 'You two were certainly hungry. I'm not surprised, with everything you've been through today.' She picked up the tray and moved to the kitchen.

Brooke frowned. 'How do you know what we've been through?'

'Has Willow been here?' Dale added.

Jayne returned to the fireplace and knelt to drop another log into the flames. Brooke noticed the hem of her dress was spotless, even though they'd been walking through the woods for a while. Her own boots had picked up a thick coat of mud between the clearing and the hut.

'No, Willow hasn't been here,' said Jayne. 'I haven't seen her in quite some time, actually. But I expect she'll pay us a visit very soon.'

'You know each other?' said Brooke.

'Oh yes, everyone around here knows Willow. As a matter of fact, I'd say she's fairly familiar to many throughout Uland. And don't worry,' Jayne added, anticipating their next question, 'she's a Woodsperson, so she'll be just fine out there tonight. I'll be rather shocked if she doesn't knock on my door first thing in the morning.'

She removed her spectacles and began to clean the lenses on her sleeve. Light from the fire flickered in her brown eyes as she watched them, waiting for the next question.

'Are you the Seer?' asked Dale.

Jayne smiled and nodded, just once. 'Some call me that.'

'Is that how you know about us?' said Brooke. 'How you know what's… happened to us today?'

'I only know some things,' Jayne replied, replacing her spectacles. 'For instance, I know you arrived through a portal earlier today, and you were with Willow at the time, but you parted ways afterwards. I had an inkling you'd come across the Fairy Ring and – '

'Fairy Ring?' interrupted Dale.

'Of course,' said Jayne patiently. 'Who do you think you gifted your torch to?'

'Those were *fairies*?' Brooke exclaimed. 'They didn't look like any fairies I've ever seen!'

Jayne grinned. 'Interesting – how many fairies have you seen in your time?' Brooke opened her mouth and closed it again. 'Fairies are very particular about their sacred places, especially their trees. I know them well – we have an understanding. But those who don't often fall prey to their tricks and are never seen again.'

'They seemed nice,' said Brooke. She was very sleepy.

'When treated properly, they usually are.' Then, to Dale: 'This will be your final question of the evening, young sir.'

Dale, who was about to ask a series of important questions, hesitated. 'Just one?'

Jayne nodded. 'Tomorrow, before you leave, you can ask more and I'll do my best to answer them.'

'Ok.' Brooke saw Dale's brow furrow as he considered which question to ask – when he spoke again his choice surprised her, and she was ashamed she hadn't thought of it herself: 'Where's Charlie?'

'Charlie Flint.' Jayne looked into the flames. 'I know he's alive. But he's moving further from my sight with each passing minute, and the darkness around him is growing. I'm afraid I can't tell you any more than that.'

'It's ok,' said Dale quietly.

'And that's that,' said Jayne. She clapped her hands and they both jumped. 'More tomorrow, much more. For now, you two need your rest. Sweet dreams, Brooke Woods and Dale Reed.'

'But how – ' Brooke started.

Jayne Butterfield snapped her fingers and they both fell asleep.

<<>>

Brooke ascended the stairs, her footfalls reverberating round her. There was the door again, closed, foreboding. That feeling of anticipation muddled with fear.

You choose well.

The symbol on the door was clear this time - a tree, branches extended to the sky, roots spread below. She reached out to touch the door, expecting it to spring open by itself, hoping it would.

Instead, her fingers brushed on rough wood. It was somehow warm to the touch, thrumming almost imperceptibly. She wanted to know what was on the other side, *needed* to know, but the fear remained. Tangible, thick in the air.

Come.

Brooke reached down and grasped the door handle. It was ice cold and she almost jerked her hand away.

COME.

She twisted it and the door swung open.

A blaze of light met her, engulfed her. She was in the room now, though she didn't remember stepping inside. It could have been small or huge, she couldn't tell. There was only the searing red light and the pulsing, thrumming sound.

She squinted, trying to shield her eyes. Someone else was in the room, close by. Two people? More than two? Her eyes burned, silently shrieking for relief from the scarlet light.

A figure darkened into view. She saw a hand, reaching towards her.

Take your reward.

In her dream, Brooke screamed. Then the light was gone and she sank into merciful darkness.

Chapter Seven: A Journey with Trolls

The road through the woods was peaceful, bathed in the soft grey light of dawn. Foxes and badgers had long since returned to their homes underground; the birds hadn't yet begun to sing. Somewhere far off in another forest entirely, Brooke and Dale slept peacefully in Jayne Butterfield's house.

Then, *thwack*. The quietness was broken.

Thwack, thwack, thwack.

'Hurry up!'

'I'm going…' – *thwack* – '… as fast as I can…' – *thwack*.

'Chop faster!'

'Why don't you have a go?'

'It's *your* axe.'

'Stop complaining and keep a lookout.'

The *thwack*ing sound continued, then became a low creak.

'That's it – push!'

The low creak became a high whine of tearing wood, and with a crash, a rotting oak tree toppled across the road. Two trolls emerged from the undergrowth, one with an axe over his shoulder.

'That'll do the trick, old sport' he said.

'And not a moment too soon,' said the other, peering up the road with beady black eyes. 'Here they come. Everyone – take up your positions!'

The trolls disappeared back into the woods

Daylight broke as the black-armoured horses came within sight of the tree, drawing the rickety wagon behind them. A pair of soldiers trudged on either side, weary from the night's journey; a lone driver seated atop the wagon held the reins. It swayed violently each time a wheel dipped into a pothole in the road, jostling its passengers inside. Hardly anyone had slept since they left the village.

'Whoa,' called the driver, tugging on the reins to slow the horses. 'What's that up ahead?'

One of the soldiers shielded his eyes and squinted up the trail.

'Tree's come down,' he said. Then, to the others: 'Come on – sooner we shift it, sooner we get back.'

The wagon trundled on as the four soldiers ran ahead of it, approaching the tree. In the woods around them, the trolls waited.

'Right lads, put your backs into it,' said the soldier, crouching by the tree. 'Ready? Heave!'

A stone whistled out of the woods and struck him on the side of the head. He went down instantly.

'Shields!' yelled one of the others. Each of the remaining soldiers fumbled a small round shield off his back and onto his forearm, desperately trying to keep an eye on the woods around them. Shapes moved among the trees, slipping in and out of view. Another stone hit one of the soldiers on the thigh – he cried out in pain and turned towards where he thought it had come from and was struck on the forehead, collapsing in a heap on the road.

'Where are they?' demanded one of the remaining pair, brandishing a sword with a lion's head pommel as he turned on the spot. 'Who's doing this?'

'Trolls!' shrieked the wagon driver from not far away, pointing into the woods.

Two, three, then four of the creatures emerged from where they'd been hiding in the bushes; they were shorter but stockier than the soldiers with skin the colour of granite, dressed in sackcloth and leaves over brown leather armour, armed with clubs and axes.

'We can handle this lot,' growled the soldier with the lion's head sword. 'Four filthy cave-dwelling cannibals are no match – '

He was cut off mid-sentence as a heavy wooden club crunched down on his helmet from behind. As he fell, the last soldier spun round just in time to see a pumpkin-sized rock sail out of the woods, straight for his face.

The black-armoured horses snorted and whinnied in fear, pawing at the ground as the trolls – six of them – closed around the wagon. The driver trembled like he was made of jelly. One of the trolls approached, studying him with onyx eyes, trailing his club.

'P-p-please!' stammered the driver. 'I-I… I'm unarmed. I'm j-just the… driver. You can take whatever you w-w-want…'

The troll listened curiously for a moment, then grinned, baring two rows of yellow teeth. He slung his club over his shoulder and patted one of the horses on the side. It snorted again but ceased whinnying.

'Jolly good show, chaps,' said the troll to the others. 'Looks like we've got ourselves a negotiator.'

'Indeed, sir.'

'Always easier when they're cowards, sir.'

'What should we do with the others, sir?'

'Same as always,' said the troll leader, 'strip their armour and tie them up. We'll leave them here and someone'll see to them, one way or the other. Remember lads, we aren't killers.'

'Think I might've killed this one, sir,' said another troll regretfully, crouched over a crumpled soldier.

'Ah well, hard luck. We can't not kill them *every* time.' The troll leader reached up and grabbed the driver's boot, causing him to squeal. 'Say now, driver, where are you off to this early in the morning?'

The driver's eyes rolled in his head and he slumped over, unconscious.

'Damn, another fainter. Oh well, tie him up too. Come now, chop chop.'

Then, a voice from inside the wagon: 'Help!'

'What the dickens was that?' said the troll leader.

'Believe it came from inside, sir.'

'Should we open it up, sir?'

'Yes, yes, jump to it.'

The doors of the wagon were flung open, and those within immediately began to scream.

'For crying out loud,' sighed the troll leader. He walked to the rear of the wagon and looked inside. The passengers were bunched at the far end, their eyes wide with horror. 'Good morning... yes, yes, calm down... are you all prisoners, then? Of course you are, your hands are bound. Well, you're all free to go. I expect you'll want to head in that direction, back to Birchfell, or some such place. Off you go, then – you've been rescued.'

'It's a trick,' cried one of the prisoners, a skinny man with a tear-stained face. 'As soon as we set foot outside, they'll eat us.'

'*Eat* them?' cried one of the trolls in disgust.

'Yuck!'

'Gon' be sick...'

'Dear boy,' said the troll leader, 'if we wanted to eat you, you'd be eaten already. But we're not that way inclined, you see. Now, if you don't get out, we'll simply bar the door again and be on our way.'

When still nobody moved, a pair of trolls began rocking the wagon from side to side. Crying out in fear, the prisoners leapt out and took off down the road without looking back. An elderly woman, heavily wrinkled with age, accepted a hand down from the trolls and waddled off into the woods.

'Excellent work, chaps,' said the leader. 'Get that armour gathered up and loot those storage chests, and we'll be on our way.'

The trolls made quick work of the soldiers, stripping them down to their undergarments and tying them up with rough rope from the wagon. They bundled their armour and weapons onto a large wheelbarrow hidden in the bushes, then unhitched the horses and sent them galloping back the way they'd come. The still-unconscious soldiers were left tied to trees by the road.

Lugging their spoils, the trolls started up the road. Sunlight streamed through the trees and birds chorused on their branches. One of the trolls whistled tunelessly.

'Um, sir?' said one after a while. 'Something's following us.'

The troll leader glanced back. A boy was trailing along behind them near the tree line, keeping his distance. His black hair was a tangled mess and his face was drawn with weariness.

'Never mind him,' said the leader, 'he'll stop following once we're in the woods.'

But he didn't. Even when the trolls left the road and began making their way through the trees, the boy continued to follow, sticking close enough to keep them in sight but far enough away if a quick escape was needed.

Finally, the troll leader sighed and motioned behind him. One of the trolls bounced off into the trees and returned a minute later with the boy under his arm. He was struggling furiously.

'Get off! Let me go!'

'Drop him,' said the troll leader. The one carrying the boy set him down. 'Cut him loose.' Another troll produced a knife and moved to cut the rope binding the boy's wrists – he held up his hands reluctantly, and the troll sliced the rope with one fluid move. The boy rubbed his wrists, which were red raw.

'What's your name?' asked the troll leader.

'Charlie,' replied the boy, glancing nervously at the other trolls gathered nearby. 'Charlie Flint.'

'And why are you following us, young sir?'

Charlie studied the face of the creature before him, trying to read signs of trickery in its expression. The last time he'd been questioned, he'd ended up in the back of a prison wagon. "I… don't have anywhere else to go right now.'

The creature cocked its head slightly, meeting Charlie's gaze with eyes that were black as the night. Like the others, it was just a few inches taller than him with grey skin and almost no hair. Its nose was bulbous and drooped down to its lips, behind which were large yellow teeth. The creatures wore clothes covered in leaves that Charlie suspected was camouflage, and each of them carried either an axe, a club or a slingshot.

'I see, I see.' The creature's voice was deep but it spoke well, unlike the ghouls. 'And why were you imprisoned by the Doomgaard?'

'Doom-guard?'

The creature grinned, not unkindly.

'Why yes, those ponces with their shiny black armour and fancy swords. Daresay we'll make a pretty penny or two on their gear up north.'

'They… the Doomgaard… captured me back at the mountain, took me down to the village. It was all… on fire. And the others were…'

'The lad's confused,' said one.

'Looks well sleepy.'

'Needs a bite to eat.'

'And we'll oblige him,' announced the leader, with some gusto. 'Come, boy – when's the last time you breakfasted with trolls, eh?'

The fact that these creatures identified themselves as trolls simply washed over Charlie – all he and his empty stomach really took in was the word 'breakfast'. The trolls headed deeper into the woods, and he followed.

<<>>

Brooke drifted gently out of sleep to find she was still curled up on the armchair by the hearth. The fire had long since died out; the room was now warm with morning sunlight, and birds trilled melodiously outside. She sat up and stretched, yawning loudly. For the moment, her dream was forgotten.

On the other armchair, Dale woke with a start. His cheek was wet with drool and his hair stuck up crazily on one side. Brooke looked at him and giggled.

'What?' said Dale, frowning. He made a half-hearted attempt to smooth down his hair. 'Where are we?'

'Still in Jayne's house,' said Brooke, standing. 'But she's not here.'

The inside of the hut was unchanged from the previous night, except the dining table was now set with plates, bowls and cutlery, and every other available space on it was occupied by a covered silver platter. They padded over to the kitchen – their boots, now scrubbed clean, were neatly lined up next to the door.

'What's that smell?' asked Brooke, sniffing. Dale lifted the lid of the nearest platter and she gasped. 'Oh wow!'

The platter was stacked high with crispy bacon, plump sausages and chargrilled tomatoes, all piping hot as though they'd just been lifted from the pan. Dale lifted another lid, revealing thick slices of toast, fluffy pancakes and potato bread. A third platter contained all manner of eggs: fried, boiled, scrambled, poached. There were jugs filled with juice and milk, and wooden bowls piled high with seemingly every cereal imaginable. Just as they drew back their chairs, a big copper kettle on the stove began to whistle.

'Is this all for us?' Brooke said, her mouth watering involuntarily.

'Must be,' said Dale, bringing the kettle to the table. 'I don't think we should question it. I'm *starving*.'

'Me too,' said Brooke, pulling a plate towards her.

They ate until they felt they were going to burst. Brooke slumped happily in her chair, watching as Dale wiped egg yolk from his plate with a piece of pancake.

'We should wash up.'

Dale made a face, stuffing pancake in his mouth. 'You sound like my mum.'

Mum. Brooke wondered if their parents were worrying about them right now. A pang of guilt tingled somewhere inside her.

Suddenly, the door of the hut swung open, sweeping the thought from her mind. Jayne stepped inside, golden sunlight streaming around her. She now wore a sky blue dress and had a wicker basket filled with carrots and parsnips on one arm.

'Ah, awake at last I see!' she said, beaming at them. 'Come outside at once, it's a lovely day.'

Tipping the vegetables into the kitchen sink, she ushered them outside. Brooke blinked rapidly as her eyes adjusted to the warm, bright sunshine. There was a little garden outside Jayne's hut, overhung with boughs from the trees above, and Brooke was sure it hadn't been there the night before. A low stone wall formed a rectangle adjacent to the hut; to the left was a raised vegetable patch which Jayne had clearly been working on, and to the right, a small tree supported about a dozen bird feeders, covered in twice as many twittering birds.

In the centre of the garden, near a wooden gate leading into the forest, was a round cast-iron table and four chairs – Willow was perched on one, cradling a mug in both hands.

Brooke was instantly glad to see she'd made it through the night in one piece. Then, just as quickly, her relief gave way to a surge of anger as she pictured Willow disappearing into the darkness, abandoning them to the ghouls.

She left us.

'Let's have a seat,' said Jayne, gesturing towards the table. Biting her tongue, Brooke chose the chair furthest from Willow, who stared fixedly at the contents of her mug.

'Hi, Willow,' said Dale. She looked up, opened her mouth to speak, and then just nodded in reply. Brooke didn't say anything. Jayne sat with a flourish.

'Miss Willow arrived here just after sunrise but you two needed your rest, so we've been enjoying a nice chat in the meantime, isn't that right?'

'Yes,' Willow said, holding her mug closer and closer to her face as she avoided Brooke's gaze.

'She also filled me in on the finer details regarding your arrival here in Uland yesterday. I knew you'd passed through a portal in the mountain – though I don't know how exactly – after Willow rescued you from – '

'*Rescued* us?' Brooke exploded, causing Dale to jump in his seat. 'She didn't rescue us. She *abandoned* us, in the middle of a dark forest, at night, with those things coming after us. We could've been… been…'

'Eaten?' suggested Jayne. 'Gobbled up? Devoured?'

'Yes, all of those,' said Brooke, setting her jaw.

'Well, the fairies helped us, didn't they?' Dale ventured.

'We just got lucky.'

'No such thing, my dear,' said Jayne. 'You stumbled into that fairy ring and met the Wee People last night by design, it wouldn't have happened any other way. Nevertheless, I believe Willow has something she'd like to say.'

She looked pointedly at Willow. An awkward moment or two passed. It was as if they were in class, seated next to the pupil who didn't know the answer to the teacher's question. Brooke crossed her arms with some finality.

'Alright,' said Willow, breaking the silence. 'I'm... sorry for leaving you both last night. It was wrong... I suppose.'

Brooke reared up at the word "suppose", but Jayne got there first.

'Thank you, Willow,' she said quickly. 'And you're right, it *was* wrong. These two are visitors in our land, and the Wraithwood is the last place they should have been in the dead of night. If Doomgaard's ghouls hadn't got them, the Puca surely would have.'

Brooke saw red creep into Willow's cheeks, and a little anger left her.

'However, it's all worked out,' said Jayne. 'No-one was eaten or went away with the fairies, so we'll let the matter drop. We've got more important things to worry about right now. For instance, how exactly do we get you two back where you came from?'

Jayne looked at them as though expecting an answer. Dale shrugged. 'We don't even know where we are now.'

'Good point.' Jayne motioned casually over her shoulder, and a roll of parchment unfurled from where it hung horizontally along a tree branch behind her. Brooke was sure it hadn't been there before. 'Let's clear that one up for starters.'

The parchment, which Brooke imagined had once been cream in colour, was now a faded beige and worn along the edges. It was an enormous map; suspended from the tree branch, it looked to be as large as Jayne's dining table. The map showed a country Brooke didn't recognise at all. She felt a little stupid – what would Mr Green have said?

'This,' said Jayne, 'is the continent of Uland.'

'No such place,' said Dale, matter-of-factly.

Jayne scooped up an acorn from the grass at her feet and tossed it at him. It bounced off his forehead.

'Ow!' he cried. 'What'd you do that for?'

'That acorn dropped from a tree that grew in Uland – if there's no such place, why did it hurt?'

'Still… seemed unnecessary,' said Dale, rubbing his forehead. Brooke saw the beginnings of a grin on Willow's face, quickly suppressed.

'As I was saying,' Jayne continued, 'this is Uland. It's where you are right now. To be more specific – ' She pointed at a patch of green on the western side of the map, not far from a little triangle that must be the mountain. ' – you're here, in the Forest of Lost Souls, as they call it. Very over-the-top, if you ask me. You arrived in the Great Cavern of Mount Aibal last night through a portal and, as destiny willed it, here we are.'

'It just doesn't make *sense*, though,' said Brooke. 'I mean, yesterday we were on a completely different mountain in our… own world, with our friends from school… and now we're here, in this place where there're ghouls and fairies, and…' – she looked at Willow, who narrowed her eyes – '…and we don't have those in our world.'

'Of course you don't,' said Jayne, 'because your world, as I understand it from your continuous surprise at everything around you, has not yet awoken to forces beyond the confines of your understanding.'

'You mean, like magic?' said Dale slowly.

'Indeed.'

'And you can *do* magic?'

Jayne's smile was warm. 'I've been gifted with an awareness of it, yes. Many of us here in Uland know it.'

'And Willow,' said Dale, turning to her, 'you can do it as well, can't you?'

Brooke watched as clear discomfort enveloped Willow, like someone had just dropped it on her from above. With obvious effort, she replied: 'I can do some.'

'Magic takes many forms,' said Jayne, overly chipper. 'My abilities are completely different from Willow's, or from those of an Elemental warlock, for example. We all have our place in this world.' She gestured at Brooke and Dale. 'And then there's you two – what will *your* places be, exactly? How do you fit into this puzzle, hmm? That's what we're going to find out.'

'How?' asked Brooke.

'By taking you north to meet the Druyads. Willow's going to lead the way, actually. We agreed that'd be the best arrangement, while you were still sleeping.'

'Agreed is a strong word,' Willow muttered.

'After all,' Jayne went on, as though she hadn't heard, 'Willow's the reason you're in Uland, and the reason you're in my garden right now. You also entered this world through a Druyad portal, so if anyone knows how to send you back to where you came from, it'll be them. Unfortunately, going back to Mount Aibal right now is out of the question, so they'll have to find another way to send you home.'

She stood abruptly, and the map rolled itself back up under the branch. The others followed her lead.

'It's time we were off,' said Jayne, looking up at the patch of blue sky protruding through the trees above them. 'I very much want to see you returned safely to your world for your own sake and, quite frankly, for mine. If the Doomgaard find you here, I'm afraid my little illusion won't be much use.

'Gather up your things and we'll be on our way.'

<<>>

'But what is it?' said Charlie, wrinkling his nose in disgust. The charred thing impaled on the stick looked a lot like a rat.

'It's breakfast, that's what,' said the troll.

They were in the trolls' camp, in a clearing not far from the road. The grass was flattened in places where tents had been pitched. Burnt-out torches lined the perimeter.

Charlie, seated uncomfortably on a rock next to the dying embers of a campfire, managed a few reluctant bites of "breakfast" while the trolls dismantled their makeshift dwelling around him, loading supplies onto a wooden cart pulled by what appeared to be a gigantic ram with curled horns. On another day Charlie might have found the creature strange, but being surprised by things felt increasingly pointless right now.

The trolls had led him to their camp and offered him a seat by the fire, which was welcome in the cool of early morning. He'd been vaguely worried they were planning to roast him over it, but instead they'd handed him food and a tankard of water, and then gone about their business in silence. As far as he could tell, the trolls were bandits, and the cargo on their cart was all stolen property.

When his stomach simply couldn't take any more of the skewered animal, Charlie set it down and took a few gulps of water. A passing troll with a sack over one shoulder snatched up the remains of his breakfast and finished it off in two bites as he walked.

'Feeling better, boy?' said the troll leader, a bundle of spears in his arms. Charlie nodded untruthfully. 'Good. Breakfast is the most important meal of the morning, after all. Now, I believe introductions are in order...'

He pointed at each troll in turn: 'That's Angus, he's Dungus, that one's Tumygus, there's Lombrigus, and Fungus, and I'm Amoogus.'

'Pleased to meet you,' chorused the trolls. Charlie offered a half-wave, still none the wiser as to which one was which.

'We're the Trolls of Wosdren Marsh,' announced Amoogus proudly, 'protectors of the poor and innocent.'

'We take from the rich – ' said one.

'– and don't eat them – ' added another.

'– and sell their stuff – '

'– and give the money to those who need it most,' finished a fourth.

'We've become quite famous around these parts,' said Amoogus loftily. 'Doing our bit for the good name of trolls across the land. A lot of our kindred haven't helped much in that regard over the years, what with the, umm…'

'Cannibalism?' suggested one, helpfully.

'Yes, that. And the general eating of people everywhere. But no more – the Trolls of Wosdren Marsh are *vegetarians* by choice. No livers and guts for us.'

'Not anymore.'

'Mostly.'

'Unless they're squirrels, or rabbits.'

'They're basically vegetables.'

'Indeed.' Amoogus shifted the spears in his burly grey arms. 'So, young sir, would you like to accompany us?'

'Where to?' said Charlie. The other trolls went back to their work.

'North, of course. We've finished our raiding and pillaging for the week, and now we're off to sell our spoils at the goblin markets.'

'The goblin – '

'If we set out now and the Stone Road's clear enough, we should be there by sundown. What do you say?'

'The Doomgaard will be looking for me.'

'Certainly, but they can't touch you on the Stone Road. It's protected by ancient magic, and violence is forbidden. We'll take you north as far as the markets, and if you want to continue on to the Kingdom of Ulandai from there, that's up to you.'

'And I can't go back the way I came?'

'You can, but you'd almost certainly be captured. Or killed. Or both.'

'Um, ok. Guess I'll come with you guys, then.' Charlie shifted on the log. 'And thanks for, you know, rescuing me and everything.'

'Unnecessary,' said Amoogus. 'Now, on your feet and start packing that cart – until we reach the markets up north, you're a troll. And an ugly one at that.'

<<>>

The woods were alive with sound and colour. As they walked, a pleasant cacophony of bird calls, insect drones and tree rustling filled the air. In daylight, Dale thought, the Forest of Lost Souls didn't seem so bad.

They followed a narrow trail between the trees, descending in places and climbing gently in others. Warm sunlight flashed between gently swaying pine trees, glinting off holly bushes and tiny pools of algae-covered water alongside the path.

Dale and Brooke walked single-file behind Jayne, whose red cloak remained spotless, even though the trail was often muddy in places. Willow ranged some distance ahead. She'd said she was keeping a lookout for danger, but Dale suspected she was still ashamed for leaving them the night before.

'What's the name of the place again?' said Brooke, abruptly breaking the peaceful silence.

'Ringmoffren,' replied Jayne. 'Nice little spot. You'll like it.'

'And we'll find someone there to take us north, to…'

'Further north, yes. Right now, we're in the Northern Barrowlands, east of the Stone Road and west of Canyon Lake, about the same distance from each. You're going as far as Ringmoffren on foot, and from there you'll find transport to the Throat. The Stone Road also leads there, but I think it's best if you stay off the main highway and keep to back roads for now. They'll be searching for you.'

'How far is it from Ringmoffren to the Throat?' asked Dale, picturing the map in his head.

'On foot, it'd take at least a day,' said Jayne, 'but if you take a peryton, you'll be there in just a few hours.'

'What's a perry-ton?' said Brooke.

'You'll see,' replied Jayne, with a knowing grin. 'Oh, here comes Willow.'

Dale peered up the trail but saw no sign of her. Seconds later, however, there was a rustle of leaves and she appeared right next to them, her golden eyes shining.

'The Puca's been this way,' she said. Dale felt a shiver run down his spine.

'Recently?' said Jayne.

'Probably just before dawn. There're tracks crossing the path, right to left, and some blood. It made a kill.'

Next to Dale, Brooke gave a barely-audible yelp.

'I think we should move faster,' said Willow.

'Agreed,' said Jayne. 'Keep an eye out for us, Willow. We'll do our best to keep up.'

With a nod, Willow disappeared back into the trees. After that, Jayne began walking twice as fast. They struggled to keep pace with her; Dale started to feel a stitch forming in his side.

They didn't see any signs the Puca had crossed the trail, but Dale hadn't really expected to – Willow was right at home in the forest and perceived far more than they did. But Jayne was clearly worried, and that alarmed him.

The trail continued on for most of the early morning, winding between more of the swaying pines in less dense areas, then on through a marshy bog from which decayed-looking white trees grew. Here, they heard the croaking of frogs and had to swat at flies swarming around their heads; the trail became muddier than ever and they lost their footing more than once.

Finally, after not speaking since Willow mentioned the Puca, Jayne said, 'I do believe we're almost there.'

'Where?' said Brooke, a little breathless. 'Ringmoffren?'

'Oh no, you've got a long way to go before then,' said Jayne. 'We're about to reach the northern boundary of the forest.'

'Great,' sighed Dale, clutching his side.

Sure enough, the forest floor began to firm up as they left the bog land behind. They were ascending again, following a leaf-strewn trail through a thick carpet of bluebells and pungent wild garlic; here, the sun found more pockets of space as the trees thinned out, dappling the forest floor. The woods around them had grown quiet, expectant.

They came over a rise, and suddenly the forest simply ended.

Ahead, it looked to Dale as though the landscape stretched on forever. Hills of green and yellow grass rolled on and on into a hazy horizon that merged with the blue sky above it; here and there, the land was dotted with rocky outcrops and trees bent double by the wind. Narrow lanes flanked by crumbling stone walls criss-crossed over the hills every way they looked, and far, far off, Dale thought he could see a lone trickle of smoke rising from a chimney.

'The Barrowlands,' said Jayne, with a sweep of her hand. 'The free region of Uland, where no king or faction reigns… anymore.'

'So much… open space,' said Brooke, one hand flat above her eyes.

'Yes, too much for my liking. I prefer the forest – it's one of the reasons why I'm now bidding you farewell.'

Brooke and Willow wheeled around and cried '*What?*' in unison.

'Gosh, that was dramatic,' Jayne smirked. 'Yes, I'm not going any further. But don't worry, you'll be better off in the open country without a tired old frump like me slowing you down. A young trio like you will cover the ground faster going at your own pace.'

'But we need you!' insisted Willow.

'And you're not *that* old,' said Dale, before quickly adding: 'I mean, I'm thirteen, so I'm basically an adult too.'

'I'm also thirteen,' noted Brooke immediately.

'Ah, to be that young again,' said Jayne wistfully. 'Unfortunately, I am slightly more than thirteen years old, so the next part of your journey will be without me. Besides, there's a very delicate balance in this forest, and if I'm gone for too long everything will go to pot. No, this is your time. And if anyone can get you safely to the Druyads, it's Willow. I trust her completely.'

Dale saw a flush of pink creep into Willow's cheeks.

'But before you go, I think a change of attire is in order.' Jayne reached inside her cloak and pulled out two others, which Dale thought couldn't possibly have been there before. She tossed one to him and the other to Brooke. His was dark navy and hers was a deep green. 'Try these, they'll help you blend in a bit more.'

'Hey!' cried Dale, after he'd put his on. 'Where's your backpack, Brooke?'

'Yours is gone too,' she observed. He twisted his arms around and felt where his pack had been, but it wasn't there. And yet…

'I can still feel it on my shoulders,' Brooke completed his thought. Jayne smiled, adjusting her spectacles.

'Special cloaks, for the journey.'

'You look less weird now,' said Willow.

'Anyway, get moving,' said Jayne. 'It's a long way to Ringmoffren from here, and it's not easy going. Stick to the roads and don't deviate for *any* reason. When you stop for a rest, you'll find fresh provisions in your bags.

'We'll meet again soon enough. You can bank on that - I'm the Seer.'

With a wink, she turned and strode quickly back into the forest, and was gone. Willow looked from Brooke to Dale, then out across the hills.

'Follow me, then,' she said.

<<>>

'You need to stop staring,' muttered Angus the troll.

'I'm trying,' whispered Charlie. 'It's hard not to.'

They'd joined the Stone Road and were travelling north. It was aptly named – every square inch was flagged with smooth stones, and every single one was perfectly intact. As they'd walked along behind the cart pulled by the giant ram – called Woolly, of course – the troll named Fungus, who had a flair for the dramatic, had given Charlie a little history lesson.

'Across the vast continent of Uland stretches the ancient highway called the Stone Road,' Fungus explained flamboyantly. 'It extends from the sun-baked grasslands of Suthdren to the rich coastal regions of Eisdren, northward through the sweeping forests and freezing tundra of Nardren, and out towards the moors and heathland of Wosdren – an unbroken circle. In places, the road is flat and easily travelled, wide enough for three, even four carts to pass unencumbered; in others, no more than one person at a time can use it. Travellers will find the road runs near peaceful villages, cuts between fields of golden corn and barley, winds through steaming swamps inhabited by monsters, on over snow-topped mountains and rocky steppes where the very air is ice, crossing rivers of raging white water and bottomless gorges. It spans woodlands and bogs and prairies, comes within sight of thriving cities and abandoned holdfasts, connecting countless other roads and lanes and trails along the way, like a mighty river feeding lesser tributaries. And every bit of it, from start to finish, is paved with stone.'

'You've rehearsed that,' said Tumygus.

'But why's it safer than other roads?' asked Charlie.

'Because it's protected by very old magic, a spell not even the Druyads know. No traveller can harm another while walking the Stone Road – if he does, he'll find himself cursed forever. And they say anyone who uses it reaches their destination faster than would normally be possible. All of Uland travels the Road, from one end of the continent to the other.'

Fungus wasn't wrong. They'd passed all manner of people and creatures throughout the morning: some looked human, but their clothes and languages were strange; others appeared humanoid but were clearly of other races, which Charlie likened in his mind to elves, dwarves and other fantastical beings he'd seen in movies.

And as each one had passed – casting nervous glances at the trolls – he'd been unable to stop himself from goggling at them.

'Stop. Staring.'

'You'd stare too if you'd just gotten here.' Then Charlie stopped dead. Lombrigus lumbered into him from behind, almost knocking him flying with his huge belly.

'What now?' sighed Angus.

Charlie's eyes widened as an enormously-tall creature approached. He guessed it must have been more than twelve feet in height. Its skin was grey-blue and covered in tattoos. Arms like tree trunks swung at its sides, and a colossal club was strapped to its back. It wore armour made from a combination of hardened brown leather and metal plating. A bushy grey beard obscured the lower half of its face, though its small head was completely bald. Other travellers on the road were quick to dodge out of its way.

'Oh, him. He's one of the giants of Golemar, from up north. Must be down for the markets.' Angus raised a hand as they passed. 'Hello, friend! Safe passage to you!' The giant grunted something in reply and strode on, his huge feet thumping loudly on the road. 'Not talkative chaps, those lads.'

'Giants,' Charlie breathed. 'That's… so cool.'

'Cool?' said Lombrigus. Charlie had learned to differentiate between the trolls based on two things: the size of their noses, and the type of weapon they carried. Lombrigus had a particularly fat nose and wielded a sling. 'I'd say it's rather warm, actually.'

'Are they all as big as him?'

Angus chuckled. 'Yes, though they used to be much, much bigger. The giants of old could have carried that fellow on one finger.'

As Charlie tried wrapping his head around that, they carried on, passing more and more travellers going in both directions. The road cut through small forests and open grassland, sometimes running parallel with (or over) streams of rushing water; they occasionally went by the crumbling remains of a building or between disused fields bordered with rotted fences. Charlie had the impression they were travelling west, and the further they went, the more dilapidated the landscape became.

Some time after they'd passed the giant, the road forked. The trolls veered right, leaving the Stone Road for a narrower, unpaved trail.

'Why're we going this way?' Charlie asked Angus.

'Because if we keep following the Road from here, we'll be in Doomgaard territory before you know it. See those dark woods up ahead? If we enter them, we'll have crossed the border.'

'But isn't the Road safe there too?'

'For most people,' said Angus gravely, 'but not for you. They'll be looking for you.'

Charlie nodded and said nothing more. As they left the paved highway, he cast a last glance towards the shadowed woods of Doomgaard, and shivered.

<<>>

Dale was uncomfortable.

Since Jayne had left them at the edge of the forest border, Brooke and Willow had hardly said a word to one another. They'd joined a narrow lane not unlike the one leading away from their campsite to the mountain trail (*back in the* real *world*, Dale thought) and had been following it for at least an hour. Even this early in the day it was already getting hot, and they were exposed in the open countryside. He found himself missing the cool shade of the Wraithwood.

'I'm getting thirsty,' said Brooke, breaking the awkward silence. 'We should stop for a drink soon.'

'We don't have time to stop,' replied Willow, without breaking stride. Dale sensed they were already moving far too slow for her liking.

'It's *important* to stay hydrated,' said Brooke prissily, and stopped. Dale hesitated, then did the same; Willow walked a few steps further before turning back with a sigh.

Ignoring her, Brooke shrugged her backpack off her shoulders - Dale marvelled at how it appeared seemingly from nowhere - and crouched next to it, retrieving her water bottle. 'Hey, there's food in here.'

Dale unshouldered his pack and opened it. Inside, he found thick ham and cheese sandwiches carefully wrapped in brown paper, salted nuts, a shiny red apple and his water bottle, freshly filled. The lunches they'd packed back at camp, squashed somewhere along the way, were gone. Dale took a grateful swig of water and said, 'Thank you, Jayne.'

Willow frowned. 'She isn't here, you know. She can't hear you.'

'No, she's the *See*-er, after all,' replied Brooke sarcastically, zipping up her bag.

Willow stared at her, then turned back to the lane. 'We should keep going.'

They started out again, with Willow several paces ahead. After a few minutes, Dale leaned towards Brooke and said in a low voice, 'You don't have to be so mean to her.'

He instantly regretted it. Brooke glared at him, her blue eyes burning.

'She *left us* in the woods. We could have *died*.'

'But we didn't.'

'That's not the point.'

'She did rescue us in the first place, Brooke.'

'I know, but still. We *could* have died.'

Dale left it at that.

They walked on. A warm breeze swept across the grassy fields around them, carrying summery smells their way. The lane dipped and rose, bending gradually left before swinging to the right again, always heading north. Dale held a picture of the map in his mind, trying to maintain his bearings. He knew there was an enormous lake somewhere to the east, and a much wider road far off to the west, across the expanse of the Barrowlands. And beyond it, the sea. *What sea, though?*

He tried tallying passers-by on the road (something he enjoyed doing to pass the time), but there were hardly any. An old man leading a donkey eyed them suspiciously, and a couple of hooded individuals brushed past from behind, so silently Dale jumped out of his skin. They passed a small wooden house with a thatched roof – smoke curled upwards from its chimney, and a fat ginger cat watched them lazily from the front step. No-one spoke to them along the way.

The sun was high in the sky when they rounded a bend in the lane and heard someone up ahead yell, 'HELP! HELP ME!'

'What's that?' Brooke said.

Hurrying round the bend, they saw a crossroads ahead. A rickety wooden signpost at the roadside pointed out the nearest villages. Just below it, trapped under the wheel of a horse-drawn cart, was a man dressed in purple.

Seeing them, he cried all the louder: 'HELP ME! I'M TRAPPED!'

'We're coming!' called Brooke.

'Careful…' muttered Willow.

Dale followed Brooke to where the man lay on the dirt road by the cart, which was loaded with small crates, sacks and bundles tied with rope. His right foot was pinned under the wheel, pressed down into the mud; he wore bright purple from head to toe, including purple boots with curled toes and a purple turban. His horse, which wore no purple, munched placidly on grass by the verge, oblivious to his predicament.

'Get this thing off me!' he cried, thumping the wheel with his hand. 'I've been stuck here for half an hour!'

'We will, we'll help you,' said Brooke. 'Dale, you push and I'll pull.'

'Hang on - ' Willow started.

'Just help!' Brooke snapped.

Glowering, Willow joined Dale by the rear of the cart.

'Please hurry!' cried the man in purple.

'Ready?' said Brooke. 'Now!'

She pulled; Dale and Willow pushed. The cart creaked, shuddered, and then the wheel began to turn.

'Ow! OW! That hurts!'

'Be quiet, we're helping you,' said Willow.

The wheel kept turning. Seconds later, it rolled off the man's foot. The horse snorted and ducked her head for more grass.

Gasping in pain, the man in purple hauled himself to his feet.

'Skies above, that hurts,' he said, wincing as he tested his weight on the injured foot. 'That'll smart tomorrow.'

'Is it broken?' asked Dale.

'I don't believe so, no.' Then he looked up and smiled at them; curls of brown hair protruded from beneath the turban. His eyes were a deep green. 'Thank you, my friends. I don't know what I would have done if you hadn't come along.'

'Willow,' Brooke said, 'can you give him one of those pills?'

'Yeah, like the one you gave me earlier,' added Dale.

Without speaking, Willow fished in her pocket and brought out one of the little purple pills she'd given Dale on the mountain. She offered it to the turbaned man.

'Ah, I know what these are,' he said, plucking it from her palm with nimble white fingers. 'Magic-infused beans from the forests of Nymm, am I right? They have marvellous restorative properties, if I'm not mistaken.'

Willow nodded. The man in purple popped the bean in his mouth and swallowed, then uttered a long sigh of relief.

'Gracious, those are potent.'

'Well, we'll be on our way,' said Willow.

'No, wait!' their new friend cried. 'You may well have saved my life today - there are wolves in these hills. And bears! How can I ever repay your kindness?'

'Oh, that's ok,' said Brooke, blushing. 'We were happy to help.'

'Nonsense!' the purple man said, turning to his cart with a flourish. 'You must have something in return.' He began rummaging through the little crates and bundles, mumbling to himself; his horse swatted impatiently at flies with her tail. Finally, he turned back with something in his hands. 'Here we are.'

He held a bulging leather pouch, jingling with coin.

'Let me give you something for your trouble. I have plenty to spare.'

'We can't accept,' said Willow immediately.

'But you must!' he insisted, undoing the drawstring. 'You did me a kindness today, a *great* kindness. Please, take a coin. Buy yourselves a pint of Blackslumber Mead at the next village. It's the least I can do.'

He held out the pouch and the coins jingled again.

'Really,' Willow said, 'we can't. We have to - '

'Friends, I insist!' he said.

His smile was warm and inviting. Dale looked at the pouch. It was bursting with money.

One little coin can't hurt, can it?

He started to reach for the bag.

'Dale!' said Willow.

'He's *offering* it to us,' said Brooke. 'It's rude to refuse a gift, you know.'

'The lady speaks the truth,' said the man in purple. 'I'll be *horribly* offended if you decline to take something. For your trouble.'

'Just one coin,' said Dale. 'Then we'll get going, ok?'

He reached into the pouch and the man's green eyes gleamed. Dale felt his fingertips brush lightly over something smooth and cold, something resting on top of the coins.

'Oi! You lot!'

Dale withdrew his hand and turned towards the new voice, missing the flash of anger on the purple man's face.

'What's goin' on 'ere, eh?'

Another man was coming towards them, swinging himself over the low stone wall by the roadside. He was dressed in filthy, ragged clothes; a tangled, out-of-control beard grew down to his chest, and he wore a leather patch over one eye. The other eye, dark and cold, swivelled towards them.

'In a spot of bother, are we?'

'No no, we're just fine,' replied the man in purple quickly. 'No need to trouble yourself, sir.'

Dale watched with mounting concern as two equally-unkempt men drifted into view and came over the wall. One was bald and bare-footed; the other, short and barrel-chested, stared at them hungrily. The bald one had a bow in his hand.

'What've you got there?' said the one-eyed man.

'It's… it's nothing. Be on your way, please.'

Dale saw Brooke inch closer to him. Willow had drawn up her hood.

'Don't look like nothin' to me. Looks like a bag o'coin. A *big* bag at that.' The one-eyed man grinned, baring mustard-coloured teeth. 'What d'you think, boys? Fancy some easy money?'

'Look,' said the man in purple, taking a step towards them. 'I don't think - '

Quick as a flash, the bald one nocked an arrow onto his bow. Dale heard the string creak as he drew it back. Next to him, Brooke gasped.

The man in purple stopped where he was and instinctively held up his palms. The one-eyed man chuckled.

'Thought so,' he said, extending a hand. 'Toss it this way.'

Glaring, the purple man obeyed. Eye Patch caught the pouch and the coins jingled again. He tucked it into his filthy tunic.

'Pleasure doin' business,' he sneered. 'Let's go, boys.'

The bald one kept his arrow trained on them as they retreated back to the wall. They swung themselves over it and disappeared up the hill, laughing as they went.

As soon as they were out of sight, the purple man staggered back against his cart and moaned. 'Oh dear. Oh *dear*. That coin purse… it was all I had.'

He put his face in his hands and his shoulders began to tremble.

Dale saw Brooke drift towards him; he knew what she'd say before the words left her mouth: 'We'll get it back.'

'No,' said Willow straight away, 'we don't have time.'

'We *have* to help him,' Brooke shot back.

'It's none of our business.'

'Well, I'm making it our business.'

And with that, Brooke left the road, vaulted over the wall and ran up the hill.

'Brooke!' Dale cried, but she was already gone. He had no choice but to go after her, swinging himself clumsily over the wall. With a sigh of exasperation, Willow followed.

'Oh thank you, thank you!' the man in purple gushed as they went. 'I'll remain here until you return. My foot, you see…'

Dale sprinted up and over the brow of the hill. As it levelled out, he caught a glimpse of Brooke disappearing behind an outcrop of moss-covered rocks in a field adjacent to the road and ran towards it. Willow flashed past, easily outpacing him, her red hair spilling out from under her hood. She rounded the first of the rocks; seconds later, Dale caught up, and then skidded to a halt.

Brooke was in the centre of the outcrop, and Dale realised for the first time that it was actually the remains of a building, long since crumbled to ruin; where the foundation had once been was now all wilted grass, scattered with stones. Just a few feet away from Brooke sat the one-eyed man.

In his left hand, he held the coin purse; his right hand gripped a hatchet.

'Well, well, well,' he snarled, coarse and bitter. 'If it ain't the three wee kiddies, lost in the Barrows. Thought you might follow us.'

From behind, Dale saw Brooke clench her fists. She looked small, standing there in front of the stranger. 'Give that back – it's not yours.'

Eye Patch threw back his head and laughed, a horrible hacking sound; when he met their gaze again, his good eye burned with malevolence.

'You 'ear that, lads? She says I've got t'give it back.'

The other two appeared again from behind the eroded ruins of the building. The bald one's bow was slung over his shoulder.

Brooke took a step back. Dale and Willow moved next to her.

'I think,' said Eye Patch, 'these three kiddies have bitten off more'n they can chew. What you think, lads?'

The bald one giggled stupidly and took a staggering step towards them. In response, Willow moved in front of Dale and Brooke and pulled her hood all the way back.

'Stop.'

The bald man did stop. He stared at her green-tinged skin and golden eyes, his mouth hanging open, ape-like.

'Here, she's one o'them Woodspeople, so she is.'

The one-eyed man was no longer grinning. 'Aye, she is. And she's a long way from home. What're you doing 'ere, Woodsgirl?'

'None of your business,' said Willow defiantly.

'That right?' He slowly rose to his feet; the hatchet, rusted though it was, glinted in the sunlight. 'This 'ere's how I see it. You three kiddies stumbled into somethin' that's got nought to do with you. You came in 'ere swingin', thinkin' you were up for a fight, and now you're in some trouble. Because, see, I'm keeping this coin, and I'm takin' whatever you've got n' all. And no *magik* person that don't look right's gonna tell us to stop. You should never've left the trees, Woodsgirl – your kind ain't welcome in the Barrows, and never will be.'

Willow's jaw was set and her eyes flared golden, but Dale saw her lower lip quiver just for a second, and he felt a sudden rush of anger.

'Grab 'em, lads,' Eye Patch ordered. 'Leave the tree girl to me.'

The two other men lumbered obediently towards them. Willow made a grasping movement with her hands and a flicker of green light sparked between her fingers, but before she could do any more, something sailed through the air and thunked the bald man in the face. With a cry of surprise and pain, he stumbled backwards, clutching his forehead.

'That'll teach you!' Brooke yelled, another stone already in her hand. 'Don't you dare talk to her like that!'

The surge of anger in Dale became adrenaline and in a flash, he had a tennis ball-sized stone in each hand. 'Back off!'

Willow looked just as surprised as the bald man with the now-bleeding face. The green light continued to dance between her fingers.

'Give us the bag and get out of here!' Brooke demanded.

With a snarl, the short man started forward, heading straight for Brooke. Willow raised her hands and said '*Freymacha*', and the advancing man suddenly toppled over, hitting the ground with a wheezy bark as the wind was knocked out of him. Thick, soily roots had burst from the grass and snagged him; as Dale watched, they continued to coil around his ankles, entangling him further. The short man regained his breath and let out a high-pitched shriek when he saw the roots slithering up his legs.

The bald man was coming at them again, going for his bow. Dale hurled a stone and hit him on the shoulder – he slowed, but didn't stop. Then Brooke caught him right on the knee. He howled and grabbed at it, toppling sideways. As soon as he landed on the grass, more roots burst from the ground and pinned him.

Eye Patch roared in fury. Dale saw his arm go back and then the hatchet was flying, end-over-end, directly towards Willow. Without thinking, he shoved her hard; she tumbled into Brooke on her other side, and the three of them sprawled onto the grass. The hatchet flew well wide of its mark and stuck in the ground behind them, its shaft pointed up at the sky.

'Get up, you idiots!' snapped the one-eyed man, advancing. The other two scrambled to their feet, pulling themselves out of the roots, which lost their strength when Willow fell. But as soon as they were free, they turned and bolted from the crumbled building, leaving Eye Patch behind.

'Yeah, you better run!' Brooke shouted after them. 'Learn some respect, you... you *asses*!'

Dale was up first, already armed with another stone. Now alone and without his hatchet, the one-eyed man suddenly looked unsure. Willow and Brooke rose to their feet.

'Give it back,' said Dale.

Behind the filthy beard, he saw a sneer of mustard teeth.

'Fine,' said Eye Patch, holding up a hand. 'You win, I'll give it back. But first, think I'll take somethin' for myself, for my troubles.'

He tugged open the drawstring and reached inside the pouch.

'Probably not worth much anyway, so...' He stopped, a frown creasing his sweaty brow. 'What's this? That ain't no - '

Suddenly, his eye bulged in its socket and his entire body went rigid. The coin purse dropped out of his hand and thumped onto the grass at his feet. He uttered a choked cry and toppled backwards, hitting the ground hard. His hands remained frozen in position.

Dale and Brooke stared wide-eyed at where the thief lay, unmoving, then looked at Willow.

'What happened?' Brooke said.

'I... I'm not sure,' said Willow.

'I'll get the bag,' said Dale, hurrying towards it. 'We should take it back to - '

'No wait!'

He stopped. Willow had him by the arm.

'Don't touch it,' she said, her eyes on the pouch. 'Look what it did to him. Whatever's inside, it's cursed.'

'Cursed?' repeated Brooke. 'Like, with magic?'

'Most likely,' said Willow. 'Come on, let's get out of here. We can go cross-country for now and rejoin the road further on. I don't think we should go back to the man with the cart.'

'What about him?' said Dale, pointing at Eye Patch, who still hadn't moved.

'His friends will come back for him.'

Still gripping Dale's arm, Willow marched past the frozen thief. Brooke hurried after them, giving the one-eyed man a wide berth.

<<>>

A short time passed, and the man in purple came up the hill. He walked easily, with no foot pain. He hadn't needed the Nymm bean, of course - he'd spat it out as soon as the Other-worlders left the road. The illusion had served its purpose.

Almost, anyway.

'Bandits,' he muttered to himself. 'Simpletons.'

He saw the ruined building ahead and crossed to it, tugging the purple turban off his head as he went, revealing a tangle of greasy brown hair. He tossed the turban aside.

'Better not have gotten far,' he said, looking around.

There was no sign of the Other-worlders or the Woodsgirl. He cursed, then spotted the hatchet sticking out of the grass. Trailing his gaze to the left, he saw the one-eyed man lying on the ground, staring at the sky.

'Simpleton,' he repeated.

The coin purse lay on the ground next to the thief. Sighing, the man in purple bent to pick it up. He winced as he did so, clutching at his back.

The one-eyed man's mouth was wide open, locked in a rigor mortis of shock. But his chest rose and fell rhythmically as the purple man's shadow crept over him. His one good eye swivelled to gaze up at him.

'I have no sympathy, friend,' said the man in purple, peering into the pouch. He pulled the drawstrings tight and stuffed it into his tunic. His green eyes were already fading back to grey. 'You took something that didn't belong to you, and you suffered the consequences. Let that be a lesson.'

Eye Patch's mouth quivered but the words didn't come.

'I know, I know,' said the purple man. 'I can't just *leave* you here, can I? There are wolves in these hills, aren't there? Or is it bears? I can never remember.'

Eye Patch managed a brief moan of terror.

'What's that? You'd rather I kill you? Put you out of your misery?' The purple man grinned, and his teeth were now yellow. 'Skies above, I don't have time for that sort've thing. I've got some children to find. But you take care now, good sir.'

He winked and walked away.

The one-eyed man lay where he was and began to tremble.

Charlie blinked up at the sun, a searing disc blazing in the sky. The air had been gradually heating up all morning and now, at what must be midday, it was properly hot. Crickets chirped incessantly in the bushes on either side of the road; directly above them, a pair of black-feathered birds circled ominously. Charlie thought they might be vultures.

His legs were tired and his feet ached in his boots. The trolls maintained a relentless pace along the lane bordering Doomgaard, rarely slowing. Charlie noticed they'd largely fallen silent since leaving the Stone Road and were glancing around more than before, a little nervously, even. He wondered what they were looking out for. He also wondered when they'd last had a bath – as the temperature increased, so did their collective body odour. The few travellers who passed by gave them an especially wide berth.

'How long will it take to reach the goblin markets?' Charlie asked no-one in particular.

'Just under a day's walk,' replied Angus.

'A *day?*'

'Of course.' Angus spat a glob of phlegm into the bushes. 'The Barrowlands are real big, one of the biggest regions in Uland, in fact. And we're only covering a short distance in the north of it.'

'We shall make camp at sundown,' added Fungus, 'before proceeding to the markets tomorrow.'

'Chin up, Charlie Flint,' Amoogus called back from the head of the group. 'Once we return to the Stone Road on the other side of Doomgaard, we'll make excellent time. We trolls are faster than we look.'

'You'll like the markets,' Angus assured him, with a grin. 'Bartering with goblins is an art form - I think you'll catch on quick.'

'Sir!' exclaimed Lombrigus. 'Up ahead!'

Charlie moved to his right to see past Woolly, who took up most of the view. Further along, the lane became a wooden bridge, crossing over a creek. Standing in front of the bridge was a figure dressed in armour. All black.

'It's a Doomgaard patrol, sir,' observed Angus.

'Curses, I was afraid this might happen,' said Amoogus. 'Alright lads, keep your eyes open.'

As they neared the bridge, the Doomgaard soldier stepped forward and unsheathed his sword with a metallic *shiiing*.

'Stop right there,' he commanded from behind his visor.

'We've stopped,' said Amoogus, spreading his hands. 'You're in our way, after all.'

'Silence, troll!' snapped the Doomgaardian. Then, in direct contradiction: 'Tell me where you're going.'

'The markets, of course.'

'This road doesn't lead to the markets. Why are you in Doomgaard territory?'

'My dear boy,' said Amoogus patiently, 'we are not currently in Doomgaard. This is still the Barrowlands, as far as those trees across that field. Perhaps you require a geography lesson?'

Charlie snickered. The Doomgaardian turned his eyes on him. 'That's no troll.'

'Correct. He's an honorary troll.'

'He's an Ulander, by the looks of things. Why's he with you?'

'Merely accompanying us along the road. He's rather amusing, in his own way. Keeps us entertained.'

'He shouldn't be – '

'Nevertheless, he is,' interrupted Amoogus. 'Now, if you'll be so kind as to step aside, young sir, we'll be on our way.'

The soldier hesitated, then drew himself up to his full height, about an inch taller than the trolls. 'By order of Commander Hysst, I'm detaining you all under Doomgaard law. Surrender your weapons and cargo immediately.'

'I don't believe we will,' replied Amoogus.

'But, I'm ordering you - '

'You're trying to, anyway.'

'So be it.' The Doomgaardian whistled, and there was instant movement in the bushes around them. Several black-armoured soldiers stepped out of the foliage, armed with swords and spears. Whoolly emitted a *baaa* of alarm; Charlie shifted closer to the cart.

The trolls had reacted with lightning speed. Each now gripped his weapon in both hands, poised ready to fight.

'We have you surrounded and outnumbered. Surrender immediately.'

'Look, young sir,' said Amoogus, 'can't we discuss this like civil fellows?'

The trolls gradually reorganised themselves into a circle around the cart and Woolly, facing out towards the Doomgaardians. The distance between them and the soldiers couldn't have been more than ten or so feet on either side. Out of the corner of his eye, Charlie spotted the hilt of a sword sticking from the cart.

'There's nothing civil about *you*, monster,' spat the Doomgaardian patrol. 'We know what you did to our comrades – you'll pay for your crimes in our darkest dungeons, though you'll probably be right at home there.'

This is all because of me, Charlie thought. He inched closer to the sword.

'Ah, so our crime isn't trespassing after all, then?' said Amoogus, his club at the ready. 'Awfully deceptive of you.'

'This is your last chance…'

'Get on with it, already.'

'Wait!'

Amoogus turned back to him slowly. The trolls and soldiers were listening.

'Don't do anything to them,' Charlie said. 'I'm the one you want. I'm the prisoner who escaped.'

The Doomgaard patrol looked him up and down.

'So,' he said, 'you're the one from the mountain. You're right, you *are* wanted.'

Two of the soldiers stepped towards him. Angus moved to block their path.

'Take me,' Charlie said quickly. 'I surrender. Let them go, don't hurt them.'

The Doomgaard patrol sneered behind his visor. 'Oh, you will indeed be coming with us. As for these beasts, well… they've sealed their own fate.

'Men – take the boy. Kill the trolls.'

Quick as a flash, Charlie reached up and snatched the sword from the cart, and then everything descended into chaos.

The Doomgaardians lunged at the trolls. Shouts, screams and the clanging of metal filled the air. Charlie turned on the spot with the sword in his hands, suddenly wishing he'd grabbed a shield instead. He saw Angus swing his club and a soldier went sailing into the bushes. A spear flew through the air and *thunked* into something.

One of the soldiers came at him, his black armour shining, his sword raised. Charlie let out a cry and stumbled backwards, holding his own sword up in defence, his eyes half closed. He was about to be cut in two, straight down the middle like a loaf of bread.

Then something happened. The Doomgaardian blade, heavy and double-edged, came down on his sword with a *clang*… and stopped. Charlie opened his eyes. He was holding his sword horizontally across himself, blocking the Doomgaardian blade. The soldier's eyes widened in surprise. He drew back and swung again, right to left, aiming for Charlie's neck. But Charlie had already leaned backwards in anticipation of the move; the blade swished past above his face, an inch from his nose. The breeze that followed in its wake ruffled his hair.

Charlie straightened up. His sword was in his right hand and he slashed it across the soldier's middle. The man bawled in pain and staggered backwards. Angus was waiting; his club connected with the soldier's head and he hit the ground.

All of the Doomgaard soldiers were down, sprawled on the road, some half in the bushes. Around Charlie, the trolls dusted themselves off, as though they'd just arrived home from a long day at the office.

'Are you guys ok?' Charlie said breathlessly. 'They didn't hurt you?'

'Oh, they hurt us,' said Tumygus. 'But not much. These chaps hurt more, I suspect.' Charlie looked at the upended soldier at the troll's feet, and winced.

'Just a minor inconvenience, lads,' announced Amoogus. He was standing on the bridge gripping the Doomgaard patrol by the throat, his boots dangling above the wooden planks. 'I daresay these fellows will think twice before ambushing us again.'

With that, he tossed the soldier over the wooden rail of the bridge. Charlie heard him splash into the rushing water below.

'I think we should get back to the Road as soon as possible, sir,' advised Dungus.

'Indeed,' replied Amoogus, walking back over to them. 'Ah, looks like our travelling companion has selected a weapon for himself. Where did you learn to fight like that, young sir?'

Charlie looked down at the sword in his hand. The wooden hilt was cracked in places, and the blade, not much longer than his forearm, was rusted. *How did I fight with this?*

'I… I don't know,' he admitted. 'I've never… used a sword before.'

'Well, you did a fine job,' said Dungus.

'And you defended us,' added Lombrigus.

'The actions of a true troll,' finished Fungus.

'Certainly! But enough chatter for now,' said Amoogus. 'Time we made haste to the Road. Leave these chaps here, I'm sure their comrades will be along soon. Let's get going, and keep that sheep moving!'

Charlie slipped the sword into his belt, stole a last glance at the dispatched soldiers of Doomgaard, and hurried after the trolls.

Chapter Eight: The Scar-faced Knight

The sun rode high in the sky, beating down on Uland. Beneath the shade of an old sycamore tree, the black-armoured knight with the scar on his face cleaned his sword. The blade gleamed in the light of midday.

A small group of people huddled before him, flanked by more soldiers in black armour. The people wore plain clothes and held no weapons. They stared at the grass, afraid to look up.

After a minute, the knight spoke again. His tone was smooth and deliberate: 'How long have you lived here?'

The oldest man in the group raised his eyes, blinking rapidly to keep the sweat out.

'All our lives, sir,' he stammered. 'This farm's been in our family for… for generations, it has.'

The knight didn't respond straight away. He continued to clean his blade, running the cloth carefully over the metal. The old man returned his gaze to the ground.

'And in all that time,' continued the knight, 'you've seen no humans?'

'No, sir. No humans. Wouldn't even be sure what they look like, to be quite honest.'

The knight sighed. 'If you don't know what they look like, how can you be sure you haven't seen one?' The old man opened and closed his mouth, once, then twice. The knight put away the cloth. 'As it happens, they look rather like you and your family. Almost indistinguishable from your own children, in fact. One might be forgiven for thinking them Ulanders in foreign clothes. An easy mistake to make, maybe'

Clearing his throat, the old man ventured: 'Pr'haps they did pass by here, sir, and we thought nothing of it. If, as you say, they look like us – '

'You've lived here your whole life,' the knight cut in. 'How many travellers pass by this farmstead on a daily basis?'

'I… I'm not sure, sir, to be frank – '

'Humour me and hazard a guess.'

'Um… well, we're a bit off from the main byways here, so anyone passing through would have to know where they're going. There's not many villages nearby, and the Road is – '

'How many?'

'Some days we see no-one,' the old man said quietly.

The knight met his gaze and held it with ice blue eyes. A smile slowly turned up the corner of his mouth, making the scar even more grotesque.

'You're lying to me,' he said softly.

'He ain't lying!' cried a boy next to him. In a flash, one of the soldiers slapped him across the face; a woman next to him moaned.

'Please, sir,' implored the old man, his eyes brimming with tears. 'We've seen no-one, no humans here. We're just farm folk, we don't trouble anybody. I'd tell you if we'd seen who you're after, swear it on my mother's grave.'

The knight considered him for a moment, then rose to his feet. Sycamore leaves cast dappled shadows across his face.

'I believe you,' he said, raising a black-gloved hand in the air.

Beyond the tree behind them stood a farmhouse, an old but well-kept home with a thatched room. Surrounding it were neatly ploughed fields, with the expanse of the Barrowlands extending in every direction around them; a grey mare stood patiently in one, waiting to get back to work.

A soldier approached the farmhouse and tossed a flaming object through the window. The old wooden building went up with a *whump*. The woman's moan became a scream of despair. Tears burst from the farmer's eyes.

'I believe you,' repeated the knight. 'Decymero, however, may be less eager to trust the words of Barrowsfolk. Tell your tales to him, and pray for mercy.'

At the name *Decymero*, the old man's face flooded with fear, then melted into rage.

'So they're right about you!' he yelled, shaking with fury. 'We heard what you did to Birchfell, and t'those in the mountain. You *are* the Betrayer! You were supposed to protect them, but you're just... criminals, murderers, traitors. They'll come for you, they will!'

The knight grinned, turning away. 'I'm counting on it.' Then he motioned to the soldiers nearby and added, 'Take them.'

'NO!'

Before anyone else could react, the boy snatched a dagger from the nearest soldier's belt and lunged at the scar-faced knight. His mother screamed again. He reached the knight, swung his arm with a cry of rage, and plunged the blade high into the man's back. It went in between the armour, right up to the hilt.

No-one moved. The farmer's family gaped in shock. The Doomgaard soldiers watched, unsure, hands on their swords.

The scar-faced knight reached behind him and grasped the hilt of the dagger. With a grunt, he tugged the blade free from his back. It came out red.

He turned to face the boy, who stared up at him, horrorstruck. The knight held up the dagger.

'Brave,' he said. 'And foolish.'

'Please!' the woman cried hysterically, straining against the grip of the soldiers around her. 'Please don't kill my boy! He didn't know what he was doing.'

'I think he did,' said the knight, grinning again. He flipped the dagger over and offered it back to the boy; his blue eyes flashed. 'Try again.'

The boy gawked at the dagger. He looked from it to the knight, and back to the blade.

'Go ahead,' said the knight softly. *'Take it.'*

Trembling, the boy started to reach for the dagger. His mother sobbed and slumped against the old farmer, who watched it all, ashen-faced and silent. Behind them, the soldiers threw uncertain glances at one another.

The knight's grin widened as the boy's fingers wrapped around the hilt. He took the dagger from him, staring at the blade as blood dripped to the grass. Then his eyes filled with tears, his hand began to shake, and the dagger dropped from his grasp.

'Please don't kill him,' his mother repeated in a despairing, monotone voice.

The knight looked at her. His smile faded.

'There are worse things than death,' he said.

He motioned again and one of the soldiers grabbed the boy, dragging him back to where his parents stood. The woman threw her arms around him, pulling him close.

As the old man, his family and his farmhands were herded off, the knight sheathed his sword and watched the burning house billow smoke into the sky. Another soldier with long blond hair approached cautiously, carrying his helm under one arm.

'Commander Hysst.'

The scar-faced knight continued to gaze at the fire. 'What news?'

'The ghouls returned from the Wraithwood, attacked by ferocious beasts, they claim. The two humans and the Woodsperson escaped.'

'Did they leave the forest?'

'No, Commander. Not before nightfall, anyway.'

'If they were there after dark, they're likely already dead.' Hysst started across the field towards his horse, hitched by the lane. 'Still, we'll keep looking. I'd rather they don't leave the Barrows alive.'

'We've been tracking the other one since the ambush at dawn. Think he's being escorted north. Sent a squad to the border road to intercept. Waiting to hear back.'

'Inform me when you've recovered him.'

Hysst braced one foot on the horse's stirrup and swung himself into the saddle. He looked up at the sun, unblinking, then out across the Barrowlands. Smoke from the burning farmhouse spread through the air.

'Where to now, Commander?'

'I have business in the north,' said the Betrayer. 'Take your men and pay a visit to the nearest village, and the next after that. Perhaps we'll have better luck there. The Ulandai will be here soon, no doubt seeking justice, as they call it. Keep your eyes open and be ready.'

'And if the villagers won't talk?'

'Burn their homes to the ground.'

Commander Hysst snapped the reins and galloped off, northward.

Chapter Nine: Flight of the Peryton

'So, it's like a cart,' Willow said slowly, 'that leads itself?'

It was mid-afternoon and they were just a few miles away from Ringmoffren, continuing along country lanes over rolling hills. The air was dense with the smell of grass and flowers in bloom.

'Well, not quite by itself,' said Dale. He was sticky with sweat in the humid air. 'Not usually, anyway. But they don't need animals to pull them, that's what I mean.'

'That's weird. And you came to be near the mountain, in your world, in one of these... ca-ers?'

'Sort of,' replied Brooke, wiping her brow. 'We came in a bus - like a big car, but for more people.'

'Bus.' Willow tasted the word. 'I think I saw it, when I was near your camp. You had... many friends there.'

'Classmates,' corrected Dale. 'Some of them are friends.'

'How long were you in our world?' asked Brooke, watching a massive bumblebee dance across their path, trying to ignore the ache in her feet.

Since their brief encounter with the man in purple earlier, Willow had been more talkative. Dale deduced that whatever icy tension existed between her and Brooke had finally begun to thaw.

'Not long,' Willow replied. 'A day, maybe. The ghouls chased me down from the mountain and I lost them in the woods. I saw you there, at your camp. And when I followed you all back up the mountain, the ghouls tracked me. I think I led them to you… sorry.'

'It's ok,' said Brooke. 'You saved us in the fog. I just hope Charlie's alright, wherever he is now.'

'Jayne said he's alive, so that's good.' Dale looked westward but saw nothing except endless hills. They were all green, yellow or brown. 'Knowing Charlie, he's probably made friends with a pack of elves, or something.'

'Willow, how did you get into our world, anyway?'

'Through the portal,' she replied, brushing a few locks of red hair from her face. 'I was in the Great Cavern, serving the Druyads, when the ghouls came.'

'Drew-adds,' Brooke pronounced. 'Who are they, anyway?'

'The most powerful beings in Uland. Keepers of ancient knowledge, wielders of deep magic. There aren't many left now. Everyone reveres the ones who remain because they ended the Age of Giants, a long time ago. They're the only Faction that knows how to use the portals, so they can travel across the continent quickly between each one.'

'What happened to them?' Dale said. 'It looked like a bomb exploded back there, in the mountain.'

Willow's face darkened. 'We were attacked. The Betrayer – Commander Hysst – let the ghouls inside. He was duty-bound to protect the Great Cavern and the Druyads, but he turned on them. The attack was sudden. No-one stood a chance.'

She was silent for a few moments. Dale and Brooke waited, walking on.

'My master, Everin, opened a portal so we could escape, but the ghouls… got to him. He pushed me through, told me to get help, wherever I ended up. But some of them followed. I tried to stop them with magic, which you're not supposed to do in the portal, and I think it sent us into your world by mistake. I thought I was still in Uland until I saw all of you, and your… bus. Even afterwards, I still wasn't sure.'

'It's not easy when you lose someone,' said Brooke quietly. 'I'm sorry, Willow.'

'For what?' Willow replied. She frowned, then seemed to realise what Brooke meant. 'Oh… thanks.'

'When we get to… wherever it is we're going,' said Dale, 'will there be other Druyads who can help us?'

'Oh yes. They weren't all in the Great Cavern, thankfully – I served the Lesser Druyads, but the Master Druyads are in another place to the north, where we're going. They'll be able to help us.'

'Good,' said Brooke. Then, 'Am I the only one who's hungry right now?'

'Yes, I'm *famished*!' said Willow immediately. Brooke and Dale burst out laughing, and she grinned.

They left the road and settled down under a nearby clump of trees, tucking into the lunches Jayne had prepared ("Magicked", Brooke clarified) for them. Dale hadn't realised how hungry he was until the first few bites of sandwich reached his empty stomach – he finished the rest in less than a minute. Willow ate some strange-looking fruit and a handful of nuts, which she cracked open expertly on a stone. Brooke let her try a bite of her sandwich, and the face she pulled sent them into a fit of laughter again.

After eating, they returned to the road and carried on towards Ringmoffren. Any weariness they'd felt before their break was extinguished by a combination of Jayne's delicious lunch and Willow's growing interest in what she called "the other world" Brooke and Dale had come from.

Dale found this amusing because Uland, with its magic and monsters, was so other-worldly to him – he had a long list of questions about it, but Willow always seemed to have more: 'Why do you wear those clothes? Why can't you do magic? What do you mean you've never heard a banshee? What's a *why-fy* signal?'

They forgot to feel tired in spite of their already-long journey, and spent the rest of the walk to Ringmoffren swapping stories and jokes. Willow tried showing them a few tricks, causing dandelions to leap from the verges by the road and whirl like catherine wheels, and summoning a swarm of multicoloured butterflies to land on their heads and shoulders - Brooke giggled happily at that while Dale forced a toothy grin, afraid to move.

Finally, with the orange sun dipping closer and closer to the horizon, they came within sight of the village: four roads converged at its centre, around which a collection of wooden houses had been constructed. Even from distance, Dale could see what must be a market square complete with a fire pit, casting a warm glow on the buildings. Ploughed fields surrounded the village, and people were still working them as they drew closer. No-one paid them much attention.

'It's pretty,' said Brooke. 'I wonder if they'll have... what was *that?*'

She and Dale ducked as something big swooped past just above their heads, their cloaks flapping in its tailwind. Enormous feathered wings cut through the air as the thing glided down to the village, where it disappeared.

'Peryton,' said Willow, with a grin.

'*That's* what's taking us to the Throat?' exclaimed Dale. 'A gigantic bird? I thought a peryton was like a, a...'

'A bus?' suggested Willow, then sauntered on.

They reached Ringmoffren and headed straight for a tavern called *The Cheerful Goose*. As they entered, a rosy-faced man slumped next to the doorway gave them a friendly wave, and then promptly passed out.

The sharp, sweet smell of beer hit them as they stepped inside. The tavern was low-ceilinged, warm and noisy, filled with raucous laughter and music from the fiddle. Yellow-orange flames crackled in the fireplace, giving the interior a homely feel. Willow led Brooke and Dale to a table in the corner, which had just been vacated by a trio of old men with forked beards and pointed ears. They warbled to one another in a foreign language as they passed by.

'Wait here,' Willow said, and headed for the bar. Brooke and Dale pulled out rickety wooden chairs and sat, scanning the room.

'I've never been in a place like this,' said Brooke, watching two men arm-wrestle while their friends cheered them on.

'Me neither,' replied Dale. Willow was talking to the bartender, a huge bald man with a handlebar moustache. 'First time for everything, I suppose.'

Brooke looked at him. 'Are you… alright? With all this, I mean?'

'Do we have a choice?'

'Probably not.' Brooke poked at the wax of an almost burned-out candle on the table. 'It feels like we're just sort of… accepting everything, you know? And it's almost starting to feel… I dunno…'

'Normal?' suggested Dale.

'Yes!' Brooke said, suddenly animated. 'Normal! As if there've always been fairies and ghouls and magical things in our lives. We've just been going along with it all like we're used to it.'

'Maybe we're actually still on the mountain,' said Dale slowly, 'and we've just bumped our heads, or something. Maybe it's all a dream.'

'Then how are we dreaming the exact same thing, together?'

Willow returned to the table and set a tankard down in front of each of them. Brooke stared, wide-eyed, at the steaming brown liquid hers contained.

'Drink up,' said Willow, taking a seat. 'There's food coming.'

'What is it?' asked Dale, sniffing his tankard.

Willow took a swig of hers, wiping foam from her lips. 'Beer.'

'We can't have beer!' exclaimed Brooke. 'We're thirteen'.

'Why not?'

'Because… because we're too young. We can't drink alcohol.'

'What's al-co-haul?'

Brooke and Dale looked at each other, then raised the tankards to their lips. The beer tasted sweet and warmed their insides as it went down.

'It's wonderful!' said Brooke, taking a bigger gulp.

'I don't think this is like beer from our world,' added Dale.

Willow smiled, then cast a cautious glance around the room. 'We should be safe here, for now. Our peryton will be ready by sundown, and then we can go.'

Their food arrived a few minutes later, delivered to the table by a grumpy old woman who rolled her eyes when Dale asked for more beer. She took their empty tankards back to the bar while they tucked into bowls of thick brown stew and hunks of buttered bread.

As the late afternoon wore on into early evening, more and more people entered the tavern, greeting each other loudly and cheerfully. Dale saw a woman in the far corner with burgundy-coloured hair and extremely pale skin, watching some men in blue cloaks play cards. Her black eyes never left them. A few people threw curious looks towards the table in the corner where two teenagers and a Woodsperson sat, but no-one said anything to them other than the grumpy old barmaid, who muttered 'Ye done yet?' twice as she passed with meals and drinks for other tables.

Finally, Willow set her empty tankard down, wiped her lips again and said, 'I think we should go.'

'Why can't we stay here?' asked Brooke.

'It's too busy. Everyone's travelling north for the goblin markets. We'll find somewhere quieter for a while.'

'I'm pretty sleepy,' said Dale. He burped and Brooke made a face, then giggled.

At that exact moment, the door to the tavern opened and three men walked in, their boots thumping on the floor. They were soldiers, all clad in black armour, with swords sheathed at their sides. The general din inside the room dropped noticeably.

Dale stared past Willow's shoulder and she turned to look. As soon as she saw the men, her eyes flared golden – Brooke grabbed her arm to stop her from standing up. The barmaid, who was standing near their table, saw the movement. Dale's throat had gone dry.

One of the soldiers removed his helmet, revealing a head of thick blond hair, and approached the bar. The other two walked towards a table, which was quickly abandoned by those sitting at it.

'It's *them*,' hissed Willow.

Brooke could feel her arm trembling with rage. 'Don't do anything,' she whispered. 'Don't - not here.'

Almost everyone in the room had stopped talking. The blond soldier noticed and turned from the bar.

'Don't mind us,' he smirked. 'Just passing through.'

Someone muttered something; Dale heard the words 'Doomgaard scum', but nothing else.

'Nice little place you've got here,' the blond soldier said to the tavern owner, loud enough for everyone else to hear. His boots were caked with mud, and something else.

'Is indeed,' replied the bartender coldly, pushing a tankard towards him. 'Never have any trouble here.'

'And you won't tonight.' The soldier took a swig of beer and smacked his lips. 'Damn, that's good stuff.' Then, addressing the now-silent room: 'We're looking for some people. Three of them. They might have been here today.'

Dale saw the barmaid step casually to her left, blocking their table from view.

'They might be dressed in foreign clothes,' continued the blond soldier, beer in hand, 'and they might look like Ulanders. Young ones.'

Brooke continued to grip Willow's arm. She felt some eyes in the room slide their way. The fireplace crackled and spat embers.

The blond man sipped his beer, waiting. When no-one answered, he slammed the tankard down on the bar. The other two soldiers stood again.

'We'll be outside,' he announced. 'If anyone has anything to say, I suggest you do it quickly. There'll be coin in it for you.'

As they moved to go outside, the tavern owner said, 'S'pose you'll be paying for that drink now?'

The soldier turned back and glared at him. 'These old wooden buildings burn easily, don't they?' he said. 'So I suppose that one's on you.'

The tavern owner's face went red but he said nothing. The soldiers left, laughing, slamming the door behind them. The patrons started back into conversation; abruptly, the old barmaid swung round.

'They're looking for you three, aren't they?' she said in a low voice. 'You better leave, right now.'

'But how?' said Dale. 'They're waiting outside.'

'There're loads more out there,' added Brooke.

'How do you know that?' asked Willow, frowning.

'I… I'm not sure – '

'Back door,' the woman cut in.

Flustered, she led them towards the bar. The tavern owner looked them up and down, and seemed to understand.

'This way,' he said, gruffly.

They all followed him through a doorway behind the bar into the kitchen. Dale caught a glimpse of a startled-looking girl chopping onions before they were ushered out a rear door into the cool evening air. The dusk sky was dark blue.

'Listen,' said the tavern owner, a hulking shadow next to them. 'I don't want to know why them'uns are after you. Ain't none of our business.'

'Those were Hysst's men, weren't they, Hugo?' said the barmaid, his wife.

'Bloody traitors, Martha.' Hugo spat on the ground. 'Meant to be protectin' that place, and here they are runnin' round the Barrows in Doomgaard armour. Folk say they've been burnin' up villages and killin' anyone they please.'

'They'll be hanged, when they catch 'em,' said Mary.

'Aye.' Hugo looked at them again. 'You know, I could turn you all in right now,' he said slowly, an edge to his voice. 'Make some coin, save my tavern for sure. Not really my problem, is it? Shouldn't have to suffer for it.'

'Hugo!' Martha exclaimed.

'Well, it's true enough.'

'I'll pay extra,' said Willow quickly. 'Here.' She fished inside her cloak and brought out a fistful of silver coins, which she handed to Hugo. He squinted at them in the low light.

'Aye, that'll do,' he grunted. 'You'd better get outta here quick. Peryton lander's that way – he'll likely be tired, but he'll get you where you need to go. And stay out of sight.'

'Druyads protect you,' Martha whispered, and they went back inside. Dale heard the door lock.

'Come on,' said Willow.

Together, they slipped through the village towards the peryton lander, weaving between little houses and shops, smithies and woodworkers, keeping to the shadows as much as possible. Inside the homes of Ringmoffren, children laughed and babies cried as parents tried to quiet them, perhaps aware of the black-armoured men near the tavern. The smell of roasting meat and broiling vegetables wafted from windows, mixing with the fragrances of dusk. Dale thought it would have been nice to stay in Ringmoffren, if they'd been able.

'The lander's close,' whispered Willow, as they crept along in the shadows between two buildings. Up ahead, they could hear voices in heated discussion. 'When we get there, I need you to… oh, blast!'

The lander was a raised stone platform on the edge of a small, paved square. It was roughly rectangular in shape with a stone pyre at each corner, lighting the area around it and, presumably, providing some warmth for the creature now resting on the platform itself.

They ducked down into the shadows and Dale whispered, *'That's* a peryton?'

The animal on the lander looked like a stag, except it had two enormous feathered wings protruding from its shoulders, and its hind legs were scaly like that of a bird. Instead of hooves, its back feet ended in three toes with ferocious talons, and a long plumed tail draped over the rim of the lander behind it. When it turned its antlered head, Dale saw deer-like ears cocking towards distant sounds coming from across the village. Its black eyes caught the light from the pyres and flashed with an awareness that was more than animal.

And between them and the peryton, a very short man in a top hat was arguing with a group of Doomgaard soldiers.

'…no jurisdiction here,' he was saying, from behind an impressively-bushy beard. 'This transport is open and available to anyone with coin. You've got no right to – '

'Orders is orders,' replied one of the soldiers. Another was guarding the peryton nervously – the creature's black gaze had locked on him.

'Yes, but who's giving these orders?' Between the beard and the top hat, very little of the short man's face was actually visible. 'This is the free land of Barrow, no outsiders can tell us what to do. So I ask again: whose orders are you following, sir?'

The soldier sighed. 'Commander Hysst. You got a problem, you take it up with him. But he ain't here.'

'Then I shall speak to your superior. Still at the Goose, yes? I'll be right back. And no-one touch my peryton, unless you rather enjoy being impaled.'

The short man marched off up the street and out of sight.

'Bleedin' country bumpkins,' muttered one of the soldiers. 'Won't be so high n' mighty when this place is ash. Oi, don't touch it! He weren't lyin' about the antlers.' Dale saw the soldier nearest the peryton back away; there were four of them in total.

'They're guarding it,' Willow whispered. 'We have to leave.'

'But we'll never get to the Throat in time,' Brooke replied. 'Jayne said it's the fastest way.'

'We don't have a choice. Come on, we can go through the woods – '

'Hang on,' whispered Dale. 'What about, you know... magic? Can't you do something, like before?'

Willow studied the soldiers, considering. 'Well... there's something I could try.'

'Do it,' said Brooke, glancing behind them. 'I don't think we have long.'

The peryton uttered a bark-like noise, and the nearest soldier jumped.

Willow sighed, rising. 'Ok, here goes.'

She stepped out of the shadows, her hands outstretched, familiar green light sparking around her fingers. The soldiers turned to face her, automatically reaching for their swords.

'Halt!' said the one who'd been speaking to the short man. 'Who are you?'

'It's a Woodsgirl,' observed another, before adding: 'Wait – it's *the* woodsgirl! She's the one we're after!'

'Grab her before she can – '

Before they could finish, Willow clapped her hands together and said '*Seileed*', and the little square exploded with emerald light. Dale threw his hands up, shielding his eyes from the glare, but it vanished just as quickly as it appeared.

The peryton blinked at them from the lander; all four soldiers were gone.

'Where'd they go?' said Dale as he and Brooke emerged into the square.

Willow lowered her arms. 'Uh oh – wrong spell.'

Then they saw - where each of the soldiers had been standing just seconds before, there was now a fat, green slug.

'That, umm, wasn't supposed to happen,' Willow admitted sheepishly. 'It's ok, they'll change back soon… I think.'

'What's going on here now?'

The short man had returned, striding purposefully into the square. 'Who are you three? And where have those soldiers – '

'Wait!' cried Brooke.

Squelch.

'Good heavens! What's that?' he exclaimed, lifting his boot. Brooke covered her mouth.

'Are you the Keeper?' Willow asked urgently.

'Why, yes I am.' He squinted at her, then at Brooke and Dale. 'Ah, you're my next passengers, aren't you? Splendid! Quick now, let's get you on board before those vagabonds come back – '

Squelch.

' – with more fake orders. You have my coin, yes?'

'Yes.' Willow handed him a shiny piece. He inspected it briefly before pocketing it. 'More than enough. Well, come on then!'

He marched over to the peryton while Willow, Brooke and Dale carefully stepped after him. Brooke's hand remained clamped to her mouth.

'This is Percius,' said the Keeper proudly. 'He'll take you where you need to go, and he'll get you there fast.'

Dale looked uncertainly at the creature, which regarded them with what was either curiosity or hunger. It seemed much larger up close.

'We're going to the Throat,' said Willow.

'Ah, of course. For the markets? Naturally.' He leaned close to the peryton's stag-like head. 'You hear that, Percius? Crookedstone, ok? No more detours.' Percius snorted. 'Hop on, then.'

With an overabundance of caution, Brooke and Dale followed Willow up onto the creature's back. The hair of its light brown coat was short and soft, but they were able to grip a longer mane running along its back between the wings. Brooke had ridden a pony when she was younger and thought the peryton felt similar, though it was much larger. She sat behind Willow, with Dale behind her, holding tightly to her cloak. Percius remained perfectly still until they were seated.

'Excellent,' said the Keeper cheerfully. 'All set? Off you go, then!'

Percius stood, and suddenly it felt like they were on a camel's back instead of a pony. Dale instinctively clung tighter to Brooke, then loosened his grip, blushing.

The peryton's enormous wings fanned out with a rustle of feathers and a *whump* sound, like a duvet being spread over a bed. Its three passengers hunkered down along the creature's back as it manoeuvred on the lander, turning ninety degrees to face into the square; Dale noticed the feathers of its wings were tawny like that of an owl, and each one was longer than his arm.

Surely an animal this size can't get off the ground without a runway? he thought.

But it could. The Keeper leapt back as the peryton's wings *whumped* faster and faster on either side of its passengers until, in a seeming defiance of physics, it began to rise off the lander, vertically upwards. Up and up it went, its wings beating harder, until the square came to look like a framed picture beneath them. Brooke whooped in delight; Dale dug his legs tighter into the peryton's body.

And then they were flying, sailing over Ringmoffren in a wide arc, the wind whipping at their faces and hair as the peryton's long feathered tail fluttered in the breeze. They could see the whole village below them now, a collection of little wooden buildings and orange lanterns and cobbled streets; they even caught a glimpse of *The Cheerful Goose* and the handful of black-armoured soldiers outside it, nothing more than dots now. Just a few seconds later, Ringmoffren was gone, and they were flying high above fields and trees, all shrouded in darkness.

'This is amazing!' yelled Brooke gleefully, followed by another whoop. Willow leaned forward and patted Percius on the neck. He immediately began to fly faster – which Dale hadn't thought possible – until the land was simply a blur beneath them and the cool evening air nipped at their cheeks.

They climbed higher, passing through clouds. For a few moments, nothing was visible beyond the peryton's antlered head; they felt the air grow thinner as they ascended further. Then they rose out of the cloud bank into a blaze of golden-tangerine light.

Brooke ceased whooping and all three gazed off to their left, where the last embers of the sun cast a spectacular evening glow across the sky. Percius beat his great wings and flew on, skimming the clouds just below them. Dale grinned in spite of the queasy feeling gathering in his stomach, staring at the fiery sky as Brooke's hair flapped in his face.

It's like a painting, he thought.

'It's incredible! I love this,' said Brooke, echoing his thoughts. 'We should have perytons back home. I don't want to leave this place.'

As the sun dropped below the clouds and the sky filled with stars, they flew on, northward.

Back in Ringmoffren, a cloaked man left *The Cheerful Goose*, passing by the Doomgaard soldiers still gathered outside. He'd long since discarded his purple turban and they paid no attention to him. He was just another traveller.

The tavern owner had given him everything he needed, and there was no time to spare.

He headed for the road.

Chapter Ten: A Meeting in the Markets

Goblins, as it turns out, come in all shapes and sizes.

Some are tall and skeletal, others are short and stocky; many are hunched, as though always stooping to pick something off the ground, while others walk with a straight back, almost noble. Some goblins inherit lime-green skin from their ancestors, and others are quite grey in appearance. But all goblins share three common features: long, hooked noses; long, pointed ears; and unchanging facial expressions that are an exact combination of glee and deviousness.

Of all the creatures she'd encountered in Uland so far, goblins were Brooke's least favourite. After ghouls, anyway.

She hadn't been fully awake when Percius dropped through the clouds shortly after sunrise. The first thing she heard that morning – their second in Uland – was Dale's yelp of surprise as he woke behind her to find they were swooping rapidly downwards.

'We're here,' Willow informed them.

As the peryton circled down in wide arcs, they got their first glimpse of the Throat. Brooke wasn't sure what she'd been expecting (a big dark hole ready to swallow them up, maybe?), but what lay below looked very much like a cliff face, immense and sheer, reaching vertically towards the morning sky. The cliff stretched all the way across their horizon, and for the first time, they'd been able to see water at both ends; the water on the left was sea, and on the right it was a river. This was the northernmost point of the Barrowlands – the Throat acted as a barrier, blockading everything else beyond it.

A settlement, much larger than Ringmoffren, sat squarely in the centre of the cliff face, walled in by a semi-circle of reddish stone at odds with the almost glassy greyness around it. As they drew closer, dozens of thin smoke trails became visible rising from chimneys within the town; a smooth, wide road sloped down towards it across the surrounding fields, already occupied by travellers going both directions, insect-like from this height. Several other roads also converged on the town, like roots spreading from the base of a tree.

'It used to be a weapon,' Willow called over the wind as they descended. 'It belonged to a giant from long ago called Skorvoluc, back in the third age. A hammer or a club, or something. When he fell, his weapon landed here, just as you see it, separating the Barrowlands from Ulandai.'

'It's huge!' Brooke said.

'Yeah, and it takes a long time to get around. So the Stone Road builders dug a passage under it instead and built up the town, Crookedstone, to help protect it.'

'A giant's weapon,' Dale said in a voice that was far off. 'He must have been… *really* gigantic.'

'All the ancient giants were,' said Willow. 'And now they're all dead.'

As Percius descended in tightening circles, Cookedstone grew larger below them, filling up with houses and shops and buildings of trade. Hundreds of people milled about the streets, drifting to and from the market. Brooke could see it now: an expansive area in the heart of the town where no buildings rested, a chaotic-looking palette of movement and colour.

Then the peryton stopped its descent and flew level, heading straight for a tower near the centre of town. It was all stone with a slated cone-shaped roof and looked like it could topple over at any moment; there were openings in the walls at random intervals, as though someone had poked sections out to see if it would still stand. Brooke thought it looked like a giant Jenga tower.

Other perytons were coming and going from the openings, swooping in and out with passengers on their backs. Percius made for a vacant space and, despite seeming much too large for the gap, slowed to a stop with a beat of his enormous wings and landed gracefully inside the tower, his antlers just missing the ceiling.

They were now in a circular room with a stone floor and a door at one end. Other than a few small bales of hay and a wooden trough, the room was empty. As the peryton settled gently into a sitting position, a small man came through the door and hurried towards them – he looked exactly like the Keeper in Ringmoffren, complete with top hat and overgrown beard. Brooke wondered if he could somehow be the same person.

'Welcome to Crookedstone,' he declared, in an identical voice to the man from Ringmoffren. 'Glad to see Percius came *directly* here this time. Please, watch your step as you disembark.'

Percius snorted indifferently and began munching on a hay bale. Willow slipped lightly to the floor; Dale and Brooke followed, less gracefully. Dale was a little green.

'Thanks for the ride, Percius,' he managed, patting his neck. The peryton snorted again but didn't raise his head.

They followed Willow out of the lander room and down a steep spiral staircase, passing doors to other rooms on their descent. Through one open door, Brooke caught a glimpse of a burly two-headed man in heated discussion with another peryton Keeper – from the snippet she heard of their conversation, it seemed the little man in the top hat was trying to charge his customer for two spots on the creature's back instead of one.

The tower opened right into the centre of Crookedstone onto a busy boulevard, filled with a variety of travellers: men and women who appeared human (though Brooke and Dale had come to learn they were not), some in ragged clothing, others in exquisite and colourful attire; creatures who were far too tall, others who were far too short, still others with too many limbs, wings, tails or mandible. Brooke even saw something that looked like a cat with a woman-shaped body, impatiently pawing at its fluffy ears while it stood in line. Many of them were pushing or pulling carts loaded with crates, sacks and, in some cases, cages containing even stranger creatures which squawked and hissed from behind bars.

They joined the throng and made their way through town, following the Stone Road that Jayne had told them about. After walking over miles and miles of rough, uneven countryside for the last two days, Brooke found the flat stones now underfoot to be soothing on her throbbing soles. Willow had mentioned that people travelled faster on the Road; Brooke wondered if it also healed weary feet.

Further ahead, the Road bottlenecked under an archway carved into an interior wall. Here, travellers began bunching up into a queue. Directly beneath the archway were two wooden barrels, one balancing on the other, and seated precariously on top of them was a goblin.

It had bright green skin and long, thin ears jutting out from its head like handlebars. Its arms, folded across its chest, were much too long for its dumpy body. It wore a dark leather doublet, baggy grey trousers and no boots, and it regarded each traveller with calculating yellow eyes as they passed under the arch.

'Where you off to, then?' it sneered in a high-pitched voice at a man with blue hair in a blue cloak.

'Passing on, northward,' he replied curtly. The goblin waved its clawed hand dismissively and addressed the next traveller in a similar way.

'He never asks the same question twice,' Willow whispered as their turn drew near, 'and if he doesn't like your answer, or if you're rude, they make things difficult for you.'

Brooke wondered what sort of difficulties goblins might create. Then they abruptly found themselves under the archway, scrutinised by the sentry on the barrels.

'Here for the markets?' it asked through its permanent, devilish grin. 'Or for something else?'

'We're passing through, to the north,' Willow replied.

Brooke had expected the goblin to wave them on, as it had done with those ahead of them in the queue. But as its yellow eyes roved over them, it continued, 'And what are these? Ulanders?'

Willow faltered, clearly surprised at being asked a second question. 'Um, yes… they are. Ulanders. Returning home.'

Brooke studied her feet, but she could feel the goblin's eyes on her. Dale shifted uncomfortably on her right. And when the goblin asked a *third* question, they heard surreptitious whisperings in the growing line behind them.

'What's a Woodsperson doing in the Barrowlands with two Ulanders?'

Willow hesitated fractionally and the goblin's eyes gleamed. It had them right where it wanted them – difficulties were on the way. But before she could answer, someone behind them interjected with, 'Could we get a move on, please?'

The goblin's eyes jerked from Willow to whoever had dared interrupt its line of questioning. Its contemptuous grin widened, revealing two rows of pointed white teeth.

'In a rush, are we?'
'No, I was just – '

'We've got our eye on you, friend.' The goblin, now with someone else in its crosshairs, waved them on. They hurried under the archway as the impatient traveller behind them protested in vain.

'That was close,' Willow said. 'I've never heard them ask more than one question before. Ever.'

Then they were inside the central walls of the town, and goblins were everywhere. They leered at passers-by from the doorways of houses, inns and merchant stores with their malevolent yellow eyes, taking note of the contents of their carts, tracking those with bulging coin purses; their high-pitched voices and tittering laughs punctuated the general din around them, and many travellers gave them a wide berth by keeping strictly to the Stone Road, which was much narrower here. And yet, Brooke saw people playing cards and clinking tankards with goblins outside taverns, exchanging news and jokes on street corners, mock-fighting with wooden weapons. Not everyone minded them, it seemed. But they creeped her out.

The Road sloped gradually downwards through the town. Further on ahead, the clamour of the markets was growing louder.

'There're a *lot* of people here,' commented Dale, watching a four-armed juggler toss glowing eggs in the air while a small crowd cheered and applauded.

'Exactly, so don't wander off,' warned Willow, 'or we'll never find you again. And watch out for pickpockets.'

'The goblin at the gate,' said Brooke, as they wove their way between travellers on the Road, towards the markets. 'Why did he ask three questions? Were we in trouble, or something?'

'I'm not sure. Maybe. I think something weird's going on.'

The clamour grew and grew. Then the rows of buildings ended, and they found themselves on the perimeter of the markets.

'Bloody hell,' Dale exclaimed.

The market area was enormous, taking up what must be at least half of the space within the town walls. The Stone Road wound its way on through the centre towards the Throat itself, a black hole at the base of the cliff face; on either side of the Road was a sea of market stalls, tents and pavilions in a multitude of colours, all manned by vendors, all of whom were doing their best to out-yell their neighbours.

'Fresh fish! Fresh fish, straight from the sea!'

'This way for mud-fired marbles!'

'Gorgensnozzlers! Get your gorgensnozzlers here!'

'Musical shells, straight from the Crystal Coast!'

The noise was deafening, but Brooke thought something about it was strangely wonderful. As they passed along towards the Throat, an intense blend of smells filled the air, some so tantalising they made her stomach rumble, and others so foul she had to briefly hold her breath until they'd moved on. Everywhere she looked, merchants were yelling cheerfully to passers-by about how utterly *fantastic* their goods were. The further they descended into the markets, the noisier it became.

'Maybe we could look around a bit?' suggested Dale, craning his neck every which way. 'That food looks *amazing*.'

'No, there isn't time,' said Willow, raising her voice so they could hear her properly. 'We have to stay together and keep moving.' The curious, chatterbox Willow of yesterday seemed to have disappeared for the time being. *She sounds like Miss Harington now*, Brooke thought, smiling to herself.

All around them, goblins patrolled the markets, keeping watchful yellow eyes on customers and merchants alike. Some of them manned their own stalls, but for the most part, they merely supervised. Brooke accidentally met one's gaze and looked away quickly.

'I've a question,' said Dale. 'Why didn't we just take Percius all the way to the Druyads? I mean, couldn't he have just flown over all this?'

'The Ulandai don't allow magical creatures within their borders,' Willow replied. 'If Percius had crossed the Thunderflow River, he could have been shot down.'

'That's awful!' cried Brooke, aghast.

Willow shrugged. 'It's in their law now. The Ulandking doesn't like magic, never has. He's tried for years to get rid of all magical people and beasts in Ulandai. That's why we have to stick to the Road from now on, otherwise even *I* could be arrested.'

'They could arrest us too though, couldn't they? We're not Ulandai.'

'No, but you *look* like them. That's enough, as far as they're concerned.'

'I'd rather be magical,' said Dale. 'It's boring being human.'

They continued on through the markets along the Stone Road, winding and narrow here, drawing closer to the gaping black maw of the Throat. From this close, Brooke saw that it sloped downwards into darkness under the sheer cliff above it, which at this angle seemed to hang over them dangerously, just waiting to topple and crush the markets beneath. Birds circled and cawed along its ridge top, scanning with keen eyes for scraps far below. Those who were done trading (or were simply passing through) carried on into the tunnel, disappearing into the black.

As they approached the entrance, Brooke was alarmed to see another goblin in their path; it was at least a head shorter than they were, so she hadn't spotted it over the crowd. When it's yellow eyes fixed on them, she shuddered.

'You three,' it said, pointing a gnarled green finger. 'Where're you off to?'

Other travellers glanced curiously at them as they passed by on either side, like water flowing around a rock in a river. Willow marched right up to the goblin and replied, 'Northward.'

'Not yet, you ain't. Got some questions for you first.'

'What? Why?'

'You'll find out.' The goblin motioned and two more appeared from nowhere. 'Follow my associates, if you please.'

'This way,' croaked one, heading off to their left.

'Willow?' said Brooke uncertainly.

'We'll go, for now,' she said, glancing coldly at the goblin in their path. It grinned back.

They left the Road and followed the first goblin into the maze of vendor stalls while the second trailed close behind (too close, for Brooke's liking), weaving their way deeper into the market, easing past merchants bartering excitedly with perusing customers, moving further and further from the safety of the Road.

'Boy!' cried a man with an oily, curled moustache, 'can I interest you in these delightful Sugar-filled Snail Shells?'

'No thanks!' Dale gulped, flinching away.

'Perhaps some Jellied Earthworms, then?' he continued, but the goblins had already ushered them on.

They came at last to a large marquee striped in purple and gold, looming over the stalls surrounding it. Their goblin guides stood sentry at the entrance, one on each side. Brooke wondered what would happen if they tried to run away.

'Pop in there,' instructed their goblin guide, with a nod at the curtained doorway.

Willow looked as though she was, in fact, steeling herself to run, or fight, or at least argue with the goblins. But she didn't. She simply cast a grim smile at Brooke and

Dale, and pushed her way into the marquee. They hurried after her, and one of the goblins snickered.

Inside, the marquee was spacious but dimly lit and the air was stuffy, like there wasn't enough oxygen for all of them. An earthy scent met Brooke's nostrils and she stifled a sneeze. Ornamental rugs covered wooden boards on the floor, but apart from a table, four chairs and a couple of candelabras casting a flickering glow around the room, the marquee interior was empty.

Almost empty.

A man sat on one of the chairs with his back to them, his black cloak draped over the chair obscuring most of his body. But Brooke could see his left leg, coated in black mail, and one jet black boot, muddied from travel. And there was a sword across his lap.

'At last.'

Next to her, Brooke felt Willow stiffen, as if an electric shock had just passed through her bones.

Suddenly, the inside of the marquee wasn't just stuffy. It felt too small - claustrophobic - like it was tightening around them. Brooke's heart, which had been pumping steadily harder while they followed the goblins, was now jackhammering in her chest.

The man in black stood, leaning his sword carefully against the edge of the table. He turned towards them and smiled, spreading his hands. 'Good to see you, Willow.'

It's him, Brooke thought instinctively. *This is the Betrayer, the one we saw after leaving the mountain.*

Commander Hysst.

Without thinking, she took Willow's hand to stop her from lunging at him again, but the Woodsgirl's grip was limp, almost lifeless. Brooke looked and saw tears welling in Willow's eyes. Dale had taken her other hand.

'I'm so stupid,' came Willow's shuddered whisper. 'I led us straight to him.'

'Come now,' said Hysst, smiling. He gestured at the table. 'Sit.'

They approached the table as one. Brooke was vaguely aware her legs had turned to rubber. As soon as they moved away from the marquee entrance, two Doomgaard soldiers stepped inside to block their escape, their boots clunking heavily on the floorboards.

The goblins betrayed us, Brooke thought. *And we were so close to safety*. She glanced at Dale as they pulled out chairs to sit – he was very pale.

Hysst remained standing, one black-gloved hand resting on his chair. From below, the purple scar running along his jaw and throat was hideous.

'You three travelled far, didn't you?' he said. 'All the way from the Druyad mountain, across the Barrows, to here. That's quite a journey, especially for two *visitors* to our lands. You must have had help.'

It wasn't really a question, and none of them answered.

'Of course you did. I suppose word's gotten round about what happened, and there'll be plenty who're sympathetic to your cause. What exactly *is* your cause, anyway? Why are you helping them, Willow?'

Willow's mouth remained shut; her tears had dried before falling, and flecks of gold in her hazel eyes were beginning to shimmer.

Hysst grinned down at her, his ugly scar contorting further. 'Do you want to know what I think, friend? I'll tell you. I think you're trying to get them to the Druyads because you mistakenly believe they'll help you. But they won't. And here's why – ' He leaned closer. ' – Druyads help no-one but themselves, and they definitely aren't interested in participating in the misadventures of their *slaves*.'

'I'm not a slave,' Willow replied through gritted teeth.

'That's right, she's not,' added Brooke.

Hysst shifted his gaze towards her, and she felt her blood run cold. Suddenly, she was more aware than ever of the two soldiers standing at the marquee entrance, and of the swords strapped to their sides. They were big men in heavy armour, and they were just kids.

'And what's your name?'

Brooke considered returning to her no-response policy, but some part of her knew if she didn't answer now, Hysst might do something terrible to them.

'My name is Brooke Woods,' she said defiantly.

'Well, my dear Brooke, I'm afraid you don't know Willow as well as you think you do.' He scraped back his chair and sat, resting a hand on the pommel of his sword. 'The Woodsgirl does not serve the Druyads by *choice*, as she may have you believe. She's been exiled from her people, you see. Cast out like some unwanted animal.'

'That's not true,' said Dale. 'You're lying.'

'Am I?' Hysst's grin widened, repulsive now. 'Why don't you tell them the truth, Willow? For a change.'

Brooke and Dale looked at her. She was staring fixedly at the table.

'My people… sent me away,' she said slowly. 'They didn't want me around because I… can't do the things I'm supposed to be able to do, by now.'

'What things?' asked Dale.

'Magic.' Her voice began to rise in volume. 'Haven't you realised yet? I'm *not good* at magic. I never have been.'

'But, you are,' said Brooke. 'You rescued us on the mountain in our world, and from the robbers on the road.'

'And you turned those soldiers into slugs,' added Dale.

'Not on purpose!' Willow cried. 'My magic barely worked with the robbers, and I didn't mean to turn the others into slugs. I was trying to do a disarming spell. And on the mountain, that wasn't even…'

She lowered her head. Hysst watched the exchange in silence, that ugly smile still twisting his lips as candelabra light played across his face. Brooke reached for Willow's shoulder. 'Listen – '

'No,' Willow snapped, jerking away. 'I'm not *good* at magic, at controlling it. That's why I'm with the Druyads. He's right – I'm not there by choice, as their servant. I've been exiled. And now look where I've gotten us – I'm going to get you both *killed*.'

'Killed?' Hysst said bemusedly. Then he laughed, and Brooke thought her blood might have frozen in her veins at the sound of it. 'My dear Willow, none of you are in any danger of that. Well, depending on the choices you make now, of course. You can be wise or you can be foolish, that's up to you. But admitting to the reality of your situation is the first step, and – '

'What about you?' Willow cried, furious now. 'What about the reality of *your* situation? You say I was bound to serve the Druyads, but you were bound to them as well, to *protect* them. What you did was just… just the *worst thing* imaginable!'

Hysst held her golden gaze for a moment before speaking again. When he did, his tone was softer.

'There's so much you don't understand, Willow. You call me a liar, a betrayer… but they've been lying to you from the very beginning. I believed them too, of course, for most of my life. I would have died in their service if I'd had to. I was *willingly* duty-bound to them, don't forget – I *chose* to serve. And I probably would have continued to do so, maybe forever, until someone revealed the truth to me. He opened my eyes and helped me see things for how they really were. After that, I knew exactly what I had to do. Don't get me wrong, it wasn't easy, not at all. But it had to be done. It was *necessary*. And now he wants to meet you, too.'

For what felt like the longest time, no-one spoke. Outside the marquee, the noise of the market was strangely dimmed. When the silence finally broke again, it was Dale who asked the question. 'Who is he?'

Hysst spoke the name reverently: 'Decymero.'

'It can't be,' Willow breathed. 'That's impossible. He... he doesn't exist.'

'He does, and always has. He's been aware of you all since you came back through the portal, even before I knew about you.' Speaking directly to Brooke and Dale, he added: 'And he wants to help get you back home.'

'He does?' said Brooke. She felt Willow's eyes turn on her.

'How?' asked Dale.

Hysst spread his hands again and smiled. 'There's only one way to find out – you'll have to meet him, in person. Face to face.'

Brooke jumped as Willow slammed her fist on the table.

'NO!' she yelled. Hysst didn't flinch. 'These are just more of your lies. He doesn't *exist*, not anymore, if he ever did. He's just a name, a word, a *swear* that people use when they can't think of anything worse. Don't pretend you're on some sort of noble quest for the truth, or something like that. You *murdered* innocent people and you're still doing it – there's nothing noble about that.'

'You don't know as much as you think you do, Willow.'

'I know enough! I know what's right, and what isn't.'

'Willow,' said Dale, 'maybe we should, you know... hear him out, at least? I mean, if this Dess-a-mero person can help us get home – '

'He can't, because he isn't real,' she spat. 'You're new here, you don't know what you're talking about.'

Dale's face reddened. 'Well, it sounds to me like you don't, either.'

Willow's mouth dropped open; the golden flecks in her hazel eyes rapidly gathered around her pupils.

'Listen....' Brooke began again.

'It's your choice, then,' said Willow, to both of them. 'You can come with me, or you can go with him. I won't make you. But I promise, if you go to Decymero, you'll die. That's the way it is.'

'The choice is yours,' Hysst echoed, drumming his fingers on the pommel of his sword.

Brooke and Dale stared at one another across the table. Willow sat back in her chair, arms folded, trembling with rage.

'Dale, are you serious?'

'I don't know. Maybe. I mean... we have to get home, Brooke. We've been gone too long already. Everyone will be worried about us.'

Brooke felt her gaze drawn back to Hysst. He watched them in silence, waiting. His icy blue eyes seemed to pierce right into her soul.

We've been gone too long already.

'How do we know you're telling the truth?' she said to Hysst.

He shrugged. 'You don't. But how do you know she is, either?' Brooke glanced at Willow, who was now staring at the floor.

Everyone will be worried about us. But we can't leave Willow here. And we can't go back without...

'Dale, what about... you know...'

She didn't see Hysst's eyes flash across the table in that moment, but it didn't matter. A second later, there was a commotion just outside the entrance to the marquee. Hysst turned in his chair, just as the two guards were yanked bodily out through the doorway. Their shouts of surprise were immediately cut off.

'What was that?' Dale said. From her side of the table, Brooke saw Hysst's face harden.

All four of them rose to their feet as a dark-haired boy burst into the marquee. He had a sword in his hand.

'CHARLIE!' Brooke cried.

He levelled the sword at Hysst and said, 'Let them go.'

The Betrayer's face lit up with malevolent satisfaction. His sword was already in his hand.

'So good to see you again, Charlie Flint. I thought we'd lost you.'

'Let them go,' Charlie repeated.

'My boy,' Hysst said, 'this isn't what you think. Your friends and I have been enjoying some lively conversation here. We're getting to know each other. Why don't you put your weapon away and join us?'

'Last chance.'

At that, Hysst's expression darkened. His grin vanished.

'I admire your bravery, boy,' he said, 'but I don't mind bringing you back to Doomgaard in two pieces, if I have to.' His own sword, double-edged and ferociously sharp, glinted in the amber light from the candelabras.

'Come on, then,' Charlie shot back. 'What're you waiting for?'

'Charlie, no!' Brooke cried.

The Betrayer shifted his feet and spun his sword with casual expertise in one hand; it emitted a metallic humming sound as it cut through the air. *Whuumm, whuumm.*

'Alright then, boy,' he growled, both hands going to the hilt. 'Let's see how that toy blade holds up against real steel.'

He stepped forward, raising his blade. Charlie held his sword up to block the imminent blow. Brooke shut her eyes.

The clash of metal on metal was tremendously loud inside the marquee. Brooke had expected to hear Charlie scream, but the only sound that followed was a grunt of surprise. She looked.

Some creature was between Charlie and Hysst. It held an axe, sturdy as a roof beam, just above Charlie. The axe head was locked with Hysst's sword.

'Step back, chap,' it said. Charlie obeyed.

The sword and axe came apart with a piercing metallic screech. A half-second later, the walls of the marquee crashed inwards as more of the creatures, bulky and grey-skinned, burst inside brandishing axes and clubs and slings. Brooke, Dale and Willow darted to the far side of the table, out of Hysst's reach.

The scar-faced knight moved back a pace, readjusting his feet.

'Ah yes, the trolls,' he said, his voice thick with hate. 'Just as ugly as they say.'

The trolls lined themselves up on either side of Charlie, weapons in hand. Onlookers from the markets were gathering outside, peering through the destroyed walls of the marquee.

'Happen to think we're rather dashing, in our own way,' said one of the trolls.

'It's what inside that counts,' added another.

'Unless you're a mud-eating Swamp Licker…'

'…then it's *all* bad, really.'

'This fella looks like he's licked a few swamps in his time – '

'Enough, monsters!' Hysst pointed his blade at Charlie. 'Let the boy go and I promise he'll live.'

'Let me go?' Charlie said. 'I'm not their *prisoner*. They're my friends.'

'And comrades,' said one of the trolls.

'Also, we've recently dealt with your sort,' said another, patting the head of his club against his palm. 'And there were a lot more of you then, too. So my good fellow, I suggest you sheath your weapon and leave this place in short order. You are, after all, rather outnumbered.'

The horrible grin broke out on Hysst's face again.

'Outnumbered? You're very much mistaken. Men!'

Instantly, several people in the crowd stepped forward and threw off their cloaks, revealing black armour underneath. Onlookers scattered in alarm as Doomgaardians brandishing swords, spears and crossbows encircled the marquee. Brooke guessed there might be at least twenty of them. The goblins, she noticed, did nothing to intervene.

'Foolish monsters,' sneered Hysst. 'My men underestimated you once before – they won't do so again. You bandits will pay for your crimes in Doomgaard before Decymero himself, and – '

'Twice,' interrupted Charlie.

The Betrayer glared at him. 'What?'

'Your men underestimated the trolls *twice*.' He counted on his fingers. 'Once, when they raided your wagon and freed your prisoners, and twice, when they kicked your butts at the bridge. That's two times since yesterday. Not bad, for monsters.'

The troll with the club grinned. 'Third time's a charm, eh?'

Hysst's face flushed red in fury. But before he could speak, someone else stepped out of the crowd and addressed him in a quavering voice. 'You can't say that name.'

Brooke recognised the man. He was dressed in plain clothes, and had been standing next to a stall – just a merchant, there for the markets. He was the one who'd offered them Sugar-filled Snail Shells. When Hysst replied, his tone was ice: 'What name?'

'Angus,' Brooke heard the troll with the club mutter, 'take them and go.'

'You know,' the merchant said. His legs trembled, but he stood tall. 'We don't speak that name, sir. Not in the Barrows, not anywhere. That's a foul word, a *Doomgaard* word, and it isn't allowed. You should go, right now.'

For a moment, no-one spoke. The Doomgaardians stared at the merchant, and for one hopeful second, Brooke thought they might actually leave. There were after all, hundreds, maybe thousands, of people in the market – the odds were stacked against them.

Then Commander Hysst rolled his eyes and motioned with his sword. A crossbow discharged with a *thwap*. The merchant gasped once, and went down.

'No!' Brooke cried.

In almost the same moment, the soldier who'd fired the arrow toppled sideways into a fruit stall with a stone lodged in his skull. Apples and pears rolled into the Road as the troll reloaded his sling.

'Angus, GO!' yelled the troll with the club.

Before Hysst or the Doomgaardians could react, the trolls grabbed Willow, Brooke and Dale and flung them towards the marquee entrance. Angus scooped Charlie up in one burly arm and, as the other trolls launched themselves at the soldiers, shepherded all four of them away into the crowd.

Behind, they heard the *thwap thwap thwap* of crossbows and the clash of metal. And with it, several dozen voices, all screaming.

<<>>

Angus the troll barged his way through the markets, Charlie under one arm, shoving past any unfortunate travellers who got in his way. Most scattered when they saw him coming but several were sent flying. Dale, Brooke and Willow stuck close by, following in his wake.

The marquee (or what remained of it) was already far behind, but they could still hear the noise of the skirmish: blades clashing, bowstrings twanging, stalls getting smashed to pieces in the melee. Visitors to the market were either fleeing the area or running towards it for a better look.

'Will they be ok?' Brooke gasped, struggling to keep up.

'They'll be fine,' replied the troll, but there was little conviction in his voice.

They reached the Stone Road again and made for the Throat. This time, the goblins simply stepped aside and allowed them to enter the tunnel - it seemed they weren't keen on picking sides once the element of surprise was gone.

And now they were in the Throat, leaving Crookedstone and the markets behind, descending into darkness. Here, the footsteps of travellers on the Stone Road made muted echoes off the earthen tunnel walls, creating a new kind of noise. It was claustrophobic in the tunnel, just like the marquee had been once they realised Hysst was there. The Stone Road was still beneath their feet.

'Alright, put me down,' said Charlie.

'We should keep going,' said Angus.

'Yeah but I *can* walk, you know.'

Angus set Charlie down and they all stopped to catch their breath. Other travellers in the tunnel passed by without a word.

'So,' Charlie said finally, straightening up. 'How're you guys?'

In response, Brooke threw her arms around him. Surprised and a little embarrassed, he awkwardly hugged her back; Dale made it even more awkward by embracing them both. They drew apart quickly when Angus started to move in. Willow watched in silence, her eyes glowing like headlights in the gloom of the tunnel.

'We're so glad you're alive!' exclaimed Brooke.

'We thought you'd been eaten by now,' said Dale, glancing at Angus.

Charlie laughed. 'I thought the same about you, squirt. I had trolls for company, so I was fine. Right, Angus?'

Angus nodded but said nothing. Brooke noticed he was wringing his big grey hands.

'We were ok too,' Dale said. 'We had Willow...' And then, remembering their last exchange in the marquee, he stopped talking.

'Hi, Willow,' said Charlie, with a nod.

'Hello,' she replied. Then: 'The troll's right, we need to keep going. Come on.'

She turned and stalked off down the tunnel.

'Charming,' said Charlie.

They had no choice but to follow, hurrying after her.

The Throat was illuminated by little orbs of multi-coloured light – reds, yellows, blues, greens, purples – which jumped from spot to spot on the walls, droning like bees. In places, they went out altogether, briefly plunging them into darkness, before reappearing again.

'Fire-fairies,' Angus explained, pointing at the orbs of light. 'They live in the walls. Best not to touch them.'

They walked on, never slowing. Travellers continued in both directions; dozens of conversations reverberated around them. After a time the Road levelled, then began to climb very gradually upwards. Brooke pressed at a stitch in her side.

'So what happened?' she said to Charlie, doing her best to keep pace with Willow. 'The last time I saw you was on the mountain, when the ghouls grabbed you.'

'Oh yeah, those things,' Charlie said with disdain. 'They dragged me through the portal and the next thing I knew, I was inside that big room.'

And as they went on, Charlie recounted for them the events of the last two days, from his capture by the ghouls to being rescued by the trolls and his encounter with the Doomgaard, right up until they'd reached the markets that morning.

'We were unloading Woolly when we saw them, the Doomgaard soldiers. They were disguised but they're not hard to spot, even in a crowd. We followed them to where you were, and once we realised what was happening, well…'

'You were very brave,' said Brooke.

'Anyone can be brave when they have trolls as backup,' Charlie said dismissively. 'Plus, I hate Hysst - he's burned down farms and villages all over the Barrowlands, for no reason. And they've taken loads of people away to Doomgaard as prisoners.'

'Are you sure?' said Dale. 'I mean, maybe people were just saying that. You know how stories change, by word of mouth.'

Up ahead, Willow scoffed bitterly.

'I'm sure,' said Charlie. 'I saw it for myself: villages in ruins, fields burned black. The Doomgaard don't care who they hurt, and no-one's doing anything to stop them.'

'Well, maybe someone can help where we're going,' said Brooke.

'Where *are* we going? And what happened to you guys, since the mountain?'

Now it was Brooke and Dale's turn to tell their story. Charlie and Angus listened as they told them about the ghouls and the Wee People and Jayne and Percius. The fire-fairies buzzed over the walls around them, winking in and out; Willow moved through the shadows further along the tunnel, her cloak billowing behind her.

'And then you appeared,' Brooke finished.

Charlie nodded. 'I've heard them mention Decymero before. Only the Doomgaard, though - no-one else will say it.'

'It's a foul word,' said Angus, wrinkling his over-large nose.

'The Doomgaard – they'll stop chasing us when we're out of the Barrowlands?' asked Dale, stepping aside as another traveller hurried past them. Many of those coming from the market side of the cliff seemed to be in a rush to leave.

'I think so,' replied Angus. 'Doomgaard soldiers haven't been seen in Ulandai for a *long* time. Besides, they're afraid of the High Druyads, the ones you're going to see.'

'Afraid, because of their magic?' said Brooke.

'For many reasons. But yes, their magic, too.'

'Good, I'll be glad when… hey, Willow, wait up!'

The Woodsgirl hadn't slowed at all since they'd entered the tunnel, weaving between travellers going in both directions.

'Willow!'

'It's no use,' panted Dale, side-stepping a man with several birds perched across his shoulders. 'She's mad at us.'

'At you, looks like,' Charlie clarified.

'She's going to lose us,' said Brooke, 'and I don't want to get lost in here, underground!'

'It's a tunnel, there's only one way out,' said Dale. 'And look!' They missed his pointing finger in the shadows. 'There's light up ahead – I think we're almost at the end.'

'That's a relief. It's creepy down here.'

Dale was right. Further along, the Throat began to slope upwards and they could see the first suggestions of sunlight on the tunnel walls. The fire-fairies became fewer in number as they drew closer to the exit.

'Hey, Willow,' Brooke called, 'can we take a break when we get out? Please? My feet are aching.'

'Same here,' said Dale.

Willow glanced back over her shoulder, then abruptly spun round and yelled, 'LOOK OUT!'

Dale and Brooke turned just in time to see a massive dark form barrelling towards them, its head brushing the tunnel ceiling. They leapt aside, narrowly avoiding the enormous feet of a giant as it thundered past. Willow and the other remaining travellers in the tunnel pressed themselves to the wall, giving it plenty of space. It thundered on up the slope, vanishing into sunlight.

'What was *that*?' cried Brooke.

'Just a giant,' said Charlie. 'First time seeing one?'

'What was it running from?' Dale said, but if anyone replied he didn't hear it. More travellers were following the giant, going for the tunnel exit. As they passed, they picked up snaps of conversation.

' – you see them? Must've been fifty or more…'

' – definitely Doomgaard, with that dark armour…'

' – didn't know trolls could talk!'

' – heard what he said, right? Decymero – '

Suddenly, Willow was there, earnest. 'Let's go, now!'

They followed the other travellers, running for the way out. The light grew brighter as they neared the end of the Throat. Dale had never felt more relieved to get out of a place.

'As soon as we're outside,' Willow said, 'we're going straight to the bridge. It's right ahead, just down the hill. Don't stop until we're across the river.'

And just like that, the tunnel came to an end, and they were outside once again. They all raised their arms to shield their eyes from the harsh light. The daylight was intensely bright after being in the darkness of the Throat.

'Alright, straight for the bridge,' Willow repeated. 'And remember, keep going until we're all…'

She stopped.

'Oh no.'

The bridge over the Thunderflow River could be directly in front of them just down the hill, but they would have no way of knowing for sure - everything up ahead was completely obscured in a wall of thick white.

'Fog,' whispered Dale.

'Ghouls,' said Brooke.

'Run!' cried Willow.

They ran, straight into the fog. The Road - they could only see some of it ahead - sloped down the hill towards where the river must be. The fog quickly enveloped them, as it had done back on the mountain; inside the white, the sound of their breathing seemed louder, as though they were trapped in a very small room. They could see no other travellers now, not even the giant who'd blundered past them not so long ago.

'Stay focused!' Willow shouted. 'If you start to forget, just keep saying your name.'

I'm Brooke Woods. I'm thirteen years old. I was on a class trip…

The roar of rushing water came to them from somewhere further down the hill. They were close now. Behind, the enormous cliff face - once the weapon of Skorvoluc the giant - had vanished in the fog.

'I see it!' exclaimed Brooke. 'I see the bridge!'

'Me too,' Charlie said. 'We're almost - '

The ghouls came from nowhere, dark shapes in the fog. They saw their eyes first, glowing red, speeding towards the Road to block their path.

'Weapons!' barked Angus, reaching for his club. Charlie drew his sword.

'We don't have weapons!' cried Brooke.

'Get behind me,' Willow ordered, arms spread, palms facing down.

The bridge was indeed visible now through the fog. The end nearest them was flanked on either side by weathered stone statues that could have been wolves or bears. Just beyond them, silvery water rumbled by from right to left. They were agonisingly close to safety.

But the ghouls, many more than before, had them surrounded. Their black-haired bodies whipped in and out of view as the fog swirled around them, and they spoke to one another in their horrible snarling drawl. Only their red eyes were clear, stabbing through the white, watching them hungrily.

'There're too many,' said Dale, turning on the spot. 'They're everywhere.'

'We'll fight,' said Charlie, trying to mask the fear in his voice. 'We can't let Hysst win - we're so close.'

'What are they waiting for?' said Brooke.

As if in response, the ghouls charged.

Charlie and Angus raised their weapons; Willow lifted her hands. Brooke screamed and ducked down.

A crackling sound filled the air. With a *whoosh*, orange flames leapt up from the ground and exploded out towards the onrushing ghouls. Those who were closest were thrown back, singed and shrieking. The others staggered away from the fire, covering their ugly faces with sinewy black arms. The fog around them began to disperse.

Brooke stood and looked about in amazement. 'Willow, was that you?'

'No, I - '

'Who cares!' yelled Charlie. 'Look, there's a gap right there - run!'

They made for the bridge, passing through a break in the fire wall. The flames were red hot on either side of them.

'Get across!' Angus shouted.

The ghouls were coming at them again, manoeuvring around the circle of fire, which was already diminishing. They were going to cut them off, just a few feet from the bridge.

'Back, you beasts!' Angus roared.

The troll swung his club, clobbering the nearest ghoul. The creature howled in pain and stumbled back into the thinning fog. Charlie swiped at another with his sword, slashing its arm; it retreated immediately.

'Come on!' cried Dale, who was already between the statues. The waters of the Thunderflow rushed past nearby. 'Get onto the bridge!'

Dale didn't see it coming.

The ghoul had been waiting behind one of the statues, hidden in the fog. Just as Dale stepped onto the bridge, it dropped towards him, eyes red, teeth flashing.

'DALE!' Brooke screamed.

They saw him go down under the ghoul, but something else was already happening. The Road beneath their feet had begun to tremble.

A dark figure materialised out of the fog, barrelling towards them from the far side of the bridge. Brooke caught a glimpse of hooves and a mane, and saw light flare on steel. Then the ghoul who'd landed on Dale was tossed aside, smashing into one of the statues. Brooke saw it had been cleaved in two.

The horse, huge and dark and sleek, galloped past on their left, just missing them. It was instantly followed by another, which passed on their right. More were coming, charging over the bridge out of the fog.

'Get Dale!' Charlie shouted over the rumble of hooves.

Angus bent low and came up with Dale. Brooke's heart skipped a beat - his body was limp in the troll's arms.

The remaining ghouls scattered or were mowed down by the riders, who chased them off into the fog. Brooke and the others hugged the statue opposite the dead ghoul until the last of the horses had ridden past and the bridge became still again. Finally, as the last of the ghouls were chased off into the abating fog, one rider doubled back, cantering his enormous horse up to them. He was armoured from head to toe in polished silver-blue steel and his sword dripped with black blood.

Before he could lift his visor, Brooke cried, 'Our friend needs help!'

The knight studied them for a moment as his mount pawed at the ground.

'Who are you?' he asked in a deep voice.

'We need passage to your healer,' Willow said. 'Right away. He's injured.'

The knight glanced at Dale, who appeared lifeless in Angus's arms.

'Indeed he is.' He pushed up his visor, revealing green eyes and bushy eyebrows. 'But the nearest healer is in the city. He may not make it there.'

'Please,' Brooke pleaded, her voice cracking. 'We have to try. Please help us get there.'

Other riders were approaching now, resheathing their swords. The knight considered it for a moment longer, then seemed to make up his mind.

'We'll bring you to the city,' he said, 'but the troll can't come.'

'What?' Charlie said, indignant. 'We're not leaving him behind. He's our friend!'

'It's the law.'

'Don't worry, Charlie,' said Angus, 'these lads can take it from here. I'll be getting back to Crookedstone anyway, need to see how the others fared. Daresay there'll be a tale or two about it tonight.'

Charlie looked from Angus to the knight, then back to the troll.

'We'll meet again,' Angus assured him. 'Now, help me get this one onto a horse.'

Willow gave Dale another one of her purple pills and colour returned to his cheeks, but his clothes were bloodied under his cloak. One of the riders lifted him carefully onto his saddle, cradling him in one burly arm. Charlie got up behind the rider, while Willow and Brooke took positions behind another. The horses were enormous.

'Fortune smiled on you today,' said the green-eyed knight. 'We were on our way to the Barrows - there's much to be dealt with there.' He gestured at the riders. 'These two will bring you safely to Hammerfall. When you arrive, go straight to the House of the Healer. Don't delay or your friend will die, if he doesn't before you get there.'

He turned his steed and galloped off towards the Throat, followed by the other riders. The fog had now cleared, and they could see the bodies of ghouls scattered over the hill among dozens of hoofprints. Gaping travellers gathered near the mouth of the tunnel moved aside to let the riders pass.

Brooke's rider snapped the reins and their horse bulleted forward. Angus the troll waved as they crossed the Thunderflow River and rode on into the Kingdom of Ulandai, leaving the Barrowlands behind.

Chapter Eleven: Fort Hammerfall

If you'd asked Charlie Flint what the landscape of Ulandai was like - how much of it was ploughed field and how much was forest, how many villages there were, whether it was largely flat or dominated by hills and viewpoints - he wouldn't have been able to tell you. Their journey from the bridge to the city was a blur to him because, like Brooke, he was exhausted.

Hours of non-stop travel over the course of two days had left him with blistered feet and wearied muscles. The trolls seemed to be capable of almost relentless movement, trudging along on their short legs at a constant pace over any type of terrain, but Charlie, athletic though he was, wasn't built for such journeying. He desperately missed his own bed, and his games console, and above all else, cheesy deep-pan pizza.

The Ulandai riders drove their horses on all morning without stopping. Charlie sat behind the knight who held the now-unconscious Dale, doing his best to stay awake and not tumble from the saddle. Riding alongside them, Brooke and the girl with the greenish skin seemed equally tired - Brooke was slumped forward in front of their rider while Willow fought to keep her eyes open behind him.

Charlie looked across at Brooke, his classmate, who he'd assumed he'd never see again. Her blonde hair, normally pristine, was tangled and greasy, and the green cloak she wore was caked with mud; there were dark rings under her eyes and her skin was pale, though not as alarmingly white as Dale's. Charlie hadn't gotten a proper look at the squirt's injury, but his glimpse of the blood soaking through Dale's sweater told him enough.

He was equally worried about the trolls. There'd been a lot of Doomgaard soldiers in the market and many of them had crossbows. The trolls were a tough bunch but the odds hadn't been in their favour there.

Is it my fault? Charlie thought. *Did I lead them into a trap?*

It didn't matter though, not really. Even if he hadn't rushed off at the sight of Brooke and Dale, they would probably have gotten caught up in Hysst's violence anyway. He wasn't sure exactly what happened in that marquee, but from what they'd told him about their adventures so far, the Woodsgirl could've given Hysst a run for his money.

He watched her for a moment. Her hood had fallen back and her red hair whipped about in the breeze. She must be around the same age as them... but heck, for all he knew she could have been younger, or a hundred years older. She clearly wasn't human, though only her strangely-tinted skin and golden-flecked eyes betrayed her in that respect. He realised with a start that those eyes were on him, and he looked away quickly.

The sun was high and hot when the horses began to climb steadily uphill. Now Charlie did begin to take in their surroundings: they were in a vast open expanse of green grass and the Stone Road was curving gradually up towards a rise stretching across their view; lone trees were dotted here and there, and creatures that looked like cows (though they weren't) grazed lazily nearby. Other travellers on the Road moved aside as the Ulandai horses thundered past.

'Are you awake back there?' the rider called. It was the first time he'd spoken in a while.

'Yeah, just about,' Charlie replied. On the other horse, he saw Brooke sit up, roused awake by their voices.

'We're almost there,' said the rider. 'Your friend doesn't look good.'

Charlie leaned around him, clutching the saddle for support. Dale was paler than ever and his face was slick with sweat. Bizarrely, Charlie wondered how much detention he'd get if his classmate didn't survive the trip. He shoved the thought aside.

'There's a healer, right? He'll be able to help him?'

'We'll see. There's the city.'

Charlie squinted ahead. They were coming over the grassy rise and the summit of a mountain had appeared, looming impressively in the distance. But as the horses galloped further and the rise levelled out, he realised that what he thought was the peak was only part of the mountain slope, a craggy outcrop of rock, towering high above the surrounding plains. The mountain continued growing to the east, rising and rising, its summit cloaked in white cloud. The sheer size of it took the breath from Charlie's lungs and made his heart pound in his chest. He'd never seen anything that size before, and the effect was potent.

The city itself rested about halfway up in a sort of plateau, as though it was being cradled by the mountain. A series of high walls of ashen-coloured stone ran in concentric circles around the city buildings within, becoming more sheer as each level rose above the last; towers in their dozens or even hundreds jutted up from behind each wall, making the entire settlement look like some sort of spiny animal. The Stone Road curved around the lower reaches of the mountain, with another highway snaking off from it up the slopes to colossal gates set in the first wall of the city. A river, sparkling blue in the midday light, cascaded down in waterfalls from the far side of the mountain and off towards the sea, just visible on the horizon.

'Fort Hammerfall,' said the rider, 'the capital of the Kingdom.'

They'd already begun to descend towards the plains around the mountain, which were really an enormous valley encircling it. A number of tributary roads on the plains branched off from the Stone Road, connecting it to small villages and fields lying in the shadow of Hammerfall.

Charlie tried to remember what the trolls had told him about the mountains in Uland.

'It used to be a giant, right?'

'Yes - Bornak the Brutal. They say he once devoured an entire army that dared attack him. Just scooped them into his mouth as they charged.'

'That's... pretty nasty.'

'The ancient giants were cruel,' agreed the rider. 'They loved war and death and enslavement. So yes, pretty nasty.'

Charlie shielded his eyes, tracing the Road as it wound across the plains ahead.

'So the giant died,' he said, 'and turned into a mountain over time - '

'Over thousands of years, yes.'

' - and they just... built a city on him?'

'That's right.'

'And that's the same for all the mountains in Uland?'

'All the biggest ones, yes.' The rider glanced over his shoulder. 'Why, what are the mountains made of where you're from?'

Charlie shrugged, mostly to himself. 'I dunno. Stone, I guess.'

Maybe I should've listened in Geography...

Fort Hammerfall grew larger and more imposing as they crossed the plain, passing travellers and villages and Ulanders, all of whom looked entirely human to Charlie. Many eyed Willow suspiciously as they blurred past, but if it bothered her, she didn't show it. They were quickly lost in the dust kicked up by the horses.

They left the Road and began to ascend the mountain, riding into the shadow of the city itself. The riders' steeds never slowed, even when galloping uphill. *These aren't like our horses*, Charlie thought.

The lower walls of Hammerfall towered over them as they approached the gates. Like Crookedstone, the city used the mountain as natural cover at one end and the walls as a highly defensible position at the other to keep enemies out (though that hadn't stopped the Doomgaard waltzing right into Crookedstone, Charlie noted to himself). But these walls were something different entirely, rising high above them, many metres thick. This really was a fortress, built to repel even the most fearsome assault.

The gates stood open as they arrived. Guards on either side waved them through without question, and the riders thundered on into the city.

Much like the landscape of Ulandai, most of Hammerfall passed Charlie in a blur, one of bricks and cobbles and thatchwork this time. The knights rode single-file through the city streets, barking out 'Move! Make way!' to anyone in their path. Charlie caught glimpses of storefronts and taverns, blacksmiths and armourers, apothecaries and alchemists, banks and guildhalls; the horses cantered along narrow, rough-cobbled streets between houses and galloped through wide spaces where citizens of Hammerfall congregated to dance and sing and eat and drink, and in some cases, to brawl.

They passed through inner gates on the second and third walls, always ascending, before the riders finally reined in the horses, which were now slathering at the mouth.

'This is where we part ways,' said the knight holding Dale. 'I'm taking this one to the House of the Healer. You three go with Falton there, he'll bring you to the Citymaster. Druyads protect you.'

Charlie slipped down from the saddle onto the cobbled street. His legs were weary and he almost collapsed when his feet touched the ground. The other knight, Falton, also swung off his horse. Brooke and Willow followed his lead and Brooke actually did collapse, her legs folding like an accordion. Falton helped her up with a chuckle.

'Granted, it was a long ride,' he said, as a stableboy led his horse away. 'But we'll go on foot from here. Don't worry, we're close. Let's go.'

They followed him deeper into this new district of the city. Here, the streets were much narrower and nearly deserted. The buildings were also noticeably grander and better maintained than those in the lower sections of Hammerfall. Citizens they passed here wore fine clothes and looked at them with unconcealed distaste.

After a time, they arrived at the town hall, an imposing marble building surrounded by neatly-trimmed grass and beds of indigo-coloured flowers. The flower heads turned towards them as they approached and followed them as they walked by, and Charlie was certain he saw their petals actually waving at him when he looked their way. Brooke and Willow were too tired to notice.

Falton escorted them into the town hall and straight to the office of the Citymaster, a tall, skinny man with a hooked nose and spectacles. He wore an elaborate gold chain around his neck, and he peered at them across his desk as they told their story, sipping from a comically-small china teacup. Willow did most of the talking, omitting quite a few portions of her account along the way. Charlie explained his side of things, finishing with the ghoul ambush at the bridge and Dale's injury.

'He's been taken to the healer, sir,' added Falton, who stood behind them, helm under one arm. His sandy hair was streaked with grey and thinning on top.

The Citymaster nodded and sipped his tea, extending his little finger as he did so. His wood-panelled office was spacious and smelled of tobacco, or something very much like it. Charlie's hand went unconsciously to the hilt of his sword each time the man spoke.

'Quite the journey you've had,' the Citymaster observed, with practised eloquence. 'I must say, I'm impressed you've made it this far on your own. The Barrowlands are lawless and untamed...'

And free, Charlie thought.

'... and dangerous for any traveller, especially non-natives such as yourselves. You were fortunate to have such a guide with you. And trolls! One can only imagine what that must have been like, journeying with wild beasts.'

Charlie bit his lip.

'We will of course accommodate you here in the capital. There are those on the council who will wish to hear more of your story, and of the land you two come from. Despite what many say about us across the continent, the Ulandai are welcoming and hospitable to all, even folk of magical persuasion.'

'Thank you,' said Willow, with some restraint.

'What about our friend?' asked Brooke. 'Will he be ok?'

'Oh yes, certainly. Our healer is very good, the best in the land, actually. She'll see to him right away. Sadly, it's not the first ghoul-related wound we've encountered of late. Those monsters are becoming more bold with each passing day.'

He beckoned a servant over. 'Make preparations for our guests, please.' The servant hurried off.

'You'll have the freedom of the city while you're here, naturally. The timing of your arrival is actually most fortuitous. As you may know - or not, as you're from a foreign country - the Summit of Uland is due to begin tomorrow. Quite the event, really. All rather last-minute, too. The heads of each region are arriving this evening for the Summit Banquet, due to be held in the Throne Room, and I'm certain you'll be invited, given the nature of your being here. In fact, as Citymaster, I'm taking it upon myself to *ensure* you're there. The feast alone is worth your attendance. It's a sight to behold.'

Charlie's stomach growled at the word 'feast'.

'The Summit's been called?' said Willow. 'By who?'

'The Ulandking, officially. But the Factionheads are required to gather in the event an act of war takes place. And as of this week, it has. It's in the Agreement and must be adhered to, as long as the Pact remains in place.'

'An act of war,' Charlie said. 'You mean, what happened at the mountain?'

The Citymaster's demeanour changed.

'Regrettably. Doomgaard's outright dereliction of their duties - let's not mince our words, their *treachery* - in attacking the Druyad site on Aibal was effectively their declaration of war on the other Factions. Of course, their recent aggressive movements across Suthdren had been cause for alarm anyway, but assaulting a sacred place was a step too far. The Faction leaders were alerted immediately by the Druyads themselves - some sort of magical correspondence, I suppose - and hastened here, to Hammerfall, the nearest capital to Doomgaard, to discuss the best way to respond. Hence, the first Summit called in over twenty years.'

'Will the Woodspeople be here?' Willow asked quietly.

'Certainly. Each of the factions will be represented. We expect the High Druyads to attend too, of course.'

Willow breathed an audible sigh of relief at that. 'Good, we need to speak to them as soon as possible.'

'And you will.' The Citymaster clapped his hands together. 'But for now, I insist you rest from your long journey. Falton here will see you to your quarters, where you'll find lunch and fresh clothing have been prepared. And tonight, you'll dine with dignitaries.'

<<>>

They were escorted from the town hall and up the street to another grand-looking building in the Royal District with smooth stone walls and turrets. It was attached to the innermost ring wall of the city and, like the other buildings in the area, had a pair of guards in full silver-blue armour guarding the main entrance.

Falton, who seemed to have become their designated chaperone, led them inside to an ornate entrance hall and up two flights of stairs; here, he ushered them into a living area from which several doors opened. A fireplace on the far wall was set and ready to be lit later that day. Before it were several plush armchairs and footstools. A long dining table laden with food took up the centre of the room, and candelabras burned in each corner.

It's like a blown-up version of Jayne's hut, Brooke thought.

'Food's on the table,' said Falton, unnecessarily. 'You can choose whichever room you like. Someone will come back when there's news about your friend.'

'What is this place?' Brooke asked, staring at a painting on one wall featuring a king riding a white horse into battle.

'It's one of the royal suites. It was meant for one of the Factionheads and his entourage, but luckily for you they won't be coming, so it's all yours. If you need anything, just speak to the guards.'

He closed the door. They drifted over to the table and sat down.

'I feel bad for Dale,' Brooke said. 'He should be here for this. I hope he's ok.'

'He'll be fine,' said Willow, looking with distaste into one of the silver dishes on the table, which contained a variety of cold meats. 'The healer will take good care of him. We were fortunate, they're not always around - he could have ended up in the city infirmary and probably wouldn't have survived.'

'Cheery,' said Charlie, shovelling food onto his plate. Willow glanced across at him, unsure how to respond.

Brooke was fighting sleep, but continued: 'What happened at the bridge, with the fire? You said that wasn't you?'

'No.' Willow selected some fruit from a crystal bowl. 'I don't know who did that. Could have been some freak magical event. It happens sometimes.'

'Saved our bacon, anyway,' said Charlie through a mouthful of bread.

'Bacon?'

'Just an expression,' explained Brooke. She looked at Charlie, at his tousled black hair and dirt-stained face. 'Glad you're alive, Charles.'

'Me too. Surprised we haven't all been eaten or turned into frogs already, to be honest.'

They ate the rest of their lunch in silence then retired to their chosen bedrooms, dumping their cloaks and backpacks. Brooke found that her room was enormous and lavishly decorated in rosewood and velvet, with a four-poster bed against one wall, another plush armchair in the corner and a private bathroom through a side door. Through her window, she could see a walled courtyard with a little garden in the centre and beyond it, an enormous castle built into the side of the mountain, topped with a blue flag bearing a hammer and stars.

She ran a hand through her hair and grimaced. *I should wash up - I probably have ghoul blood on me.*

But tiredness drew her over to the bed, which was at least three times the size of the one she slept in at home. She knew she desperately needed to sleep, but vague memories of the dream - the nightmare about the spiral staircase, and the door, and the figure in the red light - filled her with fear. Maybe it was over now, though. Maybe it wouldn't happen again now that they were safe in the city.

I'll just rest my eyes. Just for a minute.

Brooke lay down and promptly fell asleep.

<<>>

The mid-afternoon sun beat down on the mountain. Far below her, the city bustled with anticipation. The Summit of Uland was a rare and important event, and the atmosphere in Hammerfall was electric.

Willow pushed a strand of red hair from her face. Perched on the rim of a turret, she could see a procession making its way through the city streets towards the Royal District, flanked by Ulandai guards. A flag borne at the head of the procession featured a diamond divided into four sections, each a different colour: green, red, blue and purple. The Elementals.

She looked down at her hands, turned them, studying her long green fingers. Her nails were chipped and dirty.

Why hadn't she done anything at the bridge? Why hadn't she reacted in time? She'd seen the ghoul drop from the statue, saw it knock Dale flat on his back and swipe at him with one clawed hand. It was a bad wound, she knew that, right across his chest. Ghoul claws were deadly sharp and often tipped with poison.

Why hadn't she done something? Was her magic really so weak?

If anyone can get you safely to the Druyads, it's Willow. I trust her completely.

She wished Jayne was here. The Seer would know what to do, she always did. Everin, her master, would also have known, but he was dead now. She was more alone than ever and the responsibility was becoming too weighty, even though they were close now to reaching their goal.

She would pass the Other-worlders on to the Druyads and they'd help them get home, and then…

Then what? What was next for her? With Everin gone she was without direction, without purpose. She'd been assigned to assist him, and that'd been a lifelong commitment. And she couldn't go back to her people, not now. She doubted they'd welcome her with open arms, anyway. She dreaded running into them here.

I hope Dale's ok.

It was strange, really. She shouldn't have to care about them, these children from another world. Yes, she'd brought them here, but she'd had no other choice in the moment - the ghouls would have taken them instead. Even those monsters could recognise an opportunity to impress (or appease) their master with a gift from beyond their realm. Or they'd simply have killed them.

And because of Jayne and her bothersome *belief* in her, she couldn't step away from the situation until they were with the Druyads. She was duty-bound to them, as she'd been to Everin.

But she knew it was more than that. She understood that she liked being around them, liked their company. She liked *them*, as a matter of fact, even though they didn't seem to know anything at all. They'd stood up for her against those bandits on the road - that was a kindness she rarely experienced from strangers, or even from people she knew.

Were they her… friends?

The Elemental procession was almost at the gate to the Royal District now. She could see their representatives, all clothed in brightly-coloured robes with staffs in hand, staring straight ahead as they walked. There were four of them, and each appeared to have at least ten servants trailing behind.

Maybe we should hear him out, at least? I mean, if this Decymero person can help us get home…

She shivered. That'd been a bad moment. She'd known exactly what Hysst had been doing and they'd sunk straight into it, like quicksand. The lies, the deception. Tools of the enemy. Everin had been right about that.

Hysst's words reverberated through her mind. *There's so much you don't understand, Willow. They've been lying to you from the very beginning.*

No, that was their way. The Doomgaard way. And Hysst was with them now, irrevocably gone, lost to the darkness.

She stood, the breeze catching her cloak. Something within her clicked into place. It had been there all along and it was becoming clear, slowly but surely.

Whether she was duty-bound or free, whether she owed it to them or not, it no longer mattered. The evil was there, waiting to snap them up. If she and Jayne and those who were left didn't intervene, they'd be lured into it, as Hysst had been. She didn't believe someone called Decymero was behind it - that was impossible, surely - but the darkness was alive and real in Uland. She knew *that* for a fact.

As the Elemental procession entered the Royal District below, Willow dropped from the turret and slipped back through her window.

Charlie looked down at the clothes laid out on his bed and sighed.

Falton had delivered them late in the afternoon. Like Brooke, Charlie had been unable to stay awake after going to his room - he was out as soon as his cheek touched the cool pillow on his bed and slept dreamlessly until the Ulandai knight knocked on his door.

'Your banquet garments,' Falton had said, handing him the neatly-folded set of clothes.

'You can't be serious,' said Charlie as he took them.

A half-grin played at the corner of Falton's mouth. 'Deadly serious, young sir. You're dining with the Factionheads, you've got to look your best.'

'And you'd wear this?'

'I don't have to, I'm a knight.'

He'd left at that, and now Charlie found himself staring at his outfit for the evening: a white shirt (laced, not buttoned), a deep blue tunic, slate-coloured trousers, a black leather belt and matching boots, and a blue cloak with a silver fastener shaped like a hammer.

The trolls would find this hilarious.

Charlie removed his filthy hiking gear and tossed it in the corner, then washed and dressed in front of a tall mirror in the bathroom. The Ulandai clothes fit surprisingly well (even the woollen socks and undergarments) but he still felt deeply uncomfortable in them. Fortunately, the cloak covered most of it.

He considered bringing his sword, but imagined the aged, rusty blade would look pretty feeble alongside the weapons carried by the Ulandai knights. He left it under the bed, out of sight.

Stepping out of his room, he found Brooke and Willow already in the living area of their quarters. They were both wearing dresses and blue cloaks, and they'd had their hair styled.

'They sent someone to do it,' said Willow sullenly.

'It took *ages*,' said Brooke.

'Well you both look great.'

'Shut up,' the girls said in unison.

Falton returned a few minutes later and led them from the building. It was now early evening; birds sang in the parapets, and the scent of lavender was in the air. They followed the knight along the wall of the inner courtyard - on the other side, the castle leered down at them, huge and foreboding, though it was dwarfed by the bulk of the mountain behind it. Its peak was lost in white cloud, far above them.

'Aren't we going to the banquet?' asked Brooke, doing her best to keep pace with the knight while hitching her dress up.

'Taking you to see your friend first,' replied Falton. 'He's awake now and asking for you.'

'For me?'

'For all of you, I think.'

'Oh, yeah, of course. That's what I meant.'

Even in the diluted colours of twilight, Charlie saw Brooke blush.

They entered the House of the Healer, set into a different section of the wall. There were a lot more people inside, hurrying along its halls, bundles of linen wrappings or medical instruments in their arms.

Falton led them up two flights of stairs and into a square room with tall windows overlooking the city below. There were six beds in the room, three of which were occupied. In the one furthest away, propped up on two pillows with a mug in his hands, was Dale.

His face broke into a weary grin as they approached. 'Hey guys.'

'Hey Dale,' said Brooke, returning his smile.

'Good to see you awake, squirt,' said Charlie.

'Thanks. Nice clothes.'

'Nice bandages. You know, if you're hurt pretty bad, maybe I can call it even on the whole getting-you-back thing. Just let it slide this time.'

'I only told Mr Green because you and Noah dumped me head-first into a bin, remember?

Charlie chewed on that for a moment. 'Even so, I'll let it slide.'

An elderly nurse shuffled over with a bowl of fruit. She took the mug from Dale's hands without speaking and replaced it with the bowl.

'Do I have to?' he asked.

She nodded and shuffled off. Dale sighed and lifted the fork in the bowl.

'Fruit's good for you,' Willow explained. 'It'll help you recover faster.'

'How are you so... recovered... already?' said Charlie, frowning. He could see that Dale's chest was bandaged beneath his infirmary gown, but his skin was rosy and his eyes were bright. 'You looked like a zombie last time we saw you.'

'Gee, thanks.' Dale speared a piece of melon. 'They gave me some weird potion, and then the healer person was here for a bit. She held her hands over the wound and they glowed, then my skin got super hot, and then it felt fine again. She said I'll be ok by tomorrow.'

'That's great,' said Brooke. 'I thought you were... I mean, we thought...'

She flushed again. Charlie smirked; Dale cautiously slipped the fruit into his mouth, pretending not to notice.

Falton cleared his throat and said, 'We should go to the banquet now.'

'Banquet?' said Dale, spraying melon.

'Yeah,' replied Charlie. 'Don't worry, we'll save you some leftovers.'

Dale made a face and dropped his fork with a *clink*.

'Alright, let's go,' said Falton, turning away.

'See you tomorrow, Reed.' Charlie held out his fist and Dale gave it a light punch, pleased.

'Feel better,' added Brooke, following quickly after Falton.

'I'll catch up,' said Willow.

The others looked at her. Charlie noticed a flash of something in Brooke's eyes, gone in an instant.

'Do you know where to go?' said Falton.

'Yes,' said Willow.

'Good. Don't be long.'

Charlie and Brooke trailed after him and the door closed. Willow moved to sit on the bed, then thought better of it and remained standing. She folded her arms.

'What's up?' said Dale, watching her closely.

Willow glanced at the nurse, who was across the room tending to another patient. When she spoke again her voice was lowered. She met Dale's gaze and held it.

'At the bridge, with the fire,' she said. 'That was you, right?'

Dale looked puzzled. 'Me? What do you mean?'

'I think you know,' said Willow, 'or at least, you suspect. Because it wasn't me, and it wasn't the troll. And I don't think Brooke or Charlie have magic - '

'You think I have *magic?*'

'Keep your voice down.' Now she did sit, right on the edge of the bed. 'Look, I saw you, when the ghouls came at us. You were down, but your hands were up, like this.' She held out her palms. 'And then the fire appeared. I don't think you realised you were doing it.'

'Doing what?'

'It's called Elementascia. Creating something out of nothing using magic.'

'But I can't - '

'No, *I* can't,' said Willow. 'My magic... what little I have... is from nature. I can summon a little, but mostly I draw from what's already there. But you formed from what isn't, from the elements themselves, without spellwords. Only a sorcerer can do that.'

'A sorcerer?' Dale whispered.

'Yes, and a good one, too. Plenty of sorcerers struggle with Elementascia, especially with fire. I also think you might have turned the Doomgaard soldiers into slugs, but I'm not sure.'

'Oh.' Dale looked at the bowl of fruit.

'We'll keep it between us for now,' said Willow, standing. 'I need to talk to the Druyad first. And... I'm sorry for before, back at Crookedstone. I misjudged you.'

Dale shook his head. 'Don't be sorry.'

Willow smiled and patted him once on the arm. 'Just get some rest. Maybe we'll bring you something from the banquet. And try not to start any fires, if you can.'

'But... how?'
She was already out the door.

Chapter Twelve: The Banquet

'Welcome, welcome! Right this way, please.'

Hammerfall Castle sat at the highest point of the city, embedded into the mountain, a great impenetrable structure carved from granite, marble and bronze. Its towers, of which there were many, reached up towards the white clouds that seemed to rest continuously on the mountain summit, shrouding it from view. Falton said there was another tower up there but didn't say what its purpose was, or to what height it extended.

The knight led them through the walled courtyard outside the castle, passing through the sweet-smelling garden Brooke had spotted from her window, and into its vast, circular entrance hall, lined all the way around with statues of heroes and kings from long ago. There, the Citymaster welcomed them afresh and directed his chief servant, who introduced himself as Zapharous, to escort them to the Throne Room, where the banquet was about to begin. At that point, Falton bid them a gruff farewell and left.

'This must be so *exciting* for you,' Zapharous exclaimed, guiding them along a corridor already bustling with banquet guests. 'Your first ever visit to the city and you're attending a royal event. I lived here more than a decade before I even set foot in the Royal District!'

The Citymaster's chief servant was a skinny and sallow-skinned man with dark eyes and an oiled goatee; he wore a crisp navy tunic with silver trim and had a refined, intelligent air about him, but his smile was warm and his enthusiasm infectious as he escorted them through the castle.

'Be sure to bow when the Ulandking arrives, won't you?' he said. 'He always notices those who don't. It's quite amazing, actually.'

They came to a set of huge, ornate double doors carved with the hammer-and-stars insignia of the city. Armoured guards pushed the doors open and Zapharous ushered them inside.

Brooke had once visited Westminster Abbey during a school trip to London and spent most of it with her head bent back gazing at the beautiful architecture of the ceiling, and she found herself doing so again. The Throne Room was simply colossal. Enormously-thick marble pillars, carved with images depicting ancient battle scenes and key moments from Ulandai history, ran down both sides of the room towards a set of steps, at the top of which sat a throne made of pure gold, studded with precious stones that glimmered in the candlelight. Four banqueting tables extended from one end of the room to the other, ending at a fifth table positioned horizontally in front of the throne, with seven golden chairs behind it. One chair was much larger than the others. All of the tables were laden with sparkling silver cutlery, bronze dishes piled high with food, crystal decanters filled to the brim with blood-red wine, and candelabras burning hot and bright; hundreds of people, all dressed in colourful (and often bejewelled) finery, were already seated, chatting and laughing and toasting one another. The room echoed and rang with merriment, all the way to the shadows of the ceiling far above.

'Here you are,' said Zapharous, waving them into three empty seats near the end of the second table, almost as far from the throne as they could be. 'Please, fill your glasses and enjoy the hospitality of the Ulandking.'

Brooke, who rarely wore dresses, manoeuvered awkwardly into the seat between Charlie and Willow. Charlie seemed to be just as uncomfortable as she was, restlessly tugging at the collar of his tunic; Willow kept her head down, avoiding eye contact with those around them.

'What do we do?' said Charlie, raising his voice over the din. 'Do we drink this stuff?'

'I don't think we should,' replied Brooke. 'But look, there's water.'

Charlie filled all three of their glasses. Brooke took a sip and thought she'd never tasted water as sweet and pure in her entire life.

'Darling!' cried a curly-haired lady opposite her, causing her to almost spill her drink. 'I simply *adore* your dress! Where in the world did you get it?'

'Umm, someone gave it to me.'

'Oh, an eligible suitor, no doubt,' the woman replied with an over-the-top wink at Charlie, who drank faster. 'Mine's from Alfred Seworth's place on Tailor Street, if you know it. Cost a fortune, but it's not every day you're invited to a royal banquet, is it? Coin's there to be spent, that's what I say!'

She giggled, slopping wine from her glass onto the pearl-white tablecloth. Next to her, Brooke heard Willow mutter something.

'And you,' the woman continued, brushing away a curl, 'what's your profession? Judging by your youthful yet rugged appearance, I'd say you're a knight in training, yes? For whom do you squire?'

Charlie shrugged and said the first thing that came to mind. 'I'm between squiring jobs right now.'

At that, the woman exploded into another fit of tittering giggles, spilling more wine. Those on either side of her didn't seem to notice, or care.

'Oh I say, you are a cad, aren't you? Hold on to this one, young lady.'

Brooke and Charlie averted their eyes from one another.

'And what about you?' she continued, turning to Willow. 'Are you also...'

She trailed off, finally noticing Willow's green-tinged skin and golden-flecked eyes. For the first time, she set her glass down.

'Goodness,' she exclaimed, gaping. 'You're... a Woodsperson, aren't you? From Nymm?'

Willow nodded and the woman squealed in delight. Several other table guests now looked curiously their way.

'Why, I've never met one before. This *is* a treat! I mean, I knew there'd be some here tonight but I never expected to actually *meet* one. Goodness!'

Each time she said 'one', Brooke felt a sharp stab of annoyance. She was back on the road to Ringmoffren again, facing the bandits.

But then, whether she'd sensed some coldness emanating from Brooke or simply sobered up for a moment, the curly-haired woman's attitude seemed to change.

'I'm honestly quite glad to meet you, really,' she said, extending a gloved hand across the table. 'I'm Marcy Bunski, of Redmere Grove.'

Willow took her hand and gave it a brief shake.

'I'm... Willow,' she said, 'of Nymm.'

'Pleased to make your acquaintance, Willow of Nymm. And what're your names?'

But before Brooke or Charlie could answer, all chatter was drowned out with a series of trumpet blasts. A ripple of excitement washed along the tables as everyone turned to the doors, and then silence fell in the room. The doors swung open and the Citymaster strode in, hands behind his back.

'Ladies and gentlemen,' he announced, his voice reverberating around the walls and up to the ceiling. 'I invite you to stand as we welcome our most honourable guests for the Summit of Uland.'

Hundreds of chairs squeaked as guests stood, drinks in hand.

'The most honourable Murblok of Golemar.'

There were gasps as the trumpets sounded and the Giant entered the Throne Room, stooping under the frame of the doorway. Like those they'd seen on the Stone Road and in the Throat, Murblok had grey-blue skin and a tangled bushy beard. He was, however, dressed in banqueting robes and wore a thin crown of wood on his bald head. The banqueters stared up at him as he stomped his way towards the top table. The trumpets sounded again.

'The most honourable Ravocus of Strobor.'

'A real life Pyre!' said Marcy. 'How exciting!'

Ravocus walked, or rather glided, into the room to the trumpets. His feet barely touched the floor as he breezed past the Citymaster. He was humanoid in appearance, but his skin was so pale it was almost translucent; his ears, chin and nose were pointed, and his eyes were blacker than onyx, with no light in them whatsoever. His burgundy-coloured hair was slicked back, and the dark robes he wore clung tight to his skeletal frame. Those black eyes swept the banqueters as he passed, grinning at some unspoken joke - all merriment evaporated from the room, replaced with something eerie and unsettling. Brooke shivered, holding her elbows.

Ravocus slipped silently behind the top table next to Murblok, who was seated in the overlarge chair. The Citymaster announced the next guest, Luno of Elementa, a tall woman with unnaturally bright red hair and scarlet eyes, dressed in a flowing red gown. She swept in to more trumpets and up to the top table, tracked by hundreds of admiring eyes along the way. Some warmth crept back into the room as she took her seat.

'As you all know,' continued the Citymaster, 'no representative from Doomgaard will be joining us today, or for the duration of the Summit, for obvious reasons.'

Murmurs around the Throne Room, along with a good deal of knowing looks and nods.

'But no matter. For I now have the distinct pleasure of welcoming - and for many of you, introducing - a very special guest. Please, raise your goblets and glasses to Orchidema, the most honourable and revered sovereign of the Woodspeople - the Empress of Nymm.'

Gasps erupted around the room. All heads swivelled towards the doors.

'The Empress!' exclaimed Marcy. 'I can't believe it!'

Brooke turned to Willow. 'Nymm - that's where you're from?'

She nodded, but her eyes were on the glass in her hand. Orchidema was entering the room now, her head bowed away from the trumpets, moving quickly towards the top table; she was dressed in a moss green gown with a veil of sorts covering her head, though locks of black hair were visible under it; furtive glances at the banqueters revealed eyes the colour of her dress, flecked with gold like Willow's. Her alabaster skin betrayed only the slightest hint of green.

'Oh she's *beautiful*,' gushed Marcy.

She is, Brooke agreed, *and she looks younger than us*. She glanced at Charlie and saw with amusement that his eyes were wide and glued to the Empress.

Orchidema reached the top table and took the seat next to Luno, who smiled sweetly at her. *Too sweetly*, Brooke thought.

'The most honourable Yulerin of the Druyads.'

Willow looked up sharply. An old man with long white hair and a beard tied in two plaits shuffled into the Throne Room, leaning heavily on a wooden cane that looked almost as ancient as he did. His grey cloak trailed on the floor behind him and his breathing was laboured as he made his way past the tables. A reverential silence had descended on the room, but as the old man struggled towards the top table and no-one offered any help, Brooke felt something more akin to pity than awe.

This is a Druyad?

Willow, however, was smiling for the first time since they'd been in Ringmoffren.

'I hoped it'd be him,' she whispered. 'He's the nicest of all the High Druyads.'

Yulerin clambered into his chair with a sigh of relief and all eyes turned once more to the doors. Brooke shuffled restlessly, eager to sit down again.

'And now, ladies and gentleman, we welcome our most honourable host and protector of the great city of Fort Hammerfall. Please raise your goblets and glasses to the Lord of Ulandai, defender of the people and champion of Wosdren, his majesty, the wise and mighty King Sol - the Ulandking.'

The room erupted into cheers and applause and trumpet blasts as King Sol marched through the doorway, flanked on both sides by guards brandishing silver spears. He beamed at the crowd, grinning and waving while his belly bounced under his gold tunic; his cloak, the train of which was carried by two servants, was the deep blue of the Hammerfall flag, embellished with silver stars. His face was clean-shaven and a gold crown set with precious stones sat atop a head of wispy, strawberry-blond hair. Its metal caught the candlelight and flashed spectacularly as he strode towards the top table.

'Thank you, thank you,' he said, still waving. 'You're too kind, really you are. Tremendous to have you here, truly. Thank you.'

Brooke thought his journey from the doors to the top table seemed to take an age - she wondered how everyone was able to continue clapping and cheering for so long. All she wanted to do was sit and eat.

Eventually, the Ulandking reached his seat but remained standing. He held up his hands, calling for silence.

'Friends, friends,' he boomed. 'You're all most welcome. It's an honour to host you here at Hammerfall, the greatest city in Uland, and probably the whole world. Has there ever been a place like our fair city? I think not. While you're here, our home is your home. Please, enjoy all we have to offer.'

More cheers. *Hurry up*, Brooke thought, her feet aching in the shoes she'd been given.

'I'm delighted, truly delighted, to welcome these wonderful friends alongside me here. All very wise and powerful leaders of their factions. It's especially good to welcome the young Empress of Nymm to her first summit - we're honoured to have you here, my lady.'

Orchidema smiled up at him, her cheeks flushing pink.

'Yes, I look forward to our collective discussion over the coming days as we seek a peaceful end to the troubles currently facing our great continent. I'm confident we'll find solutions together, and maybe we can even invite our friends at Doomgaard back to the table at some point, figuratively speaking.' He gestured towards the empty chair at the far end.

Friends? Brooke thought.

'But that's all for tomorrow and the days ahead. For now, let's enjoy this feast, the like of which has never been seen before. Eat, drink and be glad. Let the banquet begin!'

The king raised his tankard and the banqueters chanted 'Druyads protect the king! Druyads prosper the king!' before he finally took his seat and everyone else followed his lead. Brooke sat, relieved to be off her feet. In the corner of the Throne Room, the orchestra set aside their trumpets and started up on new instruments.

'Isn't he something?' said Marcy breathlessly. 'So majestic, so regal.'

'He's, er, something,' said Charlie.

'Do you know her?' Marcy asked, leaning towards Willow. 'Orchidema, I mean. You're both from Nymm, aren't you?'

'It doesn't mean… no, I don't know her.'

Marcy looked crestfallen. 'That's a shame, perhaps you could've introduced us. It'd be simply *wonderful* to meet royalty, especially the Empress herself. They say she's the last of a very rare and powerful bloodline.'

'A very ancient family, yes.'

'And you're sure you don't know her?'

Willow shook her head. 'No.'

'Oh. Oh well, then'

Their usefulness served, Marcy turned to the woman beside her and began to discuss Luno's dress; the woman, now trapped, could only nod and smile.

'You didn't tell us you're from Nymm,' Brooke said.

Willow shrugged. 'Would it have mattered? You wouldn't have known where it is. Besides, I'm not really from there, not anymore. I haven't been in Nymm since I was very young.'

'How old *are* you, anyway?'

'Charlie! You can't ask that,' Brooke scolded.

Willow smiled. 'I'm older than you.'

Then the food arrived, served up in silver dishes by dozens of seemingly tireless waiters and waitresses. Zapharous reappeared at that point, serving Brooke, Charlie and Willow directly. He was just as enthusiastic as ever, waxing lyrical about the dishes as he placed them on the table.

'You'll *love* this one, it's a rare delicacy in Wosdren. Oh, how I envy you right now! Delicious, delicious…'

The banqueters worked their way through five courses, starting with a luscious leafy salad (which Willow wolfed down) through to a main course of succulent meat, steamed vegetables and fluffy potatoes, all rounded off with dessert consisting of cakes, tarts and cheeses. By the time the servers had begun to clear up the last remaining dishes, it was late evening and Brooke and Charlie were slumped back in their chairs, holding their stomachs.

'I've never been so full,' Brooke moaned, 'but it was *so* good.'

'Definitely beats troll dinners.'

'How do you humans eat so much?' Willow said. Then she sat up straight as the Citymaster approached their table.

'The king would like to meet you,' he said.

Everyone within earshot turned to stare at them. Marcy's eyes almost popped out of her skull.

'Us?' said Charlie.

'Of course. It's not every day we have guests from… overseas.'

They rose, still locked in Marcy's incredulous stare, and made their way across the Throne Room towards the top table, following the Citymaster. The din of conversation diminished gradually as they drew closer to the Factionheads. Brooke felt like the journey from one end of the room to the other took forever. Hundreds of eyes tracked them all the way.

'My lords and ladies,' said the Citymaster, bowing as they reached the top table. 'Allow me to introduce our special guests.'

He stepped aside, waving them forward. They approached under the gaze of the leaders of Uland. Willow bowed, and Charlie copied; Brooke attempted a curtsy and partially succeeded.

This seemed to amuse the Ulandking, who raised his tankard to them.

'Well met, friends,' he boomed. He had the glazed look and lopsided grin of a semi-drunk man. 'I trust you enjoyed your meal.'

'Yes, your majesty,' replied Willow.

'Excellent, indeed, excellent.'

He took a gulp of wine. The other Factionheads watched them closely. Yulerin the Druyad stroked his beard, deep in thought.

'Yes, 'twas a fine feast indeed,' said King Sol, setting the tankard down, much too hard. 'My Citymaster tells me you journeyed here all the way from the Barrows? I'm impressed. I've spent much time there in days gone by, keeping the peace. Nothing keeps the peace quite like a sword, either. I'd say no-one here knows the Barrows quite like I do.'

'You're not the only one who's been there, Sol,' said Luno. 'Elementa borders the Southern Barrowlands, or have you forgotten how to read a map?'

'Certainly not!' said Sol gruffly, reaching for his tankard again.

'Tell me,' Luno said, speaking to them now, 'this foreign place you come from, is it out west, beyond the Wosdren coast? How did you come to be here, exactly?'

Brooke detected something in the way the Elemental leader spoke, something hard and cold. Her red irises burned in the warm haze of the candelabras.

'We… came through a portal,' said Brooke. 'Willow here, she brought us from our own world. Me and Dale.'

'The ghouls brought me,' Charlie explained.

'Fascinating,' hissed Ravocus, baring pointed white teeth.

'Only Druyads can use portals,' declared Sol, holding out his tankard for more wine. 'Everyone knows that.'

'Perhaps, about that, we were mistaken.'

The Factionheads looked towards Yulerin with some surprise. The old man was hunched in his chair, clearly weary after the long feast, but his eyes were alive with light.

'After all, this Woodsgirl was able to pass through it, as were the ghouls. It could be that the laws of magical travel are not as rigid as we once thought, or they're changing. You,' he said, pointed a wrinkled finger at Willow, 'were assigned to Everin, if my memory still serves me?'

'Yes, I was. He sent me through to get help. I brought these humans back instead, by mistake.'

By mistake, Brooke echoed silently.

'Humans,' rumbled Murblok. 'I know of them.'

'Yes, we've all heard the stories,' said Luno dismissively. 'Though I'm certain this is the first time any of us have laid eyes on them in the flesh.'

'They look like Ulandai,' laughed Sol. 'Maybe all humans are Ulandai.'

'So you were there when Aibal was attacked?' asked Yulerin.

Willow nodded.

'And you can confirm that the Doomgaard were responsible?'

'Commander Hysst sided with them in secret. He let the ghouls into the Great Cavern Room, and they've been raiding across the Barrowlands since then. And he almost captured us at the Throat.'

'The ghouls, at Aibal. Did they - ?'

'They killed them all.'

Yulerin's face fell further than Brooke thought possible. The old Druyad looked away, his eyes swimming, and a pang of sadness ran through her.

'My men will deal with Hysst,' said Sol confidentially. 'I dispatched them as soon as I received word about the attack. They're probably on their way back with him now, or with his head, at least.'

'Better be,' said Charlie.

'But it sounds to me like Hysst's actions are that of a rogue,' the Ulandking continued. 'Once he's been stopped, this trouble will cease.'

'Violating a sacred Druyad site is an act of war,' said Yulerin hotly, his eyes clear again.

'Of course, but who are we declaring war against? One man, I think, not an entire faction. Best to avoid all-out conflict, I say. Why end our long period of peace over the actions of one rogue and his posse?'

'But they *are* with the Doomgaard,' Charlie insisted. 'They wear black armour and use Doomgaard shields, and they *call* themselves the Doomgaard!'

'A ruse, designed to trick the feeble-minded. To lure us into attacking a peaceful neighbour.' Sol belched and wiped his chin.

'An increasingly-secretive neighbour,' put in Luno. 'One who's ignored our repeated invitations. We don't even know who leads the Doomgaard anymore, do we?'

'Decymero,' replied Brooke.

At once, all of the Factionheads stopped talking and stared at her. Banqueters within earshot turned to listen. A cold spot had appeared in the room, as though someone had opened the ceiling directly above them.

'That word,' said Sol slowly, 'is forbidden in this city.'

Brooke swallowed. 'It's what Commander Hysst said. When he had us at the goblin markets. He said he worked for… that person… and that he could help us get home.'

No-one spoke for a moment. Brooke felt like the whole room, the whole city, was watching her. King Sol seemed to have suddenly sobered up.

'Girl,' he said. 'Decymero does not exist. He's long gone.'

'It's just what Hysst said.'

'He lied.'

Brooke dropped her gaze. She felt like she was in school before the headmaster. The old tears of guilt and shame threatened behind her eyes.

'Perhaps she misspoke,' suggested Ravocus. 'She may have misunderstood Hysst's meaning. She is, after all, not from this place.'

Brooke glanced at Willow, whose eyes never left Yulerin. Charlie's hand patted the place where his sword normally hung.

'What is it you want from us?' asked Luno, finally.

'They need to get home,' said Willow, answering Luno but still looking at Yulerin.

The other Factionheads followed her gaze. Sol took another gulp of wine, muttering under his breath.

'I'm afraid I can guarantee nothing,' said Yulerin, 'except that I will do my best to assist you.'

'That's settled then,' announced Sol. 'Tomorrow, you shall leave here and travel to the Druyad temple, and there find your way home. Where's that boy with the drink?'

'Let's not be hasty,' said Ravocus, his bony white fingers steepled. 'This opportunity should not be allowed to pass us by so easily. We can learn much from these... humans.'

'I agree,' said Luno. 'They should remain here, for now. A more thorough examination by the Council is required, especially in light of this business with Hysst and his... apparent master.'

Brooke felt a surge of dread. After travelling all that time, and all that distance, were they about to become prisoners here in Hammerfall?

'My lady,' said Willow, with growing urgency, addressing Luno directly for the first time. 'It's important that my friends get back as soon as possible.'

'Why's that, Woodsgirl?' The last word was laced with thinly-veiled contempt. 'Are they leaders in their own world? Dignitaries, on whom the responsibility of governance rests? Perhaps you've accidentally hauled three members of a royal family into Uland.'

Ravocus made a sound that might have been a chuckle.

'No,' said Willow. 'But there is a... time factor. They have to get home soon, very soon. If they don't - '

'Of course we will help, Willow.'

Orchidema's voice was soft, almost timid, but it cut through the others like a familiar song. Her eyes were pools of gold.

'We wish no harm on these visitors, and if keeping them in Uland too long would cause that, then we should do all we can to see them safely home.'

Willow bowed her head. 'Thank you, Empress.'

'Yes, thank you,' Charlie added quickly, almost tripping over his own words. The Empress smiled at him.

Luno said, 'I believe this is a matter for - '

'Help the humans,' bellowed Murblok, slamming an enormous fist down on the table. Everyone in the Throne Room jumped, startled.

'Let's talk about this tomorrow,' said King Sol, who now looked like he might throw up at any second. 'I'm getting tired and I don't think best when I'm tired. We'll add it to the Summit agenda and let the Council decide. Citymaster, take them back to their quarters.'

'At once, your highness.'

They bowed. Orchidema smiled warmly, but the Ulandking scowled into his tankard. As Brooke turned to leave, her eyes met Yulerin's.

See you in the garden.

The voice was clear and unmistakable. The Druyad winked, and then they were being ushered back across the Throne Room.

'Saying that name in front of the king, honestly!' snapped the Citymaster. 'Have you no sense at all? Your heads could be on the chopping block if you're not careful.'

He escorted them as far as the double doors, where his chief servant was waiting.

'Follow me, if you please,' grinned Zapharous, with a little bow.

Chapter Thirteen: Yulerin

Zapharous led them back through the castle to the
entrance hall, his navy tunic sweeping around his feet. It
was now late in the evening and most of the royal staff
were gone, but several members of the Factionheads'
entourages still roamed the hallways or loitered by
fireplaces in the lounges and libraries, merry on
Hammerfall's wine. Charlie was relieved to have left the
banquet - he couldn't wait to change back into his normal
clothes.

'... wonderful to see the city so alive at this time,'
Zapharous was saying enthusiastically. 'We're so rarely able
to welcome representatives from the other Factions, what
with the ongoing disagreements over how to handle the
centaurian uprising in the north and the pirate raids along
the Eisdren coast. Between you and me, I wouldn't mind a
bit of excitement round here again. It's been so boring in
Ulandai recently. Your being here has livened things up
considerably!'

They passed the entrance guards and started down
the steps. Outside, the evening air was refreshingly cool;
the courtyard was illuminated with torches made to look
like spears in the hands of statues, and above them,
billions of stars in unfamiliar constellations filled the clear
sky.

'I'll come for you all in the morning after you've eaten,' said Zapharous. 'There's a royal breakfast for the Factionheads, but I don't think you'll be - '

'Wait.'

They stopped, halfway to their building. Brooke faced towards the garden in the centre of the courtyard. It was encircled with a neatly-trimmed hedge, around which dozens of fireflies winked in and out of view.

'Can we go over there for a minute?'

Zapharous looked puzzled. 'My... orders are to escort you to your chambers...'

'Please. It won't take long.'

The chief servant hesitated, his dark eyes flicking towards the garden and back to them. Then he nodded. 'Alright, as you wish.'

'Why the garden?' asked Willow as they approached it, Zapharous tailing behind them.

'Just a feeling,' said Brooke.

The hedge hid the interior of the garden from view. Brooke led them around the perimeter to a trellis arch covered in climbing pink roses, where they were able to enter.

The garden was a circle of soft grass with colourful flower beds set along the inside of the hedge. At the end nearest the castle, water trickled down an ornate fountain into a small pond filled with goldfish; at the opposite end, the garden opened out towards the courtyard gates, now sealed for the evening. In the centre of the area was the tree Brooke had spotted from her window, old and bent and leafless, and seated under it on a stone bench, puffing on a pipe, was Yulerin the Druyad.

'Yulerin!' cried Willow, going to him. Brooke was surprised to see her hug the old man, who chuckled, trying not to spill ash from his pipe on her dress.

'Willow,' he said, 'good to see you. I'm sorry for my formality before - the circumstances called for some... aloofness. I hope I wasn't being deceptive.'

'You know each other?' Charlie said.

'Oh yes, many years. Willow's been a faithful friend of the Druyads since she was very young.' He nodded towards Zapharous, who stood awkwardly under the rose trellis. 'You may leave us, sir.'

Zapharous hesitated, then bowed and left. Charlie and Brooke crossed the grass and stood by the tree. The scent of lavender, intensified in the evening stillness, perfumed the air around them.

'So you got my message, then?' Yulerin said to Brooke. Willow and Charlie frowned.

'Yes,' Brooke replied, 'but I don't know how.'

'I have a theory or two,' said the Druyad, with another wink. 'But that'll be for another time. You're all here now.'

'You wanted to talk to us?' said Willow.

'I did, and I do. Sit.'

Willow sat next to him on the bench; Charlie and Brooke chose the grass, which was softer than a carpet.

'There've been rumblings across the continent about you,' said the Druyad, lighting his pipe again. 'Ever since you arrived here, along with your friend Dale Reed.'

'How do you - ' Brooke began.

'What do you mean, rumblings?' Willow cut in.

'Among the magical folk, those connected to the heart of Uland. The non-magicals haven't sensed it, obviously, and word travels more slowly with them. But when you came through the portal at Aibal, something shifted here. Things changed.'

He puffed on his pipe for a moment, then went on.

'The death of Everin and the other Druyads - which you sadly confirmed, Willow - should have created a void in the world, a fissure in the invisible nexus that binds us all together. That may have been the goal of those who carried out the attack. But for whatever reason, when you three Other-worlders appeared, the void was filled again.

'And because of that, you're now part of the magical network from which we all draw our strength and understanding, and those who employ magic are aware of you. Your presence was felt in the Barrowlands, wherever you were: in the Forest of Lost Souls, on the Stone Road, Ringmoffren, the Throat. Even those on the far side of the continent felt it, felt your *otherness* moving through the magical nexus. And it stirred something that had lain dormant for a long time.'

'The goblins,' said Willow. 'They knew, didn't they? Before we even got to the markets.'

'Most likely. As did your friends, that rowdy bunch from Wosdren Marsh, though they perhaps didn't realise it.'

Charlie grinned. Then a fresh thought occurred to him, bursting into his mind with sudden urgency. 'Are they alive? Do you know?'

'I believe so,' said Yulerin. 'I don't, however, know precisely where they've disappeared to. They may be in hiding after their encounter at the markets - the Doomgaard are probably hunting them.'

'And what about Hysst? Did he survive?'

'That I also don't know. He's been hidden from our sight ever since the attack on Mount Aibal and Birchfell. Something's shrouding him and the rest of the Doomgaard.'

None of them spoke for a few moments. Brooke listened to the water gurgling in the fountain. Sleep tugged at her gently.

'Ask the question you wish to ask,' said Yulerin, gazing up at the stars.

'Is Decymero real?' Willow said immediately.

The Druyad took several long puffs, then sighed, long and weary.

'Yes, he is.'

'How long have you known?'

'Not long. Not for sure, anyway. A matter of months, I'd say. We've suspected for many years as Doomgaard grew darker and more closed off to the rest of Uland, but we've only recently become certain of his existence. He is, it appears, a master of deception and disguise.'

'I wish you'd told me.'

'It was for your protection, my lady.'

'Commander Hysst said *we* were the ones being lied to, and Decymero was telling the truth,' said Brooke, absently pulling at the folds of her dress. 'And Dale sounded like he believed him.'

Yulerin smiled sardonically. 'Hysst would say that. He's been well and truly fooled by a darkness even he can't comprehend. I knew him, and I don't think there was any real evil in him, no more than a spark perhaps, but Decymero was still able to twist his mind to the point where he believed murdering Druyads and innocent villagers was the *right* thing to do. Or at least, if he knew it was wrong, he simply didn't care.'

The old man sniffed. Brooke saw his eyes glisten with tears before he blinked them away.

'The Factionheads,' Willow said, 'they don't believe us.'

'That doesn't surprise me. Why would they? These two are foreigners, new to the land and unaware of its history. And you're a servant and messenger, easy to dismiss, and they're very eager to cling to the belief that Decymero isn't real, nothing more than a naughty word the lower classes swear by when other naughty words just won't do.'

Abruptly, he rose to his feet, old joints cracking. He hobbled a few paces, leaning on his cane. They watched him, waiting.

'We're in a dangerous moment,' said the Druyad, turning back to face them. The moon, now visible in the darkening sky, cast a pale glow on the grass at his feet.

'The leaders of Uland who've gathered here this week don't believe they're under any real threat. As far as they're concerned, their armies are best suited to curbing far-off rebellions and skirmishing with savages in the wilderness, just to keep them occupied. We've been in a period of peace for many years and it's made them complacent, maybe even lazy. Acknowledging the existence of an enemy as powerful as Decymero is just too much for them. I fear this summit of theirs will accomplish nothing more than the increase of their ignorance and decrease of their trust in one another. Especially the Ulandking, who the others greatly dislike.'

Willow also stood. 'So what now? Why'd you want to speak to us?'

'Because,' Yulerin said, 'I believe the four of you represent something extraordinary. An unexpected twist in the game. That means you're both a potential helping hand to the forces of good and a major threat to the side of evil. Decymero offered you the hand of friendship already - what he truly intended by that, I'll never know - but next time, that hand will likely hold a dagger instead.'

'I've turned the Time Keeper,' Willow reminded him, as Charlie and Brooke rose to their feet, 'so we don't have long. Once the sands fall…'

'What happens?' said Charlie.

'I think we turn to stone,' Brooke replied.

'WHAT?'

'Indeed,' said Yulerin. 'Your time here is limited. However, the Druyads are able to return you to your own world, so no-one will be turning to stone.

'Here's what I need you to do. Tomorrow morning after sunrise, meet me here, packed and ready to leave, with your friend Dale. The guards won't stop us, and judging by the sound of the rabble still in there, the king will be in no hurry to start his day. We'll go to the royal stables and take three mounts, then we'll leave the city and follow the Road north to the Druyad Temple. It's perhaps half a day's journey on horseback. And once there, we'll send you home.'

'But won't King Sol and the others be angry?'

'Maybe, though they may also be glad to be rid of you. No offence, of course - your talk of Decymero made you more of a problem than you're worth, I suspect.'

'Sounds like a plan,' said Charlie.

'Then I'll see you at sunrise,' said Yulerin. 'Get some rest, my friends.'

<<>>

They left the garden and went quickly to their quarters. There was no sign of Zapharous and no-one challenged them along the way. Below, the city still buzzed with festivities organised in honour of the Summit and the castle remained full of banqueters, but the rest of the Royal District was quiet.

Charlie said good-night to Willow and Brooke and went to his room. He was pleasantly surprised to find his normal clothes neatly folded on the armchair, freshly washed and dried, and his hiking boots scrubbed clean of mud. His sword was where he'd left it, hidden under the bed.

He undressed and dumped the Ulandai clothes on the armchair, grimacing at the laced shirt.

'When this is over,' he said to the empty room, 'I'm never going hiking again.'

He climbed into bed and lay staring at the window, which looked out over the city. It would be sun-up in just a few hours, and then they would once again travel across Uland. Hopefully for the last time.

I wonder how it'd feel turning to stone.

He closed his eyes and thought of the Empress of Nymm, and slept.

<<>>

'Wake up!'

'Wha… what is it?' Charlie said groggily, sitting up.

Brooke was in his room, dressed in her normal clothes. She'd been shaking him by the shoulder. Her eyes were wide with alarm.

'Something's happening!'

'What? Where?'

'I don't know, it's outside! Hurry up and get dressed.'

Brooke left the room. Charlie struggled out of bed and into his clothes. He was dressed and in the living area in two minutes, face dripping with the water he'd splashed on it.

'What's going on?' he said, attaching his scabbard to his belt.

'Not sure,' replied Willow, standing by the window. She was also back in her normal clothes with her brown cloak wrapped around her. 'It's hard to tell.'

Charlie joined her at the window and peered out into the night. Far below, much of the city was still lit and awake; beyond the lower walls the plains around Fort Hammerfall were inky black, but something was moving in the darkness. Charlie could just make out people leaving the villages outside the city, running for the gates.

'What should we do?' said Brooke. 'Lock the doors?'

But even before she was finished speaking, the doors of the living area were thrown open. Falton stood there, breathing heavily, sword in hand.

'Come with me,' he panted. 'The city's under attack.'

<<>>

Below the sturdy walls of the Royal District, Fort Hammerfall was in chaos.

Citizens were running and yelling in the night, waking their neighbours, searching for their loved ones. The city guards gathered near the gateways between districts, ready to seal them shut as soon as the word went out; a battalion of Ulandai soldiers - swordsmen, archers, spearmen and cavaliers - had mobilised at the main entrance to the city, preparing to defend it.

Falton led Brooke, Charlie and Willow from their quarters to the castle courtyard, where squires hurriedly fitted armour to the royal knights. The soldiers, already dressed in mail hauberks, stood with their arms out while the younger men fastened on silver-blue breastplates and gauntlets and greaves. Other squires waited nearby with the knights' weapons: shortsword and shield, or two-handed greatsword, or axe, or spear. Archers already manned the outer walls of the royal district, bows in hand and quivers on their backs.

'How did we sleep through all this?' said Charlie.

'The Citymaster's ordered all civilians in this area into the castle, for their safety,' said Falton, not really acknowledging Charlie's question. 'You'll be safe in there.'

'We're not going without Dale,' replied Brooke, in an end-of-discussion sort of way.

'Someone will attend to him. You must go - '

He broke off as a horn sounded elsewhere in the city.

'Oh no…'

Falton ran for the courtyard wall, which formed a semi-circle around the front of the castle. Not knowing what else to do, they followed him. Pushing past other soldiers, they bounded up a set of steps to the parapet along the top of the wall and looked out across the city. Charlie squinted into the night.

'What is it?' Brooke said. 'What's wrong?'

'The horn only sounds when enemies are near the city walls,' Falton replied, leaning out over the crenellated wall of the parapet. 'Near enough to attack, I mean. But I don't see - '

Just then, a house in one of the little villages burst into flames. Seconds later, another one close by did the same. Before long, a whole row of houses was on fire, burning yellow and orange in the night. And in the firelight, they saw them.

'So many,' breathed Charlie.

A sea of soldiers in black armour swept towards Fort Hammerfall, setting fire to every building in the villages they passed. Homes and taverns and shops were razed to the ground as villagers ran screaming into the night, some with animals in tow. The Doomgaard army marched on, blades flashing in the fire glow, their boots thumping on the road in thunderous tandem.

Thousands, Charlie thought. *There are thousands of them.*

'Man the battlements!' someone yelled.

Another knight, already fully armoured and astride a horse, pointed his sword towards the walls. 'Archers, take your positions! Riders, prepare for battle!'

Charlie watched as archers surged towards the walls and began mounting the steps, and for the first time, he noticed Luno of Elementa standing just a short way along the parapet from them. She was wrapped in a heavy red cloak and her hair was tied back, but otherwise, she was just as regal as before. She caught his eye, her scarlet irises ablaze in the night.

'It appears you were right after all, Other-worlders,' she called.

'The Doomgaard have betrayed us,' came another voice, and they jumped as Ravocus sidled up next to them, his pointed white teeth glinting. His movements were totally silent. 'Where is the Ulandking?'

'On his way,' said Falton.

Below, they could see the Ulandai soldiers forming up on the inside of the wall, preparing to meet the Doomgaard on the slope outside the city.

'They are too few,' observed Ravocus. 'They cannot hold out against such a great force.'

'The Ulandai have faced worse odds,' replied Falton, his eyes never leaving the Doomgaard army, which flowed like a river between two banks of burning villages. 'We'll hold the city.'

'I should hope so,' said Ravocus. Like the goblins, Charlie noted, the Pyre retained a perpetual grin on his deathly-white face.

'What's the meaning of this?'

They looked back and saw King Sol stomp across the courtyard from the castle. He'd been fitted with at least half of his armour but had clearly grown impatient - his forearms were bare. A squire hurried after him carrying the king's vambracers and gauntlets.

'You're awake then, your highness?' said Luno, pointedly.

'Of course I'm awake,' snapped the king, mounting the steps. He staggered a little and had to reach for the rail to keep from tumbling - he was still a little drunk from the banquet. 'Who is it? Who's attacking my city?'

'Looks to be our friends from Suthdren,' replied Luno.

'It's the Doomgaard, sir,' said Falton.

Sol's face hardened. He climbed the last of the steps and approached the wall, staring down at the dark army now assembling into rows outside the city, just beyond the reach of the Ulandai archers. When he spoke again, his words came out in a croak. 'I can't believe it.'

Charlie couldn't help himself. 'We told you so.'

The Ulandking glared. 'Careful boy, or I'll send you and that toy blade of yours to the front line.'

'We should send for help,' said Willow, who was perched on the wall itself, perfectly balanced. 'If the city can hold - '

'*If it can hold?*' bellowed Sol, causing the squire who'd followed him up the steps to flinch back. 'Hammerfall has never fallen, not since its walls were first constructed. No traitorous horde from Suthdren will take it tonight, mark my words. The Ulandai are not so easily beaten.'

'Haven't you heard?' said Luno, and Charlie knew instantly that she'd been waiting for this moment, whatever it was. 'Word arrived from the coast not long ago. Mooncrest Harbour was taken at dusk yesterday evening, when we were feasting in the castle. The Doomgaard army must have sailed straight up the river during the night and crossed the open plain, right to your doorstep.'

Sol faltered. 'Mooncrest… was taken?'

Luno nodded. 'And most of your fleet destroyed in the process, it seems.'

'And you elected to tell me this just now?' seethed the king.

'You only just got here, your majesty.'

Before Sol could respond, there was another horn blast from below. The gates had been opened and the Ulandai battalion was streaming out to meet the Doomgaard.

'It's time to defend your city, sire,' said Ravocus. 'The Pyres, few though we are, stand with you. We will honour the Pact.'

'As will the Elementals,' said Luno.

'And the giants!'

Murblok was below them at the courtyard gate, fully dressed in armour, a tree-trunk sized club strapped to his back. He raised a huge fist into the air and bellowed, 'Less talking, more fighting!'

The Ulandking looked from the Factionheads to the armies facing off outside the city walls, then to his squire. 'What're you waiting for, boy? Finish armouring me so I can do battle.'

The Factionheads dispersed to gather their respective forces. Charlie began to drift after Falton, one hand already on the hilt of his sword, when Brooke grabbed his arm.

'Dale,' she said.

He stared back for a moment, the urge to join the battle pulling at him. Then he saw the expectancy in her eyes, and the fear, and some part of him remembered afresh that she was his classmate from school, and they were thirteen years old.

'Yeah, Dale,' he said. 'Let's go get him.'

'This way,' said Willow.

She darted down the steps and out through the courtyard gates, Charlie and Brooke at her heels. No-one paid them any attention as they raced across the Royal District towards the House of the Healer. Beyond the walls, a great warcry went up, followed by the rumble of horse hooves and hissing of arrows leaving bows.

They came to the Healer building, and finding the door unguarded, rushed inside and up the stairs. Other than a handful of fearful nurses casting sideways glances at them, the building was empty.

'When we get Dale,' Brooke panted, 'what then?'

'We'll go to the castle,' Willow replied. 'It's the safest place in the city, easiest to defend.'

'You think the Doomgaard can get inside?' Charlie said.

'I hope not.'

They came to the door of Dale's ward and pushed it open. Inside, the room was dark, lit only by a single lamp in the corner. Willow said '*Eydrom*' and snapped her fingers, and a ball of green light appeared in the air, bathing the room in its glow. Of the six beds in the ward, two were still occupied with sleeping patients.

'Oh no!' Brooke exclaimed.

Dale's bed was empty, the bedclothes thrown back.

He was gone.

Chapter Fourteen: The Druyad Tower

'Where is he?' Brooke cried, wheeling around in panic. 'Willow, where's he gone?'

'How should I know?' replied the Woodsgirl.

'Maybe he's at the toilet or something?' suggested Charlie. The other ward patients were stirring around them.

'We need to tell someone,' said Brooke, looking under Dale's sheets as though he might be hiding there. 'We should tell Yulerin, or Falton, or - '

'Falton's probably in the battle by now,' said Willow, 'and Yulerin could be anywhere.'

'Well we have to do *something!*' Brooke yelled. One of the ward patients let out a little cry, startled.

Suddenly, the door flew open. They turned, expecting to see an Ulandai guard standing there, or Dale himself. Instead, it was Zapharous. His dark eyes bulged with panic; he was still in his navy dress robes from the banquet.

'There you are!' he gasped, face flushed. 'I've been trying to find you.'

'What is it?' said Willow, snapping her fingers again to put out the green light.

'Your friend,' Zapharous said, struggling to regain his breath. 'The one who was in here, with the wound... I know where he is.'

'Where?' asked Charlie.

'How?' Willow added.

'Can you take us to him?' said Brooke.

Zapharous hesitated, trying to decide which question to answer, then waved them to the door.

'I'll show you - come on.'

They descended the steps quickly and left the House of the Healer. Outside, there was bedlam in the Royal District as soldiers bolted to their posts and civilians ran for safety. Zapharous led them to the courtyard, making for the castle. Charlie caught glimpses of the battle raging at the lowest wall of the city - clashes of steel and shouts and screams carried to them on the breeze; columns of smoke billowed into the sky, which was already beginning to lighten with the first hints of dawn.

'Man your posts!' yelled a soldier.

'Get those men to the trade district, right now!' ordered another.

'Hurry, hurry!' cried Zapharous.

They sprinted up the castle steps and into the entrance hall, once again ignored by anyone who passed by. Zapharous led them through hallways and up staircases, weaving between guards and servants and members of the Factionheads' parties. Terrified guests huddled in rooms along the way, peering round the doors. A pair of giants barrelled by in the direction of the castle entrance, almost knocking Zapharous flying.

Passing a window, Brooke saw a brief flare of light in the sky and realised the Doomgaard were catapulting fireballs into the city.

Seconds later, they came round a corner and almost collided with another group.

'My apologies!' said Zapharous, filtering between them. 'We're in a hurry.'

'Sorry, sorry,' muttered Brooke as the other group went by. She saw brown cloaks and leather armour the colour of pine trees, and then she was face-to-face with the Empress of Nymm.

The Woodsperson's golden eyes were wide with alarm. Her cloak was pulled up over her head, hiding most of her dark hair. Not for the first time, Brooke wondered how old she was.

'Empress,' said Willow, now at Brooke's side. 'You should get to safety.'

'I will,' said Orchidema. 'Come with us, Willow.'

'We have to find our friend,' Brooke interrupted.

The Empress looked at her, then stared at Willow. Something passed between them, some unspoken understanding. Then Orchidema nodded.

'Go, and Druyads protect you.'

She allowed her guards to usher her away down the hall. Charlie watched her go with something like longing.

'We're almost there,' Zapharous said, 'hurry.'

They followed him down the hall and up another flight of stairs, and then they were spiralling upwards through the centre of a tower. Brooke's lungs and calves burned from the exertion.

'Skies above,' Zapharous panted, 'we're here.'

They'd arrived outside a heavy-looking wooden door. There wasn't much light where they were, but Brooke was still able to make out the symbol on the door. It was a tree.

I know this door…

'Wait,' said Willow, 'this is the Druyad Tower, isn't it?'

Zapharous nodded. 'Yes.'

'Does that mean Yulerin…?'

Willow pushed open the door - it wasn't locked - and went inside. Brooke and Charlie followed, with Zapharous behind.

They found themselves in a large round room with a high, cobweb-strewn ceiling. There were tall bookcases on two walls filled with dusty old tomes, and opposite the door, a window looked out over the city. A table and chair rested in front of the window; a stubby candle burned on it, but aside from that, the room was devoid of anything else.

Anything, that is, other than Dale. He lay on the floor next to the table, unconscious.

'Dale!' Brooke cried, going to him at once.

She and Willow rolled him over, and they saw his face was pale like before on the bridge, and his eyes rolled blankly.

'He's alive,' said Willow.

'Zapharous,' said Charlie, 'how did you…?

But Zapharous had closed the door and was turning a brass key in the lock.

Click.

<<>>

'What are you doing?' said Willow slowly.

Zapharous turned towards them, slipping the brass key into his pocket. There was something in his face, in his dark eyes, that Charlie didn't like.

'I'm sorry,' he said, and his voice seemed different now, too. 'Sorry it had to be this way. I had to get you all together, and away from the others. It's a shame, really.'

Willow rose to her feet; Brooke remained crouched next to Dale, staring bewildered at the Citymaster's servant.

'I've been waiting, you see,' Zapharous continued, coming towards them now. 'He sent me here to wait. I didn't think I'd get here in time. But he said you'd arrive soon, and you did. And here you are now, without the Druyad. *Alone.*'

Willow moved, but Zapharous was faster. His hands were up before Charlie could blink. A flash of purple light engulfed the room for a second, then faded. And when it did, Charlie found he couldn't move a muscle. He and Willow were rooted to the spot like statues, frozen in position. Brooke remained on the floor next to Dale, one hand on his shoulder.

'Just a simple spell,' Zapharous said. 'It'll wear off soon. We don't need long, anyway.'

He grinned, but the smile didn't reach his eyes.

And as they watched, those eyes began to change. The dark in them faded, turning grey; his hair also changed, becoming longer and lighter, until it was brown. His skin, once sallow, grew pale.

Disguised, Charlie thought.

As he watched, his heart thumping furiously in his chest, Zapharous reached into his other pocket and brought out a small, dark object. It was glassy and misshapen, and it glinted in the candlelight when he placed it on the floor. As Charlie's eyes came to rest on it, something flared deep inside him; it jolted through his nervous system and went straight to his brain.

Terror.

'This,' Zapharous said, wincing as he straightened up again, 'is the Soulburn Talisman. Not many in Uland know it exists other than my master, and those who serve him. The Druyads mistakenly believe only *they* possess the power to travel by portal, but they're wrong. Bunch of old fools.'

He stepped away from the talisman, moving to Willow's side. Her golden eyes followed him, burning with anger. Zapharous caught her expression and scowled.

'Don't look at me like that - this is all your own fault. If you'd only accepted Commander Hysst's generous offer in Crookedstone, this wouldn't have to be quite so dramatic. Oh yes - ' He saw Brooke's face, ' - I know all about that meeting in the markets. There's very little I don't know, in fact.'

'Who are you?' Charlie said, surprised when his lips moved.

'No-one special,' Zapharous replied, with a shrug. 'Just a grateful servant who's been given a second chance. Someone who's seen the light, like Hysst.'

'You're... Doomgaard,' Brooke said.

'Please!' Zapharous scoffed. 'I'm an honourable citizen of Fort Hammerfall, born and raised here. I spent most of my life on this mountain, before they took me away. But unlike my fellows who wander about blind with the wool pulled over their eyes, I know what's true and what isn't. I know where true power lies in Uland.'

'Just another traitor,' said Willow.

Charlie desperately tried to reach for his sword, but his arm remained locked in place by the spell.

'I'll have you know I'm an *extraordinary* traitor. I've waited years for this opportunity, the chance to prove myself to my master. I was starting to think it'd never come. There were days when I was locked up all by myself in the darkness, far from here in that wretched dungeon across the sea, when I doubted. My faith wavered, and I'm deeply ashamed of that. But here we are, just as he said. I should have known he'd never let me down. Oh, how I'll be rewarded for this!'

'Your master,' Charlie said, 'is Decymero.'

'Of course.' Zapharous stroked his chin, where the goatee had been moments before. 'Would you like to meet him?'

Brooke took a sharp intake of breath. She could feel something pulsing from the black object on the floor, a power of some kind. She had to will herself not to look at it.

'He's eager to meet you,' said Zapharous, baring mustard-coloured teeth.

None of them responded. Brooke could see Charlie from her crouched position on the floor, straining to reach his sword. And for a split second, she thought she felt Dale stir under her hand.

'Well, whether you'd like to meet him or not...'

Zapharous pointed at the talisman on the floor. It immediately turned red and began to glow, thrumming on the floorboards like it was alive. It glowed brighter and brighter, bathing the room in scarlet light, until Brooke had to squeeze her eyes shut to avoid being blinded.

Then there was a *bang*, followed by a loud *whoosh*, like a strong wind blowing down a pipe. Brooke opened her eyes and saw that a doorway of sorts had appeared in front of them, shimmering and translucent, with ripples of red light around its threshold. The whooshing sound was coming from the other side of it, though she felt no wind on her face.

'It worked!' Zapharous cried giddily. 'I did it!'

The portal rippled and burned in the air, filling the room with sound. The floor trembled beneath their feet. *Surely someone will hear this?* thought Brooke. But she knew they wouldn't. Outside the windows, the battle for the city raged - unless someone was in the Druyad Tower itself, they wouldn't hear.

'Here he comes,' Zapharous exclaimed, pointing.

Brooke could indeed see a figure on the other side of the portal, dark but vague, like she was looking at him through frosted glass. Her heart hammered inside her and she realised for the first time she was afraid, truly *afraid*. She'd stood up to the ghouls in the Fairy Ring and faced bandits on the road, and neither time had she felt anything more than a rush of adrenaline.

But this was different - this was like staring right into the face of the monster that's been chasing you in a nightmare, one you can't wake from.

The fear washed over her in waves.

As the figure drew closer and more defined, Zapharous dropped to his knees.

'Master!' he cried. 'Decymero, the great Vessel of Truth and Power. Harbinger of Destruction and Prince of the New Age. See how I serve you.'

The dark figure reached the other side of the portal. It was now man-height, discernable in form. Sickenly-bright redness burst again and again from the edges of the portal; the floor shook beneath them and books tumbled from the shelves. Brooke felt hot tears rolling down her face.

'My master!' Zapharous went on. 'They're here, I've done it! Just as you commanded. Where others have failed, I've succeeded. What would you have me do?'

When the voice spoke from the portal, Brooke felt the whole world go cold.

'*Bring them here.*'

Zapharous remained on his knees, rigid, eyes wide in horror and awe.

Brooke understood: *it's the first time he's heard his voice.*

'*Now.*'

With a yelp, Zapharous scrambled to his feet. He grabbed Willow by the arm and tried dragging her towards the portal. But her legs were still frozen and she toppled over. He hauled her up again.

'*Not her,*' came the voice, hard and rasping. '*Not yet. The others.*'

Zapharous released Willow, who somehow stayed on her feet. He reached for Brooke. 'No,' she whispered, her lips barely moving.

The voice replied straight away, in her head this time: *Yes, Brooke Woods. You'll come to me and I'll show you everything. I know what you want.*

No, get out of my head...

But she couldn't shake him. He was in now, his skeletal fingers wrapped around her mind, piercing her thoughts with jagged nails. Decymero. She couldn't make him leave.

I know what you want, what you've always wanted. I know what you are, Brooke Woods. I'll show you. There's no point in trying to resist.

No! Get out!

She knew her nose was bleeding.

And suddenly, as though a door had been opened somewhere inside her, she heard Charlie's voice too: *Can't move... who is he... can't reach my sword... don't want to be here anymore... if only I could reach...*

And then Willow, too: *Betrayer, traitor, monster... must get free... all my fault... my fault... my fault...*

The pulsing red light washed over her relentlessly. She tried squeezing her eyes shut but she couldn't look away from the portal.

Get out get out get out get out

NO! I'M HERE TO STAY. DADDY CAN'T SAVE YOU THIS TIME. HE'S LONG GONE. I KNOW WHAT YOU ARE. I KNOW-

GET OUT!

With everything she had left - all the strength of will she could muster - Brooke pushed back against the voice. She felt Decymero resist, clawing at her mind for purchase, and then, with a rush, the darkness retreated.

<<>>

Charlie saw Brooke's head snap back and then flop forward like a dead weight on her neck. There was blood coming out of her nose and tears ran down her face. He strained to reach for her but his entire body was still immobilised.

'*Enough*,' said Decymero. '*Take her.*'

Once again - hesitant now - Zapharous reached for Brooke. Then he stopped.

Out of the corner of his eye, Charlie saw Dale stand up. The other boy was paler than ever and his legs wobbled, but he made it to his feet. The immobilising spell mustn't have worked, Charlie thought, because Dale had been unconscious at the time.

Panicked, Zapharous raised his hands to perform the spell again.

'*Wait.*'

Now he froze, arms comically outstretched, looking sideways at the portal.

'*Let him come.*'

Zapharous stepped back, and Charlie saw with horror that Dale was walking towards the portal. Tears continued streaming down Brooke's face.

'No, Dale,' she sobbed weakly. 'Please don't.'

'You can't,' said Willow.

'Silence!' snapped Zapharous. 'He's seen the light! He's going to his master.'

Dale staggered awkwardly towards the shimmering door and the dark figure beyond it. He was dressed again in his normal clothes, but Charlie could see bandages running up to his shoulder under his top. His chestnut hair stuck out in every direction.

'*Boy,*' came the voice. '*Very wise. You choose well. Come.*'

The figure moved. Now Charlie could see an arm, and then the shape of a hand, reaching out. Dale was right in front of the portal, immersed in red light.

'Take his hand,' Zapharous urged ecstatically. 'Take your reward!'

Dale stared dully into the portal. His hand came up. He stretched it out towards the dark figure.

'Dale, no!' Charlie cried. 'Stop!'

But Dale didn't stop. He stretched towards the portal with both hands, like a child reaching for the safety of his parent's embrace. The figure reached back, his hand now defined with fingers and knuckles and nails, reaching for Dale, ready to pull him in.

This is where it ends, Charlie thought.

Dale stopped reaching, and for a moment just stood there with his arms out. No-one moved. Charlie was dimly aware he was holding his breath.

'What are - ' Zapharous began.

Then Dale lowered his hands, reaching instead towards the talisman on the floor. Electric-blue light fizzled and crackled around his fingers. Charlie was sure he saw Dale's eyes glowing.

'*Boy* - ' said Decymero.

There was a flash of blue light and another ear-splitting *bang*, and the Soulburn Talisman exploded into a hundred pieces. The portal, and the figure beyond it, vanished.

'NO!' screamed Zapharous.

He lunged towards Dale, eyes bulging, fingers hooked into claws. But the immobilising spell had broken and Charlie felt control return to his body. His hand found the hilt of his sword and he unsheathed it, swinging upwards in the same movement. Zapharous shrieked as the sword bit into his torso, slashing a red line from naval to shoulder. He spun around and staggered backwards, tripped over Brooke, who was still crouched on the floor, and tumbled into the table by the window with a crash.

Dale had dropped to one knee, drained with exertion. Willow was at his side, holding his arm.

'You did it,' Charlie heard her say. 'Didn't I tell you?'

Dale was nodding, breathless but smiling. Charlie helped Brooke to her feet and she immediately threw her arms around him. Her tear-soaked cheek was wet against his.

'YOU LITTLE BEASTS!'

They wheeled around as Zapharous pulled himself up, leaning on the table. His face was manic, twisted into a deranged grin. Red pooled under his shirt.

'You'll *pay*!' he screamed. 'You fools, you children! You'll *die* for that!'

He came towards them, purple light sparking in his hands. Willow and Charlie faced him; Charlie raised his sword, Willow's fingers twitched.

The door behind them blew open, slamming hard against the wall.

'MOVE!' yelled Yulerin.

They threw themselves to either side as the Druyad hurled a blast of green light towards Zapharous. It hit him square in the chest, lifting him off his feet. The agent of Decyermo grunted in surprise as he flew backwards across the room, his shirt torn open. He hit the table again, flipped over the top of it like a rag doll and crashed through the window, disappearing into the night.

Yulerin stared at the smashed glass, then turned his eyes disbelievingly on Dale, Willow, Brooke and Charlie, panting, his ancient bushy eyebrows raised. He looked down at the talisman shards on the floor, then back at them. His mouth worked, but the question never came.

'Come with me, please,' he said instead.

They left the room and hurried down the spiral staircase.

Chapter Fifteen: The Uland Seven

'How?' demanded the Citymaster. 'How could this have happened?'

They were in the library, a lavishly-decorated room on the ground level of the castle; three of its walls were packed floor to ceiling with books, and in a fireplace set into the fourth wall, logs crackled among flickering orange flames. Under different circumstances, Brooke would have found the library and the familiar book smell comforting. She thought of her mum, and how she'd called her 'Brookeworm' when she was younger. A lump rose in her throat with that memory; she dabbed at her bloody nose with a damp cloth.

Yulerin had brought them to the library after leaving the Druyad Tower, where the Citymaster had met them in a panic - apparently the Doomgaard had breached the walls of Fort Hammerfall and the lower levels of the city were engulfed in fighting. The enemy army was much larger than first thought and there weren't enough troops in the city to hold them off for long.

And then Yulerin told him about Zapharous, and the Citymaster's panic had become hysteria.

'How?' he cried again, tugging restlessly at his gold chain. 'An enemy spy, right under my nose? How did he manage it?'

'He was an agent of a secretive nation, skilled in deception,' said the Druyad, seated in an armchair by the hearth. He looked older than ever in the firelight. 'A master of disguise, I suspect. Even I didn't recognise his true nature.'

'Even you,' spat the Citymaster. 'The wise and powerful Druyad.'

'Hey, he saved our lives,' said Charlie, standing in the corner. 'Zapharous, or whatever his real name was, would've killed us otherwise.'

The Citymaster snorted and continued pacing.

'I have a question,' said Brooke, a tremble still in her voice. She sat on the rug by the fire, hugging her knees.

'Go on,' replied Yulerin.

'Well, two actually. First of all, how can Dale do magic?'

Yulerin smiled crookedly. Dale, weakened and flopped in the armchair opposite him, added, 'Yeah, I was wondering that myself.'

'He's a sorcerer, isn't he?' said Willow. 'At the bridge, he was the one who summoned the fire ring. He knows Elementascia.'

'A *sorcerer?*' Brooke exclaimed.

'But I didn't mean to do anything,' Dale insisted. 'It just… happened. And back in the tower, I wasn't in full control either. I mean, I remember getting up and walking to where the talisman thing was, and then I just… wanted to make it stop.'

'And you undoubtedly saved the lives of your friends in that moment,' said Yulerin. 'I suspect if Decymero had gotten his hands on any of you, that would've been the end of it.'

'Decymero!' snapped the Citymaster. 'Not that again.'

'How would you explain it, then?'

'Who knows? Perhaps it was some sort of hallucination, brought on by the stress of the moment. Or a trick. But it can't have been real. *He's* not real.'

'And what of this?' Yulerin held out his palm, displaying shards from the Soulburn Talisman. 'The substance used to make this evil device is found in one place and one place only: the molten lakes of Eklabar, deep in Doomgaard territory. It takes ancient, dark magic to forge one of these. I wasn't sure it could even be done. A mere spy couldn't make this - Zaphorous was only able to handle it because he had magic in him. No, only a being of great and terrible power and knowledge possessed the necessary skill to create a Soulburn Talisman. I'm afraid to say that Decymero is very real indeed, good sir.'

The Citymaster stared at the talisman shards. His face had gone pale while Yulerin spoke, and now he looked as though he might faint.

'I need to sit,' he said, staggering over to a reading chair in the corner. Yulerin slipped the shards into his pocket.

'To answer your question, Lady Woods, I believe Dale here can do magic because he is - as Willow suggests - a sorcerer, or something like it. How that can be the case since he's from another world, I don't know. I'm starting to think I've never known as much as I led myself to believe, actually.'

He chuckled, stroking the plaits of his beard.

'Perhaps magic's always been in his blood and when you all entered Uland, it simply... woke up. You are not the same here as you were at home, in your own world.'

'Is that why I can fight here?' asked Charlie. 'Obviously, you know, I could *fight* before. Just not with a sword.'

'That may be the case, yes. It's clear you have the warrior spirit in you.'

Charlie seemed to grow an inch taller at that.

'But you said you had two questions, Lady Woods?'

'Oh, yes,' said Brooke. 'I did. My second question is about me. When we were at the banquet, I thought I heard your voice... in my head.'

'*That's* how you knew to go to the garden!' Willow exclaimed.

'And how you knew about the Doomgaard soldiers outside the tavern in Ringmoffren,' added Dale.

'Yeah.' Brooke blushed self-consciously. 'I heard your voice, Yulerin, like you were speaking in my ear. And it's not the first time this sort've thing's happened here. I've had dreams about things that've come true.'

The Druyad's eyes sparkled.

'Of course. Of course you have,' he said. 'This only confirms what I suspected when I first saw you. Long before I laid eyes on you, as a matter of fact.'

'I also heard *his* voice,' Brooke added quickly. 'In the tower. He spoke in my head, I couldn't get him out. It was... it was scary.'

She left out the fact that she'd heard the others as well. Willow gave her a small, kind smile and she swallowed hard, fighting back fresh tears.

'Master Flint, could you retrieve that book for me?'

Yulerin pointed at the bookcase behind Charlie, where an old leather-bound tome jutted out from the shelf. Brooke was sure it hadn't been like that before. Charlie pulled it from the shelf and brought it to the Druyad, who began flipping through the dusty pages.

'We don't have time for this,' muttered the Citymaster from his corner, absently cleaning his spectacles.

'There's always time to read, sir,' replied Yulerin. He flicked past several more pages. 'Ah, here it is. The Uland Seven.'

He turned the book so they could see. The text was indecipherable to them, written in a language they didn't know, but a series of drawings down one side of the page were clear enough. They depicted people, roughly sketched, in different poses. Some held weapons.

'These are the Seven Heroes of Uland. The Warrior... ' - Yulerin pointed a wrinkly finger at the top figure, who held a sword and shield - '... the Sorcerer, the Time-Bender, the Healer, the Seer, the Trickster, and the Changer.'

'Seven,' said Brooke, touching the page, 'one for each Faction?'

'Not quite, though the number seven does hold great power in Uland. These are special types of magical people who can, on occasion, rise up from among the non-magical, particularly from the Ulandai. They're often few and far between. There are a great many soldiers in Uland, for instance, but only some are *Warriors* in the truest sense of the word, gifted with inherent, unlearned ability on the battlefield.'

'That explains it, I suppose,' said Charlie, hand resting on his sword.

'Warriors are plentiful enough throughout the Factions, but there are only so many Sorcerers, those who practice Elementascia. The Elementals themselves strive after this power and many learn to harness it, but only genuine Sorcerers know it by heart.'

'Look, this is all well and good,' said the Citymaster, getting to his feet, 'but there's a battle going on - '

'Patience, I'm almost done,' Yulerin said. The Citymaster resumed his pacing. 'Sorcerers are powerful and often dangerous, depending on their persuasion. If you really do have these abilities, Dale, you must take great care to control them.'

'I'll... do my best.'

'Finally, there are those who have what's known as the Sight, the ability to perceive far beyond their natural reach. They can see what's happening on the other side of the continent, what's already taken place, and often, what's still to come.'

'The Seer,' said Brooke.

'Like Jayne,' added Dale.

'Certainly,' said Yulerin, with a grin. 'Jayne is known as many things, and the Seer is one of them. But unlike the

Warrior, the Sorcerer and the other Heroes... of whom there are often many at once... there is only one Seer.'

Now he looked at Brooke, who felt her heart flutter.

'You have the Sight, Lady Woods. Whether that makes you the Seer or just something similar to it, I can't be sure just yet. Perhaps since you come from afar, you're able to co-exist in this world with Jayne... though I know she refuses the title of Seer, in this age at least. Your meeting with her didn't come about by chance. You'll need to meet her again.'

'All of us?' said Dale quickly. Behind him, Willow rolled her eyes.

'I imagine it'll be all of you.'

'What about the other four heroes?' asked Charlie, leaning over Dale's head to peer at the book.

'I'll tell you about those another time,' replied Yulerin, turning the book back towards himself. 'We're pressed tonight, but I thought it pertinent that you have this knowledge now in case someone attempts to manipulate you in future... or in case I'm not around to tell you myself. I sense a great urgency tonight. But for the moment, our main concern is how to get out of this city alive. However...' - He stroked his beard, gazing at the book - '... there is one more thing, though I'm not completely sure - '

Suddenly, the door of the library was thrown open. Falton stood there, breathing heavily. His armour was stained with dirt and one side of his face was caked with dried blood.

'Falton!' exclaimed the Citymaster. 'What happened to you?'

'Just a little scratch,' panted the knight. 'You all have to come with me - they're sealing the castle.'

They hurried to the door, following Falton out of the library. The Citymaster shoved the knight aside and bolted down the hallway without a glance back.

Brooke was last to leave, right behind Yulerin. Just as she reached the threshold of the library door, the Druyad turned back towards her.

'Here,' he whispered, 'take this.'

It was a small, leather-bound book, wrapped in twine. Brooke took it, frowning.

'What is it?' she asked, but the old man was already out the door.

It seemed everyone who was left in the castle had gathered in the entrance hall: frightened servants and dignitaries, the few remaining guards, well-dressed people who must be members of the royal family. Everyone talked at once, a babble of fear and confusion. Outside, the noise of the battle had reached the edges of the Royal District.

Just as they arrived at the hall with Falton, the two great doors of the castle entrance swung open with a hollow *boom*.

'Make way!' yelled an Ulandai soldier, helmless and battle-worn. 'Make way for the king!'

Six soldiers, some injured and all exhausted, stumbled through the doorway into the castle. In their midst, supported by two of them, was King Sol. The crowd gathered in the entrance hall parted to let them through; whispers and gasps went around the room, reverberating off the stone walls.

'Make way! The king is wounded!'

'Sire!' cried the Citymaster, rushing across to Sol. 'What happened to him?'

'Didn't you hear? He was wounded in the fight.' Luno, flanked by Elemental guards, entered the castle behind them. Like the Ulandking, she was weary and dishevelled from battle. 'We held them outside the Royal District, but Hysst and his men overwhelmed us.'

Brooke glanced sharply at Willow and Dale.

Hysst? Here?

Luno spat blood on the marble floor of the entrance hall, her decorum forgotten. 'That beast killed three of my men himself.'

The Ulandai soldiers fanned out around the king. One doubled over, breathing hard; another collapsed and was caught by a nearby servant, who lowered him to the floor. Then Brooke saw Sol properly - his armour was freshly dented and scored, and the lower half of his face was bloodied. He clutched his side, where his mail under-armour was turning a deep red.

'Seal the doors!' someone shouted.

'Your majesty,' said Yulerin, 'I'm glad to see you're still alive.'

Sol stared at nothing in particular, his gaze far-off, as the castle doors swung shut behind him and the heavy locking beam slid into place. The king's face was set hard, but Brooke thought he looked ten years older than he had at the banquet.

'Your highness?' said Yulerin.

The Citymaster, who'd been bustling around Sol, stepped back with a scowl. The king looked at the Druyad as though seeing him for the first time.

'Hmm?'

'The city's been breached,' Yulerin said. 'We should make our escape, while we can.'

'Breached?' The word floated in front of him. Finally he grasped it. 'Breached. Yes, they're inside. More than we thought. My men... fought well.'

'They fight still,' said Falton.

'Fleeing isn't an option,' the Citymaster said. 'We must remain here in the castle, where it's safe. It cannot be taken.'

'Like the city couldn't be taken?' Luno said.

The Citymaster bristled, but the Ulandking merely nodded, then winced with pain.

'Let's get the king to his quarters,' said Yulerin. 'And someone call the Healer, wherever she is.' The soldiers obeyed, escorting Sol through the crowd with the Druyad. Willow started after Yulerin, saw the flash of alarm on Dale's face, and stopped.

'Murblok's still out there,' said Ravocus, materialising from the crowd, 'as are the other giants. They've done significant damage to the Doomgaard forces but it may not be enough.'

'It's no use,' moaned one of the dignitaries. 'The city's lost. We may as well surrender now.'

'No, we can't bow to them,' growled an Ulandai knight with green eyes, and Brooke recognised him as the rider who'd rescued them at the bridge. 'Their attack is almost spent - we just have to hold out a little longer.'

'Try, if you like,' said Ravocus, sidling off.

'Seal all passages in and out of the castle,' ordered the Citymaster. 'Hold out 'til morning. Help will arrive; the castle won't fall.'

'What about the people?' demanded Falton. 'They won't last long in their homes. The Doomgaard will kill them all without hesitation, if they haven't already.'

Brooke watched Willow throughout all this. The Woodsgirl's eyes, hazel and gold, never left the Citymaster. Next to her, Dale looked drained and out-of-place among the Ulanders around them.

We're all out-of-place, Brooke thought. *We're just kids, in the wrong place at the wrong moment. So what if Dale's a sorcerer and Charlie's a warrior and I can… what… see things? We're still just thirteen.*

Help will arrive.

She heard the words, echoing the Citymaster's, but they weren't his words. She closed her eyes.

Help us, she thought, straining, reaching. *Someone, help us. Anyone. Show us the way. Please.*

Help will arrive.

'Anyone who wants to stay and fight may do so,' announced the Citymaster. 'The king will appreciate your service. If, however, you'd rather live, follow me to the dungeons. They're dark and they stink, but they're safer than here.'

He swept from the entrance hall, and Brooke watched in dismay as most of those gathered surged after him. Within seconds, the hall had largely emptied.

'This is madness,' said Falton. 'Utter madness.'

'We can't just abandon the castle,' another soldier added.

'Nor will we.' Falton drew his sword again. 'We'll hold them here. If that traitorous rat Hysst gets this far, he'll get no further. Give all able-bodied soldiers and citizens a weapon, and prepare - '

'Hang on,' interrupted Dale. 'Where's Charlie?'

They looked around. Charlie was gone.

Chapter Sixteen:
The Battle for Hammerfall

Below the Royal District, Fort Hammerfall had fallen silent. Across the city, smouldering buildings billowed smoke into the morning air. Soldiers from both sides, wounded or already dead, lay in the streets. Civilians huddled in their homes, peering through cracks in their curtains.

The sky was streaked with pink as Charlie walked across the castle courtyard. His footfalls sounded unnervingly loud to him in the stillness. A warm morning breeze tousled his dark hair and rustled the bushes around the courtyard garden.

Moments after Luno mentioned Commander Hysst, Charlie had slipped from the entrance hall unnoticed and the doors had been shut behind him. There were no soldiers in the courtyard, and no-one clocked his absence. Now, as he passed under the rose trellis into the garden, he was completely alone. But for whatever reason, he didn't mind that at all.

Water trickled into the fountain behind him, making little *plop* sounds, eerie in the quiet. Charlie crossed the garden, his feet sinking into the soft grass, and stood in the hedge opening that faced the courtyard gates. The gates were closed over but not sealed. An Ulandai soldier lay slumped next to them, still clutching his now-useless sword.

Charlie waited, listening. He knew he had to wait, somehow.

The breeze carried through the garden hedges, pulling some leaves loose and scattering them across the ground. They skittered over the stone paving slabs and piled up near the dead soldier. And still he waited.

Footsteps.

Gripping the hilt of his sword, Charlie swallowed. The footsteps, heavy but quick, drew closer on the other side of the gates. Somewhere in the distance, a crow cawed once.

The gates swung open, creaking on their hinges, and Commander Hysst walked into the courtyard. Like the Ulandking, his armour was battle-worn and there was blood on him, but his expression was triumphant. Doomgaard soldiers followed him into the courtyard, spreading out wordlessly.

Hysst's icy blue eyes fell on Charlie and he grinned malevolently, his scar contorting.

'You.' The blade in his hand gleamed red. 'Of course it's you.'

Charlie met the Betrayer's stare and held it. Around them, the Doomgaard soldiers formed into a crescent. In his peripheral vision, Charlie saw crossbows levelled at him.

'Have they sent you as their champion?' Hysst scoffed.

Charlie grinned back. 'Suppose so.' He glanced at the Doomgaardians. 'Is this it? Where's the rest of your army?'

'Fallen,' said Hysst simply, 'as have the Ulandai. Now the city's defenceless, and I'm still standing.'

'Me too.'

Hysst wiped a hand across his mouth, pacing to the left. Charlie didn't move but kept one hand on his sword hilt. Behind Hysst, the Doomgaardians sealed the courtyard gates.

'You're a brave and foolish boy,' Hysst said. He turned on his heel and paced the other way, like a lion sizing up its prey. 'Braver than Sol was, anyway. He scurried back to his castle as soon as the tide turned against him. But I imagine I'll kill him myself soon enough.'

'That's why you're here? To kill the king?'

'To kill all of them. That's the plan.'

'Decymero's?'

'Yes. Stroke of genius, really.' Hysst's grin widened. 'We destroy the portals at Aibal and kill the Druyads, and all the leaders of Uland automatically come together in one place to discuss retaliation, as decreed in their wonderful Pact. All lined up nicely for us, without a second thought. We'd never have been able to tackle them all individually across the continent, but here they are, fattened up with their feasting, weak and slow. And when they're gone - '

'... Uland has no leader,' Charlie finished.

'Exactly. A rudderless ship sailing straight towards the reef, desperate for a captain to take charge.'

'Decymero.'

Hysst nodded. 'The All-Powerful and All-Seeing. And when he's lord of all Uland and the Factions bow at his feet, he'll make me his Chief Commander. Quite the leap from a lowly Druyad guard, don't you think?'

'Sounds pretty cowardly to me,' Charlie said. 'Siding with the bad guy instead of protecting the good ones.'

Hysst laughed. It sounded like a pistol shot in the still morning air.

'Good and bad - is that all it comes down to then, Charlie? You're just as naive as your friends. I offered them the chance to go willingly to Decymero, as *I* did, and they refused. And I'm assuming, since you're standing here right now, that Zapharous failed as well?'

'Yup, he's gone.'

'I never liked him anyway. They should've left him to rot in that prison.'

'Yulerin got him.'

'Ah, another Druyad.' Hysst's eyes lit up. 'You know, I'm getting a taste for killing them. Maybe I'll save him 'til the end, after I've finished off the Factionheads and your little friends.'

Charlie unsheathed his sword. *Shiing.*

'Finally,' said Hysst, starting forward. 'If you can land even one blow, I'll - '

'STOP!'

Doomgaard crossbows whipped in Willow's direction as she entered the courtyard garden. Her hood was down and her red hair tossed in the breeze. Hysst's lip curled back in a sneer of hate.

'So,' he said, 'in the end, all that stands between me and my goal is a boy with a glorified dagger...'

Willow came to Charlie's side, her golden eyes on Hysst.

'... and a Woodsgirl slave of the Druyads. I expected more, in all honesty.'

'You'll pay for what you did,' Willow said.

'Poor little *magik* girl,' grinned Hysst, gripping his sword in both hands. 'Always so eager to do everything by herself, all alone. And now here you are, ready to die alone, too.'

'She can't be alone when she has friends by her side,' Charlie said, glowering at Hysst. 'She has me.'

'And me.'

This time, the Doomgaard soldiers had to reposition themselves as Falton appeared to the left of the garden, sword at the ready; simultaneously, other Ulandai soldiers came around the right-hand side of the garden. Hysst's eyes shifted between Falton and the Ulandai knights, then back to Charlie and Willow. The air was thick in the courtyard.

'So be it,' said Hysst. 'You're still outnumbered, and one Doomgaard soldier is worth ten Ulandai. This pathetic display of force will only delay - '

The courtyard gates exploded behind him, ripping free of their hinges, showering them all in shredded wood. Doomgaardians standing nearby were flung aside. Willow and Charlie had to duck as one of the gates sailed over them and smashed through the garden hedge.

With a roar, Murblock burst into the courtyard, filling the space where the gates had been. Hysst dived to one side as the giant swung his club in a wide arc, scattering more Doomgaard soldiers.

'Kill it!' Hysst screamed.

Crossbows unloaded, peppering the giant with arrows. Murblock grunted in pain and lifted an enormous arm to shield himself.

'For Hammerfall!' bellowed Falton.

The Ulandai soldiers charged forward with a collective battle cry. Doomgaard archers, with no time to reload, dropped their crossbows and went for their swords. In seconds, the air rang with the clash of metal on metal.

Charlie scrambled to his feet, snatching up his sword. He saw Murblock kick the other gate across the ground, knocking Doomgaardians over like bowling pins. Then Hysst was coming at him, sword raised and eyes blazing.

'I'LL KILL YOU MYSELF!' he bawled.

The Betrayer would have reached him and sent Charlie's head bouncing across the garden, but Willow reacted quickly. '*Freymacha!*' A vine shot from the hedge and snagged Hysst round the neck. His body snapped backwards and he hit the grass hard, wheezing as his lungs emptied of air.

The Woodsgirl's hands were up, green light sparking between her fingers. Another vine snaked from the hedge and caught Hysst's ankle.

'Willow!' Charlie cried.

She started to turn, but it was too late. The Doomgaardian soldier was right behind her, sword drawn, ready to swing. Charlie did the only thing he could think of and hurled his blade at the enemy soldier. It whirled, flashing end over end in the morning light, and embedded itself in the Doomgaardian's shoulder between the plates of his armour. He went down with a shriek.

'Nice throw,' Willow shouted.

But more of them were already coming, crashing through the hedges. Willow sent a blast of green light their way, flinging them back. Charlie stumbled towards the fallen soldier to retrieve his weapon.

Suddenly, Falton was there, skillfully parrying Doomgaard blades. He backed towards them and shouted, 'Get to the castle!'

'No!' Charlie yelled back, yanking his sword free. 'This is our fight too.'

Falton dodged, parried, then cut down another black-armoured soldier.

'You have to get your friends out of here,' he panted. 'Get to the stables and take the first horse you - '

He stopped short and his eyes bulged. His body jerked, spasming.

Then Hysst's sword came all the way through his chest. Falton stood there for a moment, head back, mouth open, suspended in agonised shock.

'No…' Willow blurted. Charlie stared, aghast.

Hysst withdrew his sword with one sharp movement and Falton dropped to the grass. The scar-faced knight stood over him, grinning in maniacal triumph.

Brooke watched in horror as the battle raged in the courtyard. She stood with Dale at the top of the castle entrance steps; from there, they could see Charlie and Willow through the gap in the hedge created by the flying gate. As they watched, a vine shot from the hedge to snag Hysst's neck, then he disappeared from view.

'Dale,' she said, grabbing his arm, 'they're fighting Hysst. We have to help them.'

'What can *we* do?' Dale replied. He was still pale and weak, not quite recovered from the Druyad Tower, but he'd gone willingly with the others when they went after Charlie. Willow had ordered them to stay on the steps.

'Can't you use your magic or something, like before?'

'If I knew how I'd done it, I would.'

Brooke craned her neck, trying to see where Hysst had gone. There was movement in the garden, snapshots of metal striking metal.

'How'd he get here so fast?' Dale said. 'Last time we saw him he was at Crookedstone, fighting the trolls.'

'Never mind *that* - how did he manage to reach the castle without a scratch on him?'

Someone in the garden screamed. The sound of it punctuated the other battle noises and made Brooke's heart leap into her throat.

Was that a male voice? Was it Charlie?

An arrow fizzed by and thunked into the castle door above their heads. It could have come from a Doomgaard or Ulandai bow. The courtyard was a chaotic mix of black and silver armour, clashing blades, shouts and screams.

'We have to help them,' Brooke said again, gripping Dale's arm tighter.

'There's really nothing - ow! - there's nothing we can do. We're not warriors like Charlie.'

Help will arrive.

In desperation, Brooke scanned the courtyard - Murblok had a Doomgaard soldier in each hand and was shaking them like unopened Christmas gifts - and then looked to the pink and purple sky above the city, half-expecting to see something. Maybe Percius, leading an army of perytons to save them. Anything at all.

'Oh no!' Dale cried.

'What?' said Brooke, following his pointed finger.

'It's Falton! He... he...'

Then Brooke saw the knight, crumpling at the feet of Hysst. The Betrayer's sword was red, and even from their position on the steps, she saw his evil grin.

'Oh no, oh no,' Dale moaned, sinking to the ground.

Help will arrive.

Brooke's knees had begun to wobble and she thought she might collapse too. Falton's silver-blue armour gleamed in the morning light. She saw Hysst step over his body, advancing on Charlie and Willow. For a second, something obscured her view of them, some white thing in the garden.

The tree.

Something connected in Brooke's mind with an almost audible click.

'Dale, stay here,' she said.

'Where are you going?' he replied, suddenly alarmed.

'To get help.'

Brooke ran down the steps and sprinted for the garden.

<<>>

'You monster,' Willow said, her voice quivering. 'You horrible, evil monster.'

She was vaguely aware the other Doomgaard soldiers were closing in around them. Next to her, Charlie trembled, not in fear.

Hysst stepped over Falton's lifeless body, his blue eyes gleaming.

'It's over, Willow of Nymm,' he said. Blood dripped from his sword, pattering on the grass. 'Look around - you're beaten. I don't want to kill you.'

He was right. Most of the Ulandai had fallen or were surrounded by Doomgaard soldiers. She couldn't see Murblok.

'You can still come with me,' Hysst continued. 'Both of you. Decymero is forgiving. He'll take you in, show you the truth. You're valuable assets, you know. If you surrender now, you'll live.'

'No!' Charlie yelled.

Willow saw him lunge forward, his rusted sword swinging low. Hysst reacted with almost casual reflexive speed, blocking the attack. Then he and Charlie were duelling, their blades clanging and shrieking with each strike. The Doomgaard soldiers nearby stood where they were, watching, waiting. Willow felt like her feet had become blocks, rooting her to the spot. There were more Doomgaardians still standing in the courtyard than Ulandai. She knew if she moved, if she *could* move, they'd kill her immediately.

This was it. This was the end.

Charlie fought bravely. He held Hysst for nearly a minute, perhaps even surprised the Betrayer with his skill and ferocity. A couple of times he came close to landing a blow on the older man.

But Hysst was too strong, too experienced. Charlie made a rash stab at his chest and Hysst parried his sword aside, then knocked Charlie to the ground. The boy gasped, rolling away.

'Commendable effort, Charlie Flint,' said Hysst softly, standing over him. 'You made me work for it, I'll give you that.'

Charlie clutched his chest, winded from the blow. He stared up at Hysst.

He's only a boy, Willow thought. *Just a child, fighting a man.*

'But it seems you've made your choice,' said Hysst.

Willow saw him raise his sword above his head.

I've failed.

Then: 'Hey!'

Hysst froze. He and the Doomgaard soldiers looked past Willow. She turned to follow their gaze.

Brooke was in the centre of the garden, standing by the little gnarled tree. Everyone had been watching Hysst and Charlie and no-one had noticed her entering. Her blonde hair was matted to the side of her face, but her eyes shone with purpose. She leaned next to the white trunk and whispered something. The Doomgaardians didn't pick it up, but Willow's hearing was superior.

'Now,' Brooke said.

A beat passed, nothing more. Then, without warning, the Doomgaard soldiers around the garden began to yell and flail their arms. They staggered back, swatting at some invisible thing in the air. Some tripped and fell, others had their helmets turned backwards; a crossbow discharged on its own, shooting one of the black-armoured soldiers in the back. Within seconds, they were down.

Hysst watched it all, wide-eyed and confused. Then his sword was yanked from his hand and he stumbled backwards, sprawling onto the grass. Willow ran to Charlie and helped him up.

'What's happening?' he coughed, rubbing his chest where Hysst had elbowed him.

'We have help,' said Willow.

The Doomgaardians were already getting to their feet again, grabbing for their weapons. Brooke appeared at their side, beaming.

'It worked!' she cried. 'The fairies came!'

'Fairies?' said Charlie, looking about him.

'Enough!' Hysst was up again, flushed with fury, all his icy composure gone. 'Kill them, now!'

But the Doomgaard soldiers had stopped dead in their tracks, suddenly unsure. For even as Hysst spoke, several figures appeared near the fairy tree and stomped across the garden towards them. Their granite-grey skin, scored with blade and arrow wounds, blended with the castle walls behind them. Charlie let out a whoop of joy and punched the air.

'Well well,' said Amoogus, grinning. 'Looks like we're just in time, chaps.'

<<>>

'How?' Hysst snarled. Blood flowed from his lip but his sword was in his hand again. 'I left you monsters behind at the Throat.'

Brooke helped Charlie to his feet, keeping her eyes on the Betrayer. Willow was doing the same. She hadn't blinked since the trolls appeared.

'I believe you fled, actually,' said Amoogus, patting his club. 'Scurried off during the fight and left your men to pick up the pieces.'

'So brave,' said Fungus.

'And noble,' added Lombrigus.

'The question is, old sport,' Ammogus went on, 'how did *you* get here so fast? I doubt you had help from the fairies - they'd never deal with your sort. And how, more importantly, are you still walking? Didn't I crack you round the head with my little friend here?'

Hysst glanced at the club and sneered. 'I must be tougher than you think, beast.'

'He has something.'

Brooke jumped. Dale was right behind her, still pale, but standing.

'He's got something on him,' Dale said, locking eyes with Hysst. 'I... I can feel it. It's giving him protection. And power.'

Hysst's sneer grew wider. Brooke thought he looked insane.

'Power,' Hysst breathed. 'Boy, you don't know what *true power is*.'

Suddenly, the remaining Doomgaard soldiers launched themselves at the trolls. One of the creatures threw Brooke, Charlie and Dale to one side, blocking an incoming blade at the last second. Brooke's hand went in a patch of blood-soaked grass and she recoiled in revulsion.

The courtyard garden descended into chaos. Doomgaardians were tossed through the hedges but kept coming back, bellowing war cries; the trolls ducked and rolled, dodging swords and spears with surprising speed and agility. Some black-armoured soldiers fell under clubs and axes and stones slung with ferocious accuracy. One of the trolls was wounded and went down near the fountain. Everything was noise and mayhem.

'Dungus!' Charlie cried.

Brooke saw Hysst duelling with an axe-wielding troll, smashing his broadsword down again and again on the troll's weapon, driving him back across the grass. The troll, muscle-bound and fearsome though he was, couldn't stand his ground against the wild fury of the scar-faced knight.

He's got something on him. Protection. Power.

She saw then what Dale had seen, or part of it at least. Commander Hysst, who she knew to be Ulandai and practically human, was fighting with more than just physical strength and skill. He was fuelled with some dark magic, the same power that Zapharous had used to open the portal to Decymero. And it had driven him mad.

The talisman.

Then she saw something else. Something that made her breath catch in her chest.

Willow was walking towards Hysst.

'Oh no,' Brooke whispered.

'He'll kill her,' said Dale, noticing too.

'We have to help her,' Charlie said, struggling to his feet.

It's too late, Brooke thought. *She's too close to Hysst.*

Right on cue, Hysst knocked Dungus the troll aside, sending him crashing through the rose trellis at the garden entrance. He roared in frenzied triumph. And then his gaze fell on Willow.

'Woodsgirl!' he cried over the din of battle. 'At last. Finally ready to surrender?'

Willow looked across the garden at Brooke, Dale and Charlie. A sad smile tugged at the corner of her green lips, and Brooke heard her voice in her mind, clear as crystal: *My friends.*

'No,' Brooke whispered.

Willow met Hysst's wild stare. 'I surrender.'

'No!' Brooke cried.

All around the garden, the battle slowed, and then stopped altogether. The soldiers and the trolls froze in mid-fight, watching. Hysst and Willow stood just a few yards apart, their eyes locked. Willow's cloak, flapping in the breeze, was the only sound.

'You do?' Hysst said softly, wiping blood from his chin.

'Yes,' Willow replied, fists clenched. 'I surrender myself. Take me. I'll go willingly, as your prisoner. Just stop fighting and leave the others alone.'

Hysst broke her gaze and glanced at Brooke, Dale and Charlie - now standing - at the far side of the garden. His smile was venomous.

'Why would I do that?' he said, 'when I could take those three instead? They're far more valuable to my master than some yellow-eyed tree girl. What would the great and powerful Decymero want with *you*?'

Brooke saw Willow swallow. 'Your master,' she said, 'will know.'

Hysst's eyes flashed. For a second, and no more, Brooke could *feel* his doubt, pulsing from him in waves. He weighed the choice, staring at Willow with an exact combination of curiosity and loathing. And then, just as quickly, it all vanished.

'No,' he said, tightening his grip on his blood-stained sword. 'There'll be no surrender, no bargaining. You had your chance and you let it slip. You've been a thorn in my side for too long, Willow of Nymm. I'll kill you, and then your friends, and then every last person in that castle. And then it finally ends.'

He charged.

Brooke tried to cry out but found she couldn't. No-one in the courtyard spoke, or yelled, or tried to intervene. They could only watch as Hysst, screaming rage and madness, rushed towards Willow, his sword cutting through the chill morning air.

Something tingled in Brooke's chest; somehow, she knew Dale and Charlie felt it too.

Hysst's sword *whummed* downwards, straight for Willow's head.

And then it stopped.

The Betrayer's eyes went wide. His mouth hung open.

Emerald green light glowed along the edge of his blade, suspended an inch away from Willow's forehead. Hysst's arms trembled, straining to bring the sword down. Even from across the garden, Brooke could see his temples throb.

Willow raised her eyes slowly to meet Hysst's. They were no longer hazel, or even golden. They burned with light from the sun.

'What - ' Hysst managed.

He never finished. Willow's arms came up and blinding green light exploded from her body with a *BOOM*, surging across the garden in a rippling wave of power. The Doomgaard soldiers were thrown screaming into the air; the ground opened up to receive those who landed on the grass and swallowed them whole. The rest hit the stone pavings of the courtyard and crumpled instantly. Brooke saw one soldier land in the garden hedge - it came alive and gobbled him up, leaving only his boots behind.

Hysst, too, was tossed backwards by the blast. It snapped his sword in half like a twig and ripped most of the black armour from his body, scattering it across the garden. He slammed onto the grass with a pitiful gasp and was immediately snagged by slithering vines. In seconds, his entire body was pinned flat to the ground.

Willow lowered her arms but the emerald glow remained. It came off her in waves; with each pulse, daisies sprouted around her feet and the grass grew another few inches. Brooke could *feel* the power emanating from her.

'Wow,' said Dale.

Very wow, thought Brooke.

Willow looked over to where they stood, and smiled. The blazing light left her eyes and she dropped to her knees, exhausted.

They ran to her.

Chapter Seventeen: The King's Address

'Ow!' Brooke flinched away from the cloth. The nurse pressed it to her foot again anyway.

'It'll help, Lady Woods,' she said.

The battle had ended as soon as Hysst went down - most of the remaining Doomgaardians dropped their weapons on the spot, and those foolish enough to continue fighting had been clobbered by the trolls. It had, however, been just enough time for Brooke to get her foot stamped on by a fleeing soldier.

She winced, but the nurse was done. 'It'll be right as rain within the hour,' she promised, before shuffling off to attend to someone else.

Everyone left in the castle and courtyard area had gathered in the Throne Room after the battle. Tables used for the banquet just hours before were now makeshift gurneys for the wounded. Brooke sat on a bench by the wall, her foot propped up on a stool.

Dale came over, munching on a piece of cake. Most of his colour had returned since the battle ended.

'Where'd you get that?' asked Brooke.

'The kitchens,' Dale replied, spraying crumbs. 'They're *huge*.'

'Cake for breakfast - yuck.' Brooke pulled on her sock carefully, grimacing. 'Where's Willow?'

'Talking to Yulerin.' Dale sat next to her. 'Can you believe he missed it all? Apparently, he spent the whole time trying to convince the Factionheads to join the fight again. By the time they agreed, it was already over.'

'We didn't need them, did we?'

'Might've helped.'

'Maybe.' She thought of Falton and felt a sharp pang of sadness.

Dale stuffed the rest of the cake in his mouth. 'How did you know? About the tree, I mean.'

'I just did,' she said, easing her boot on. 'But I didn't know if it would work for sure. The trolls said Jayne sent them to another fairy tree not far from the Throat, after they'd escaped from the markets. Peter - the fairy leader - was there waiting, and he brought them here.'

'She must have known it would happen. All of it.'

'I guess that's why she's the Seer.'

Dale took another thoughtful bite of cake. 'Do you think Yulerin's right about us? It's so weird, but when he said it, it felt like...'

'Like you already knew?'

'Yeah. Part of me did, anyway.'

'Same.'

They watched as another soldier was carried into the Throne Room and laid carefully on a table. In the far corner, Murblock drank from a barrel-sized tankard and belched. An arrow was still lodged in his upper arm.

'So what's happening now?' said Brooke. 'Are we leaving?'

'Soon, I think,' Dale said. 'We should go find Charlie, the Citymaster says the king wants to see us before we go.'

'Great.' Brooke scanned the length of the room. 'Let's find Willow, too.'

<<>>

She sat at the top of the castle steps next to the entrance, hugging her knees. Her hood was up, her face hidden. In the courtyard below, the clean-up operation had begun - Ulandai servants cleared away debris, gathered up discarded weapons and pieces of armour, and tended to those too badly wounded to move. The bodies of those killed in the battle had already been taken away.

Beyond the Royal District, the citizens of Fort Hammerfall crept from their homes to survey the damage. Fires started by the Doomgaard army were mostly under control but some still burned in places, and many buildings were now smouldering ruins. The villages outside the city walls were simply gone; villagers wandered about where their homes had been, shocked and despairing.

'The toll is heavy.'

Willow looked up as Yulerin appeared next to her. The old man leaned on his cane and gazed out at the morning sky, blue and cloudless. Neither of them spoke for a moment. Then Yulerin's eyes dropped to the garden.

'Have they told him?'

'Telling him now.'

Charlie sat on the edge of the fountain, a soldier's cloak draped round his shoulders. The trolls were gathered there too, all five of them. Amoogus was speaking to Charlie.

'It was the one called Tumygus,' Willow said.

As they watched, Charlie hung his head. Amoogus placed a big grey hand on his shoulder.

'I think, perhaps, the perception of trolls in Ulandai may change after today,' said Yulerin. Willow got to her feet.

'So what now?'

'Now? They rebuild, and fortify, no doubt. The city's been terribly damaged and many lives have been lost. The other Factions are sending assistance and provisions, of course. That'll arrive in the coming days. It doesn't appear as though the Doomgaard are sending a second wave, either - they've already abandoned Mooncrest

Harbour. And the Summit will continue. They have much to discuss, now that it's a war council.'

Willow glanced at the Druyad. 'It's been declared?'

'Unofficially. But the word will be out later today, and then the whole continent will know. Doomgaard have made themselves a stench to every other Faction by their actions here. It's critical they unite against the enemy now. Commander Hysst told Charlie what their intentions had been, though I think it was obvious. He must have assumed he'd kill Charlie after telling him, or didn't care.'

'He was insane,' said Willow coldly. 'What've they done with him?'

'Put shackles on his wrists and ankles and tossed him in the dungeons, as far as I know. He'll stand trial soon.'

'And the imposter, who you sent out the window?'

Yulerin chuckled, just for a second. 'Disappeared, unfortunately. I may have obliterated him, though that wasn't my intention. Either way, there was no body.'

In the garden, Charlie rose to his feet, wiping an arm across his face. A servant approached him tentatively and said something. Charlie nodded and the servant hurried off.

'What about them?' Willow asked. 'I mean, what are the chances they'd all be… special? All three of them.'

'Remarkably low, I'd say. There are precious few sorcerers in Uland now. And if Lady Woods really does have the Sight, well… that calls for further discussion.'

'Is it because they're from another world?' Charlie and the trolls were making their way towards the castle now. 'Because they're different? Did that make it easier for them to…'

'If you're suggesting the portal activated their abilities, it's quite possible,' said Yulerin. He smiled at her. 'You have a keen intellect, Willow of Nymm. It'd be a shame to see it wasted.'

She knew what he was suggesting.

'I don't know what I'll do now. I need time. My duty was to Everin, but he's gone. I need to think.'

'Naturally.'

'I… I didn't mean to, you know. During the battle.' She shook her head. 'I just couldn't… keep it locked up any longer.'

'Yes, I heard what happened,' said Yulerin, with a crooked grin. 'Felt it, actually, too. I daresay you'd have levelled the castle if you hadn't stopped when you did.'

Willow lowered her head. Yulerin took her chin gently and raised her face to his.

'Your willingness to sacrifice yourself saved them. You know that, don't you? He would have taken them to Doomgaard, and that would've been the end of them. You're a true hero, Willow.'

Her eyes swam and he released her.

'And the Druyads will be ready to receive you again, should you decide to return. I hope you will. For now - ' He nodded to Charlie as he mounted the steps ' - let's get our friends home, shall we?'

Charlie's face was tear-stained, but Willow read peace in his eyes.

'They want us all in the Throne Room,' he said.

'Yes, I believe they do,' said Yulerin. 'Best not to keep them waiting.' He led them inside. The trolls followed.

'Congratulations,' Willow said to Amoogus, 'you're the first trolls to ever set foot in this castle.'

'An honour, I'm sure,' replied the troll with a wink.

'Friends, comrades,' announced the Citymaster.

He stood at one end of the Throne Room, halfway up the steps to the throne itself. King Sol was seated there, heavily bandaged and in clear discomfort. But he wore his crown and there was fresh resolve on his face.

Everyone in the castle had gathered - servants, dignitaries, soldiers and, off to one side, the Trolls of Wosdren Marsh. It was a warm morning; shafts of sunlight lanced through the windows near the ceiling, bathing the room in a golden hue. Brooke, Willow, Charlie and Dale stood among the crowd, craning their necks to see past taller adults ahead of them.

'It's my pleasure to greet you all on behalf of the king. He welcomes you here on this day of victory and mourning.'

Sol raised one hand and flinched. The other Factionheads were seated on either side of him on smaller, less elaborate thrones, as they had been at the banquet. Luno was resplendent in clean robes and freshly-styled hair; Yulerin's head was down, his eyes on the floor. Murblok, dosing lightly at the end of the row, had finally managed to pluck all the arrows from his thick hide.

On the far left, Orchidema's eyes brushed lightly over the crowd, but always came back to the four of them. The Other-worlders and their Woodsgirl friend.

'We are, of course, indebted to the bravery of those who defended our great city last night,' continued the Citymaster, his spectacles catching the light. 'Without you, Fort Hammerfall may not have held.'

Would have fallen, you mean, thought Brooke. *And where were you during it all?*

'I regretfully must declare what you already know - that as of now, we are in a state of war with Doomgaard. The leaders of those Factions who hold true to the Pact will meet today to agree on the next steps, but rest assured that our response will be swift and decisive. The one who now commands Doomgaard - '

'Decymero,' Dale said aloud, but only those nearby heard.

' - will be brought to justice. Commander Hysst, who led last night's assault and is personally responsible for a great many fatalities, will stand before the Council here in Hammerfall very soon. He will, at best, spend the rest of his days in our dungeon.'

A ripple of approval went through the crowd.

'Finally, the king has asked me to - '

'No.'

The Citymaster looked around in surprise. Sol was getting to his feet, grimacing in pain. His guards moved to help him but he waved them away.

'Your majesty,' said the Citymaster, 'I'm more than happy to - '

'No,' said Sol again, stronger this time. 'I want to speak.'

The Ulandking straightened up as best he could. He kept one hand on the golden arm of his throne for support, but Brooke thought he looked far more regal than he'd been last night.

'I just want...' Sol said. 'I just want... to say... that I'm weak. From my wound, yes. But also... in my kingship. I've not led you all as I should. I see that now.'

Brooke glanced at Willow. She met her gaze and gave a small shrug.

All it took was his capital city almost getting overthrown.

But as she watched, she saw something new on Sol's face now. Something that hadn't been there before. Humility.

'I haven't ruled well,' said Sol. 'But from this day on, I promise to be better. I'll be the king you deserve.'

The other Factionheads were also watching him closely. Brooke imagined they'd never heard him speak this way before.

'And as my first act of this... new era... I want to honour those who sacrificed much to protect us last night... from certain doom.'

He made a sweeping motion with his free hand.

'All of you: those who fought with bravery, those who tended the injured and dying. Those who aren't here now, who're going through the city, doing the same. My people.'

Then his eyes fell on where Brooke stood.

'And those who aren't my people, too. Those who helped defend us when they had no obligation to do so, who stared into the face of the enemy and renewed our resolve. Whose quick thinking brought help and turned the tide. Those from... afar. Please, join me in honouring these courageous young people in our midst: Lady Woods, Master Flint, Master Reed, and Lady Willow of Nymm.'

A smattering of applause went round the room, which quickly built into a thunderous roar of cheers and whoops and clapping. The trolls bellowed and punched the air. Yulerin smiled down at them.

Brooke felt heat in her face and knew she was beaming red. Charlie and Dale were also blushing, grinning despite themselves. Even Willow, with her head down, was smiling and rosy-cheeked.

'And we must not forget our friends from Wosdren Marsh, who rallied to our side in the crucial moment. And who, I'm told, have spent many productive months raiding Doomgaard patrols in the Barrowlands.'

The trolls ceased cheering and gazed wide-eyed around the room as everyone turned towards them, applauding louder than ever. Brooke, Charlie, Dale and Willow whooped and waved their arms. Amoogus raised a hand in acknowledgement, his chest puffed with pride.

'My friends,' said the king, addressing them all now. 'You have our eternal gratitude. But as much as today's a time of victory and celebration, it's also a time to mourn and repair. Let's get back to that work now - there are many throughout the city who need our help this morning. And I need to lie down again.'

Chuckles went around the Throne Room and the Ulandking smiled.

'Druyads protect us,' he said.

'Druyads prosper us,' echoed those gathered. Sol eased himself back down and the crowd began to disperse, going back to work.

'What now?' said Brooke.

'You tell us, *Lady* Woods,' replied Charlie with a smirk. She threw a punch at his shoulder. 'Ow!'

'We don't have long, children,' Willow said with mock reproachfulness. 'Yulerin wants us to meet him in the garden within the hour. We should get our stuff and go there soon.' Then, to Dale: 'Do you think it'll work?'

'How should I know? I'm just a Sorcerer, apparently.' They laughed and he grinned, then grew serious. 'I hope it'll work. Otherwise we've got another long journey ahead of us. And we might not make it in time.'

Brooke groaned. 'My feet can't take much more.'

'Me neither,' said Charlie. 'I just want to sleep for days and - '

'Excuse me.'

Charlie made a startled noise that was something between a gasp and a gulp. Orchidema was next to them. Once again, she wore a green dress and cloak, but this time her dark hair was in a plait draped over her left shoulder. Her smile was warm and strangely nervous.

'Empress,' said Willow automatically, bowing her head. The others did the same, but Orchidema waved it away.

'Please.' She wrung her hands. 'I just wanted to say thank you, for saving us. They took me to my quarters when the battle started, so I didn't see any of it. But I heard. They say it was… fierce.'

'It was,' said Dale. 'Loads of blood and everything.'

Willow aimed a kick at his foot, but Orchidema's eyes shone.

'I would so *love* to see a battle,' she said. 'I hear of them all the time, but they never let me watch, or help, even though I could.'

'You're the Empress,' said Willow. 'You need to stay safe.'

Orchidema's jaw set defiantly in a way that only accentuated her youthful appearance.

'Safe is boring. A leader should know how to fight. Soon I'll have to anyway, with the war coming. Maybe you could teach me, Master Flint?'

Charlie opened his mouth, closed it again, then blurted, 'Yeah no porblem, I mean, problem. Anytime, yeah…'

'So Nymm's joining the war?' Willow said, sparing Charlie.

'Yes. But not just because of the Pact. We want to fight, to help bring Doomgaard to justice.'

'Good.'

'What about you? Will you come back, now that… you can?'

Willow hesitated, just for a second, but Brooke sensed it in her. She didn't have to be the Seer to recognise it. In that brief moment, Willow's heart had broken, and then quickly repaired itself.

'Maybe,' was all she said.

Orchidema nodded, and Brooke saw there was pain on her face too, barely disguised.

'You'll always be welcome.' Willow bowed her head again and Orchidema smiled at them. 'For now, I'll bid you all farewell.'

To Brooke's surprise, the Empress reached up and touched her face. Her small hand was warm, and Brooke knew - could now feel - that it tingled with magic.

'Farewell, Lady Woods.' She did the same to Dale, addressing him as Master Reed. When she touched Charlie's face - and then planted a light *kiss* on his cheek - he looked as though he might collapse on the spot.

Finally, she said goodbye to Willow, then bowed herself and disappeared back into the thinning crowd.

'We should get ready,' said Willow, her voice cracking. 'Yulerin'll be expecting us soon, and... Charlie, are you alright?'

Charlie was just fine.

<<>>

The sun was high when they met Yulerin in the courtyard garden. The trolls had also been waiting for them, lazing about on the grass. Dale was surprised to see the Citymaster there, too.

'Are you ready?' said Yulerin, standing near the tree.

'We'll see,' replied Willow.

'I'm still not precisely sure what you're planning to do,' said the Citymaster curtly, adjusting his spectacles. 'We have many fine mounts in the stables, surely you'd be just as well taking some of them?'

'We have something different in mind,' said Yulerin. 'Master Reed?'

Dale, once again cloaked and wearing his backpack, stepped up to the tree. Its bark was white and dead-looking; it looked as though a strong wind could snap it in two. And yet, it had survived the night unscathed.

Cautiously, he leaned as close as he could without touching it and whispered, 'Peter.'

Nothing happened. He glanced at Yulerin and the Druyad nodded. Everyone was watching him expectantly.

Please let this work.

Dale leaned closer still. He was milimetres from the white trunk.

'Peter,' he said again.

'What d'you want now?'

Dale jumped. The Citymaster uttered a gasp of fright.

Peter, the fairy leader, was there, leaning against the tree. He puffed casually on his pipe, taking in his surroundings. Dale's torch was strapped to his forehead.

'Back 'ere again, I see. First you lot wake us up in the middle o'the night, and now this. Startin' to think you fancy our company.'

'Sorry for disturbing you,' replied Dale, 'again.'

'Thank you for helping us, Peter,' said Brooke. The fairy nodded, tipping the head torch like a cap.

'Pleasure. We could hear a right ol' commotion round our tree, even from far away. Knew we'd probably have to protect it anyway, and by the stars, weren't we right? Happy to oblige friends of Jayne too, o'course.' Peter frowned. 'What's he starin' at?'

'Don't mind him,' said Willow. The Citymaster's eyes ballooned behind his spectacles, gawking as more of the Wee People appeared near the tree, whispering and sniggering. Charlie, who'd never seen a fairy either, was just as surprised, but he did a better job of hiding it. 'He didn't know this was a fairy tree.'

Peter snorted. 'Whole place is a fairy ring. Why d'you think they had to make it into a garden? Some of them tried cutting it down when they first built the castle - they're still dancing with us now.'

Brooke shivered. Dale cleared his throat.

'Peter, can you help us again? Just one more time?'

'Depends what it is you want.'

Brooke stepped forward. 'Can you give us passage back to the Wraithwood?'

'Which one?'

'The, umm…' Brooke looked to Willow, who said, 'The Forest of Lost Souls, near Aibal.'

The fairy puffed on his pipe, considering the request.

'What's in it for us?'

'Whatever you want,' Dale said.

'If it's in our power to give it,' added Willow, quickly.

Peter grinned and snapped his fingers. The other Wee People gathered around him in the blink of an eye.

They all waited anxiously while the fairies conferred in whispers and more sniggers.

'Madness,' muttered the Citymaster.

'Hush, sir,' said Yulerin.

After a moment, the huddle broke. Peter lit his pipe again, puffed once, then said, 'I want that.'

He pointed at the Citymaster, who gasped.

'Me?'

'Not you, thicko. *That.*'

The Citymaster looked down at his gold chain. Horror dawned on his face.

'Oh no, I can't,' he stammered. 'Not my chain. This is my official seal.'

Peter shrugged. Yulerin levelled a look at the Citymaster - the other man squirmed, prepared to protest again, then slumped.

'Fine.'

Reluctantly, he lifted off the chain and handed it to Dale. He brought it to Peter, but one of the Wee People snatched it before he reached him. The chain was gone.

'We have an accord,' said Peter cheerfully. 'We'll gladly take you to the Wraithwood, so we will. Fair's fair.'

'Um, what about them?' said Charlie.

They followed his gaze to the trolls, still sprawled on the grass. They'd barely glanced over when the fairies appeared.

'We'll take whoever's coming,' Peter said. 'One journey only.'

With a grunt, Amoogus got to his feet. The other trolls began to do the same.

'I believe we'll stay here awhile,' said the troll leader. 'It's rather a novelty to be *allowed* into this city, you see, never mind as *guests*. We're going to make the most of it.'

'Got a fine-looking market,' said Lombrigus.

'And tasty-looking people,' added Dungus, with a wink.

'What'll you do after?' asked Charlie.

'Head south, back to the Barrows.' Amoogus scratched his chin. 'Plenty more Doomgaard patrols to raid.'

'And pillage.'

'And dismember.'

'Love a good dismemberment.'

Charlie grinned but his eyes strained, fighting back tears welling in his throat. Amoogus thumped a bulky hand on his shoulder.

'We'll meet again, young sir,' he said. 'Honorary trolls always find their way back.'

'Yeah, I hope so.'

'Right, let's be on our way,' said Peter. His pipe disappeared. 'If you're comin', now's the time.'

Charlie bopped Amoogus's fist and the trolls ambled back across the garden. The Wee People skipped towards the tree and vanished.

'What do we do?' said Charlie.

'Just put yer hand on the tree,' Peter said, 'and we'll do the rest.' Then he was gone.

They gathered around the tree and Yulerin said, 'Whatever you do, and whatever you *think* you see, keep following me.' He waved at the Citymaster, who half-heartedly returned it. 'We'll be out again before you know it, I promise.'

Dale's hand trembled as he reached for the tree. He stole a final glance across the city, where the people were already starting to repair and rebuild. Beyond, the plains around Hammerfall stretched all the way to the Thunderflow River, a shimmering blue in the morning light.

'Ready?' said Yulerin. 'One... two... three.'

They placed their hands on the fairy tree and fell into darkness, leaving Fort Hammerfall behind.

Chapter Eighteen: The Fairy Passages

When Charlie was ten, his parents took him and his little sister on a roller coaster by the sea. They whooped and cheered and screamed as they hurtled along the tracks, up and down, looping round tight bends and plunging into sudden drops. It had been his first ever coaster and he'd loved every second of it.

As they tumbled into pure black, the sensation in his stomach was the same as that day at the funfair. His insides felt like they were about to leap up his throat and into his mouth; his limbs flailed helplessly and his head spun as vertigo engulfed him like a wave. He could have been falling into that darkness for hours or seconds, there was no way of knowing - he was alone, disembodied, not in control of himself.

And suddenly, it changed.

The world took shape around them again, but they were now somewhere entirely different. Brooke, Dale, Willow and Yulerin had reappeared. Above and around them were walls of earth, veined with roots. It was like being in the Throat again but the space was much, much narrower, and despite the fact there was no visible source of daylight, they could see clearly.

Charlie tried to speak but found he couldn't. Or was it because he was already screaming, or laughing hysterically, or both? Were they *all* doing it?

The floor zipped past under them like a high-speed travelator at the airport. Their feet were moving, but it felt to Charlie like they were walking at a leisurely pace. And yet their surroundings went by in a barely discernible blur.

He was on the roller coaster again, following the fairy passage up slopes and around bends, dropping down deeper into the earth or climbing towards the surface. At times, he was variously alongside Dale or Willow or Brooke; sometimes Yulerin was right in front of him or far ahead, barely visible. He caught a glimpse of Dale's face, just once, and saw it was green.

Did Dale get travel sick? He couldn't quite remember. In fact, the further along the passage they went, the more he struggled to remember why they were in it. Where were they going? Where had they come from? How did they get there?

His head spun. Openings began to appear in the passage, leading off into other tunnels or sometimes into rooms where the Wee People were. He saw them dancing, jigging around to the fiddle, arm in arm; he saw them seated by fireplaces, gathered around tables at feasts, or simply waving at them as they passed, mischievous grins on their faces. More than once, he thought he saw other people in those rooms who weren't fairies, dancing and dancing and dancing while the Wee People laughed and clapped and cheered.

Then they were going up and the darkness began to close in again. The higher they went, the more disjointed his thoughts became.

Where am I? Why am I here?

Soily, earthen walls hurtled by, dissolving into nothing.

Who am I? Who am I?

They were in the black again and his insides were whirling. All of him was whirling, faster and faster, endless and out of control.

WHO AM I?

From somewhere deep in the darkness, a scream was building, long and shrill. It grew and grew, pulsating around him, until there was nothing but the sound of it and his eardrums felt like they were going to explode.

And then, it all stopped.

<<>>

Brooke opened her eyes. Her face was in the wet grass and she sat up, her head spinning. Had someone been screaming?

Getting shakily to her feet, she looked around for the others. They were surrounded on all sides by trees, pressing in on them, a wall of dark green foliage. Above, the sky was a deep blue splashed with purple.

She recognised the place. They were back in the Wraithwood again, in the fairy ring. The little ancient tree sat innocently in the centre of it, unmoving. There was no breeze here.

A rustling in the trees directly ahead of her. Dale emerged through the vines, wiping his mouth. He was very pale again.

'Are you ok?' she said as he approached on shaky legs.

'Yeah,' he replied, glancing at the tree. 'I didn't like that.'

'No, me neither. It felt like my brain was in a blender.'

Then Willow appeared, followed by Charlie and Yulerin. Charlie sat down and put his head between his knees. Even the Druyad had to lean on a tree at the edge of the clearing for a minute.

'Back here, then,' said Dale, looking around the clearing. Somewhere in the forest, an owl hooted.

Willow came over to them. 'No ghouls this time,' she said. 'It won't take us long to reach the mountain.'

Charlie staggered across the clearing 'Nice idea, squirt. Think I'm gonna be sick.'

'Beat you to it.'

'Is Jayne here?' said Brooke. Dale's head jerked up.

'Probably,' Willow replied. 'She's always in the forest. But she could be miles away. If she's around, she'll find us.'

Yulerin came over, leaning heavily on his cane, which sank into the grass.

'Heavens,' he said, 'let's never do that again.'

'Where're the Wee People now?' said Charlie.

'I think they're done with us,' said the Druyad. 'They've fulfilled their end of the deal and now I imagine they're off to eat and dance again.'

'They do like to dance,' observed Dale.

'Willow, can you lead us back to Aibal from here?'

She nodded, golden flecks swimming in her hazel eyes. 'We should get going, though. It's almost dusk.'

'Dusk?' exclaimed Brooke. 'It was morning when we left! Weren't we in there for like... about a minute?'

'Apparently, time moves differently inside the fairy passages,' said Yulerin. 'Now, as Willow suggests, let's make haste. I know there are things in this forest that would gladly make us into a four-course meal.'

Brooke shivered.

They followed Willow across the clearing and pushed into the trees through the vine barrier. As they left the fairy ring, the sound of fiddles drifted on the still evening air, and faded.

Dale's stomach was still churning from the journey through the fairy passages - just what had he *seen* in there? - but it began to settle as they made their way through the trees. Willow led the way, instinctively navigating the darkening forest. Dale remembered, all too well, what Jayne had said about the Puca, the nocturnal monster that prowled the Wraithwood - he stuck as close as possible to

Brooke, with Charlie and Yulerin bringing up the rear. For an old man, the Druyad was surprisingly spritely.

The forest thinned, becoming lighter. They began to move gradually uphill and he felt a telling strain in his calf muscles. Several days of seemingly-endless rambling across Uland had taken their toll, but he was getting used to it; whether he could keep going for much longer was another story. He'd also begun to wonder what his parents would say about the nice crescent-shaped scar on his chest when they saw it.

'I can see the path!' Brooke exclaimed.

Sure enough, the stony trail up Mount Aibal had appeared ahead. Beyond it, the Barrowlands extended westward towards the sea, many miles away. It had begun to redden as the sun dipped towards it.

They left the trees and crossed the open heathland they'd once crept through to avoid Commander Hysst, which seemed a long time ago now.

But it's been just a few days, hasn't it?

'Ah, it's been a while,' said Yulerin as they stepped back onto the path.

Mount Aibal jutted up into the sky, its pyramid-shaped peak bathed in warm evening sunlight. Ravens circled the summit, cawing in their sometimes human-like way. Looking back, they could see where the road met the edge of the forest and trailed off over the hills towards the village of Birchfell, or what remained of it.

'This way,' said Willow.

They followed her up the paved path towards Aibal, passing the strange stone statues along the way. Dale now recognised some of the creatures they depicted, having seen them in the flesh throughout the Barrowlands and at the Goblin Markets. Last time, he'd wondered why they were all running towards the mountain - now he knew.

They didn't make it, he thought.

Up ahead, the opening that led to the Great Cavern became visible. Dale felt a rush of something when he saw it: at first, it was excitement (they were almost home!), then it became something else, something that made his heart sink slowly in his chest.

Sadness?

'Wait,' said Willow, suddenly stopping. 'Do you hear that?'

'Hear what?' said Charlie.

Then the sound reached them, floating down the path from the opening in the mountainside.

Voices.

'Should we hide?' said Brooke.

But it was too late. Three figures had already appeared at the opening, striding into the evening sunlight. Each of them carried a bundle of items that blocked their faces from view as they descended the path, straight towards them.

Dale heard laughter, and something about the voice struck him as familiar.

'We'll come back tomorrow, lads,' said one. 'Loot the place good n' proper when it's full light outside.'

'Don't like being here in th'dark,' said another. 'Monsters in them woods, they say.'

'I'll show monsters what's what. Let's get this stuff stashed, and then - '

'Who's that?'

The first one stopped dead in his tracks. The second walked into him, knocking the bundle from his arms. It crashed onto the paved stones, spilling silver ornaments and candelabras and trinkets everywhere. The man, bearded and filthy, stared at them with one dark eye.

'It's them!' cried one of the others, the skinny one. Something slipped off his shoulder and slid to the edge of the path.

Charlie pointed at it. 'Hey! That's my backpack!'

The man with the eye patch looked from Brooke to Willow to Yulerin, then bared his yellow-brown teeth in a sneer of contempt.

'Well well,' he said. 'What do we 'ave 'ere, then? Looks like the kiddies and their tree girl found a way back to us, with an old geezer this time. That was some mistake, so it was.' His lip curled back further, like a dog preparing to bite. 'Dunno what you did to me back there, with that thing in the bag. But I'm still here. And that's - '

Whoomph!

Emerald light flared on the mountainside, intensely bright, then faded. Willow lowered her arm. Charlie squinted against the lingering glow in his vision.

Two of the three bandits stood there, looking around with dazed expressions on their ugly faces. Eye Patch was gone.

'Where… where'd he go?' stammered the short, stocky one. 'What'd you do to him?'

Then the skinny one let out a cry of fright and pointed at the ground, where a fat green slug with one eye now sat, quivering. That was enough for them. Swearing profusely, the two remaining bandits bolted into the heathland, skirted around their group, and rejoined the path further down the mountainside. They ran and didn't look back.

Brooke and Dale smirked at Willow.

'Meant it that time,' she said. Then she started on up the path towards the opening in the mountain, and they all followed. Charlie scooped up his backpack as he passed.

Last to follow, Dale used his toe to flick the one-eyed slug off to one side. It disappeared into the shrubs by the path, and he walked on.

<<>>

'It's bigger in here than I remember,' said Brooke, gazing about.

They'd made their way through the passage and down the very steep staircase to the floor of the Great Cavern, which was still littered with ragged chunks of stone and broken vessels. Willow had once again ignited the pyres and violet light flickered across the walls and up to the ceiling, high above them.

Presently, she approached the pedestal at the centre of the room and reached for the Time Keeper.

'Careful,' warned Charlie, recalling how one of the ghouls had been sent flying after touching the hourglass. 'That thing's dangerous.'

'Is it?' Willow lifted the Time Keeper off the pedestal, threw a wink at Charlie, and brought it over to them. Almost all of the blue crystalline shards had tumbled from the top section.

'Looks like we're just in time,' Dale said, with a sigh of relief.

'Indeed,' said Yulerin, taking the Time Keeper from Willow to peer at the sand. 'This device protects the Great Cavern from magical interference in the absence of its guardians - Druyads, like me - but for a limited time. Once that time's passed, any misuse of the portal is rectified by removing from Uland those who most recently passed through it. In most cases, "removal" means being turned to stone.'

Dale gulped.

'But won't that mean Willow...'

'Fortunately not, Lady Woods, as her return through the portal was rectification enough. Though if she'd remained in your world for much longer, who knows what would have happened.' He set the Time Keeper down. 'Now, to the matter at hand - getting you three home. I believe this should be straightforward enough, but we should be quick about it.'

Yulerin crossed to the portal that Brooke, Dale and Charlie had come through almost three days prior, his cane clicking on the stone floor as he went. Charlie shrugged out of the cloak he'd been given before leaving Fort Hammerfall.

'What're you doing?' said Brooke.

'I think we should leave these here,' he said. 'We'd look pretty weird wearing them when they find us.'

'Good point.' Brooke and Dale removed their cloaks and folded them as best they could while Yulerin examined the portal. 'Could you give these back to Jayne, if you see her?' Brooke said to Willow.

She sighed and took the bundle. 'I suppose so.' Brooke smiled and Willow returned it, then quickly dropped her eyes.

Don't go.

The words floated clear in Brooke's mind. She watched as Willow drifted away and felt a lump rise in her throat.

'Ah, I see!' Yulerin declared, tapping the stone face of the portal with his cane. 'I believe I have this cracked. Should be simple enough.'

He came back over to them. Charlie had unsheathed his sword and was turning the blade over in his hands. Yulerin pointed at the pedestal in the centre of the room.

'Willow, could you set the Portal Crystal, if you please?'

'Already done,' she replied, stepping away from the pedestal, where a sparkling blue crystal about the size of a football now rested. It had already begun to glow.

'Excellent. You three, step over there.'

Brooke, Dale and Charlie followed the Druyad's pointed finger and crossed to the portal.

'Right up close, please.'

They stepped up to the stone face, beneath the arch. Charlie re-sheathed his sword, then unfastened the scabbard from his belt.

'Guess I won't need this anymore,' he said, laying it down next to the archway.

'You could keep it?' Brooke suggested.

'Can you imagine what Miss Harington would do if she found me with a sword?'

The Portal Crystal was now bright blue and humming steadily. Yulerin bustled around the pedestal, muttering while he made adjustments of some kind.

'I hope this actually sends us back,' said Dale, 'and we don't just get vaporised.'

'Thanks for that,' said Brooke.

Willow had been watching in silence, her arms folded. Now, as humming from the crystal began to reverberate around the Great Cavern, she walked over to them. Her eyes were liquid hazel.

'Umm… be safe,' she said, her voice catching. 'In your world, I mean. I don't know if you can come back here again, but if you do I'll, umm… be here.'

Brooke's eyes became watery. She stepped down from the portal and threw her arms around Willow; tears broke and rolled down her face. The Woodsgirl hugged her back, gentle at first, then fierce.

'I'll miss you,' Brooke said, muffled by Willow's hair.

Then Dale and Charlie were there, and all three had their arms around her. Brooke felt Willow's shoulders tremble and when they all pulled away, she was crying too.

'So you *do* like us after all?' grinned Dale, his eyes wet.

Willow smiled, and a little breathless laugh escaped her. 'Maybe you're not so bad.'

Yulerin cleared his throat. 'Sorry to interrupt, but…'

With a sniff, Willow nodded. Then she quickly hugged each of them again in turn and stepped away from the portal.

'It was good to travel and fight with you,' she said. 'We make good comrades.'

'Good *friends*,' Brooke corrected, smiling.

Willow beamed. 'Come back someday.' Then she turned and hurried over to the pedestal.

'Charlie, are you crying?' said Dale.

'No. Shut up.'

Yulerin came back to them. 'It's time,' he said. 'Ready?'

They nodded and moved back under the arch. The Druyad raised his hands and the Great Cavern suddenly began to thrum with noise. The Portal Crystal blazed on the pedestal, engulfing everything in blue light. Yulerin said something and a stream of blue bulleted along the groove of the raised section from the pedestal to where they stood; it struck the stone face of the portal and the rune in its centre glowed. Light began to spread from it, filling the space under the archway.

'Farewell!' Yulerin shouted over the roar of noise. Brooke grabbed Charlie and Dale's hands. In the pulsating blue light of the Portal Crystal, she saw Willow wave.

Then the portal opened behind them with a *whoosh* and they were jerked backwards, as though something had yanked hard on their backpacks. They were enveloped in swirling blue-white light and the roaring sound a plane makes when landing. And they were falling, weightless, but falling *upwards*, faster and faster with each passing second. Brooke had no idea how long it went on for, or if it was really even happening.

The light became darkness and the roar began to fade. The pull on their backpacks weakened; their bodies began to slow, to become heavy again. A new sound drifted to them, hollow and echoing, as if from the end of a long tunnel.

Thump.

Brooke landed on her back. Her hands no longer gripped those of Charlie and Dale - instead, her fingers closed on damp shale and clumps of grass.

They were back on the mountain.

<<>>

Dale was in a dream.

In it, he was on a plane with his parents. It was summer and they were on holiday, flying to Spain. He was seven, or eight, and it was his first plane ride. Outside the little round window to his left, white clouds swept past below the wing, growing closer as they descended. He gripped the armrests, frightened. Were they going down too fast? Would the pilot be able to land?

Next to him, his Dad told him to be quiet and stop worrying. In the aisle seat, his Mum read a novel, one of those paperbacks from the supermarket about a well-dressed lady in a village somewhere. She didn't look up.

Dale glanced out the window again. The clouds had begun to billow past, and seconds later they were in them. There was nothing outside the window but pure white.

More frightened than ever and now feeling ill on top of it, Dale stared at the cabin ceiling, at the array of lit-up icons that informed them if they needed to have their belts fastened, or if they should remain in their seats. He began to count everything there was to count, tallying the numbers in his head: sixteen icons, eight lit up; four reading lights, two on; four air vents, three twisted to the left…

'We'll be down soon, Dale,' his Dad was saying, his hands folded in his lap. His voice sounded far off. 'Are you feeling sick again? Dale?'

Dale? Dale!

His eyes snapped open. He was on the mountainside in thick, white fog. Something squirmed behind his head.

'Dale! Charlie!'

Brooke's voice.

The thing squirmed again and Dale sat up. It was Charlie's foot.

'Ugh, what happened?' Charlie groaned, rubbing his eyes.

'We're back,' said Dale, getting unsteadily to his feet. 'Back in the fog.'

'It's foggy *again?*'

Charlie grabbed Dale's extended hand and stood. The ground beneath their feet sloped steeply upwards, disappearing into white a few feet away.

'Dale! Charlie! Where are you?'

'Over here,' Charlie called.

Brooke stumbled into view off to their right. Her hair was damp and plastered to one side of her head.

'There you are,' she gasped. 'I thought I was the only one who came back!'

'We *are* back, right?' said Charlie, looking around. 'I mean, it's hard to tell…'

Just then, another voice floated to them through the fog, not far ahead. And for a moment, none of them knew how to react, because the voice was familiar. Very familiar.

'We have to get out of here, Dale!'

Brooke spoke first, almost a whisper now. 'Was that…?'

'… you?' finished Charlie.

Then, another voice: *'Brooke, behind you.'*

'That was me,' said Dale. Then he pointed. 'Look, someone's there.'

Sure enough, three figures appeared in the fog a little way ahead. Two were on the ground, the other stood next to them.

'Hang on…' Brooke whispered.

'That's you,' hissed Charlie. 'Here, get down.'

They dropped to the ground, huddled together. The three figures up ahead materialised into view, becoming more distinct. A breeze took a swathe of fog away for a second, and then they could see them.

'Oh my days,' whispered Brooke.

There she was, her borrowed backpack half off her shoulders, crouched on her haunches. Dale was next to her on the ground, holding his ankle; Charlie stood next to them. They were all looking the other way, up the slope - if they'd glanced back, they'd have seen themselves staring up at them.

'We've gone backwards,' said Dale.

Then something else was coming out of the gloom, beyond their past selves. They saw red eyes and black hair, and the stench of rotting death met them on the breeze.

'This is it!' Dale said. 'This is when Willow saves us. She must be here.'

Two more ghouls appeared, dangerously close, and surrounded the past versions of Brooke and Dale. They saw one raise its finger to its lips in a 'shhh' gesture.

'Where is she?' said Brooke earnestly. 'She should be here by now.'

One of the ghouls cocked an ear their way, picking up on Brooke's voice. It started to turn its head. They heard one snarl.

'There's no time!'

Dale stood. His heart hammered; adrenaline coursed through his veins. He could feel the power again, the same inexplicable sensation he'd experienced in the Druyad Tower, travelling like lightning from his chest and down his arms. He lifted his hands and thrust his palms forward, just as the nearest ghoul saw them.

There was a bright flash of blue and he felt the power leave his hands, as though he'd been pushing against a heavy object that finally gave way. The light, briefly tangible, hit the first ghoul and sent it howling into the fog - as it fell, it disintegrated into a burst of blue sparks.

Dale dropped to his knees again, drained of energy. Brooke grabbed his arm to steady him.

'Look!' said Charlie.

They watched as his past self was grabbed from behind by one of the ghouls and carried off into the fog.

Suddenly Willow was there, her back to them. They saw the first ghoul lunge at her before being thrown back by a burst of green light. Then she was talking to Past

Brooke and Dale; she handed Dale a purple pill and moments later they were on their feet, running off into the fog.

'Let's go!' Brooke cried.

Stumbling across the mountainside, they followed the trio through the fog. They slipped in and out of view, zigzagging towards the concealed portal entrance. Charlie led the way; Brooke gripped Dale's arm to stop him falling, staggering into him repeatedly as they went.

Finally, they saw the cluster of boulders ahead and dropped to the ground again. Past Willow said something and disappeared. Somewhere in the fog, a ghoul howled.

'*No choice!*'

'*Brooke!*'

The past version of Brooke dived into the portal, dragging Dale after her. Charlie started to stand but Brooke dragged him back down.

'Wait,' she whispered.

They waited, several minutes. Dale noticed the fog beginning to thin out and more of the mountainside became visible. *It's not making us forget this time*, he thought.

'What're we waiting for?' said Charlie.

Then the ghouls appeared, four of them, and went for the portal. One of them had a bundle under its arm.

'That's me!' Charlie hissed, straining against Brooke's grip.

The ghouls disappeared into the portal, one after the other. Then they were gone.

'We should have stopped them,' said Charlie as Brooke released him. 'They had me. And one of them'll injure Dale later.'

'No, we had to let them go,' Dale said, standing with a wince. 'If we didn't, we wouldn't be here now.'

'And you couldn't have saved us... again,' said Brooke. She was staring at him with a strange look that Dale couldn't place.

'So, hang on,' Charlie said. 'We came back *before* we'd even left? How's that possible? We were gone for three days.'

'How's *any* of it possible?' said Dale. Charlie just shook his head.

'The fog's going away,' observed Brooke.

She was right. As they looked, the whiteness lifted and the jagged summit of the mountain came into view, not far ahead. And someone else was coming towards them, meandering awkwardly down the uneven slope.

'*There* you are!' exclaimed Tonya. 'I couldn't find you anywhere. Miss Harington! They're over here!'

Miss Harington the English teacher appeared through the last wisps of fog. Her face was haggard with worry.

'Thank goodness!' she gasped. 'That's everyone rounded up, then. Are you three ok? Gracious, that mist really came from nowhere, didn't it?'

She looked them up and down, frowning.

'*Are* you all ok?'

'Of course, Miss,' replied Charlie, shifting effortlessly into Teacher Response Mode. 'Dale got a bit lost there, but he's ok now. Right squirt?'

'Right.' Dale said, returning Charlie's smirk.

'Good,' said Miss Harington, eyeing them suspiciously. 'Then let's rejoin the others and finish this hike. I don't know about you, but I've had enough excitement for one day.'

She started up the slope towards the summit and they followed. Tonya slipped her arm round Brooke's.

'What were you doing with *them*?' she whispered.

'Tell you later,' Brooke replied.

Chapter Nineteen: Back On The Mountain

The rocks were warm on the summit of the mountain. Brooke sat with her back against one, soaking in the late afternoon sun. She was in a sort of natural groove in the ground, which she thought was rather like a chair.

My mountain chair.

A pair of rooks circled the mountain lazily, content to ride the gentle breeze. Brooke watched them for a moment, listening to the sound of her classmates chatting nearby. She could hear Zak and Noah laughing like maniacs somewhere; off to her right, Tonya and Cassie were engaged in a heated debate about some reality TV celebrity. The teachers, relieved to have got everyone to the top safely, lounged on a grassy knoll after finishing their lunch.

Brooke's eyes dropped to the sweeping countryside expanse around the mountain, then to the little book in her lap, the one Yulerin had given her. She'd tried reading it once, immediately after the battle at Fort Hammerfall, but the text was in another language, and now the writing was fading fast. Soon, its brittle pages would be blank. Then, she imagined, the book would simply fall apart and disappear.

It seemed anything that had come from Uland didn't last long in their world. Leftover snacks from

Jayne's lunch had shrivelled into brown husks in their backpacks; Charlie's sword would probably have rusted orange and broken apart if he'd kept it. She wondered what might have happened to Willow if she'd stayed on their side of the portal longer than she did.

Or what might have happened to them, in Uland.

She heard someone coming and quickly closed the book, slipping it back in her bag.

'I saw that, Brookeworm,' said Dale, grinning. He sat next to her.

'You're imagining things,' she replied. She hadn't told the others about Yulerin's book. 'How's your scar?'

'Almost gone.' He pulled his collar out and leaned closer. She saw the top part of the scar, now a barely-visible mark on his skin. He met her eyes and she looked away, blushing.

'Looks a lot better,' she said.

'Yeah, my parents won't have to interrogate me after all,' he replied.

They gazed out across the countryside in silence for a moment. The rooks dipped closer but continued to circle. Some palpable but not entirely unpleasant awkwardness hung there between them.

'I wonder what's happening there now,' Dale said, finally.

'We haven't been gone long,' Brooke replied. 'I doubt much has changed.'

'Yeah. I hope Willow's ok.'

She felt the tiniest stab of annoyance and shook it off. 'I hope so, too.'

Just then, Charlie, Noah and Zak appeared a little way down the slope. Noah saw them and smirked, muttering. Charlie said something back and then, to the obvious surprise of the other boys, walked up to them and sat down. Noah and Zak stalked off.

'Careful now,' said Dale. 'They'll start to think we're friends again.'

'Don't worry,' Charlie said, 'you're going in another bin when we get back down. That'll put things right.'

They laughed easily. Brooke felt a warmth in her chest, a strange peacefulness that hadn't been there before. She couldn't put her finger on what it was exactly.

'Do you think we'll ever go back?' said Charlie, picking at some blades of grass.

'I don't know,' said Brooke. 'But part of me thinks we will.'

'If the Seer thinks so, then it'll probably happen,' Dale said, with a wink.

'Actually, I think my... abilities... are gone now. Since we came back.'

'Mine too.' Dale looked at his hands regretfully. 'I think that ghoul got the last of whatever I had left in me.'

'Good thing I left the sword behind then,' said Charlie. After a pause, he added: 'I think we'll go back, too. It'd be cool to see... everyone... again.'

'Oh yeah, *everyone*,' said Brooke, rolling her eyes. 'We all know who *you* want to see again.'

'No-one else got a kiss, anyway,' smirked Dale.

Rather than blush, Charlie seemed to puff up with pride at the observation. 'Maybe I'll marry her. Then I'd be the Emperor of Nymm.'

'Fat chance!' laughed Brooke.

Dale and Charlie joined in, and for a few minutes they could do nothing but laugh as the unreality of their time in Uland spilled out - the fright and wonder and tragedy and joy of it all. There was no need to talk about it any more. Not now, at least.

All laughed out, Brooke sighed and pushed back her hair. The warmth inside her bubbled on. Was it magic? Maybe some of the Seer remained?

'It'd be nice if Willow was here,' she said and the boys nodded.

'Oh yeah,' Charlie said, fumbling in his pocket. He pulled out a handful of fruity sweets. 'Snagged these from the goblin market - here.'

He handed one to each of them, then held his up.

'To Willow,' he said, grinning.

'Willow of Nymm,' said Dale.

'Willow,' said Brooke. They popped them in their mouths and chewed, then immediately spat them out again.

'Oh, GROSS!' Brooke cried. 'They've gone bad!'

That started another fit of laughter, which would have gone on a lot longer if Mr Green hadn't appeared on the slope below them.

'You three!'

The History teacher beckoned them over to where the rest of the class were gathering. Everyone had their backpacks on, ready to start the journey back to camp.

'Hurry up or we'll be late for dinner.'

Brooke, Dale and Charlie stood, grabbing their things. With a last glance at the view, they trooped down from the summit to rejoin their classmates.

As they left the mountain, Brooke finally understood what the feeling was inside her. It was one she'd known before, but it had never been as strong or as pure as it was now. She smiled all the way down, savouring it, enjoying its warmth.

The surety of friendship.

'I believe that's everything,' said Yulerin, standing near the pedestal. His voice carried across the Great Cavern, rebounding back off the walls and ceiling. 'We'll return for the rest tomorrow.'

The Druyad turned. Willow was by the portal, staring at the rune in the centre of the stone face. It continued to glow blue, but it had almost faded again.

'What troubles you?' he asked, walking over to her.

Her eyes remained fixed on the rune. 'Lots of things.'

'Tell me one.'

For a moment she didn't reply. He was about to ask again when she abruptly sat down on the top step below the archway.

'It's, well… everything really. So much happened in the last few days that's never happened before. Hysst, the Doomgaard. Ghouls roaming freely, goblins turning a blind eye. And the Other-worlders - '

'Your friends.'

'…yes, friends.' She twisted her hands, searching for the words. 'I always knew there was good and evil in the world, but…'

Yulerin leaned patiently on his cane, watching her.

'But I never knew it could be so… hard to see. It's like it's hidden, deep inside people. The good and the bad.' She looked around the cavern. 'I mean, Hysst did this, and I always thought he was good. And he did *this*.'

'Evil often wears a mask. Sometimes, it's among us and we don't even know it.'

'I *should* have known,' said Willow, clenching her fists. 'I was here all the time. It was right in front of me.'

'You blame yourself for things beyond your control.'

'I have to blame someone, and it should be me.'

'Why?'

'Because… because…' She stood suddenly and walked a few paces away, then spun round. 'Because there's no point blaming anyone else, is there? It *should* be me. It makes me stronger, tougher. And I have to be strong, because a day will come when I can't just hide away anymore.'

Yulerin watched, saying nothing. He could see she wasn't aware of the emerald glow beginning to brighten around her, or of the dandelions sprouting from cracks in the floor where she'd stepped.

'There's evil in the world. I always knew it - now I just have to get better at seeing it. If I can see it, I can fight it. If I can fight it, I can defeat it. And then…'

She kicked at a piece of debris on the floor. It scuttled across the stone slabs.

'Then there's no more evil.'

'It's not always so simple,' said Yulerin softly.

'Isn't it?'

'No, I'm afraid not.' The old man shuffled back towards the pedestal. 'As long as good endures in the world, evil will too. The scales can never tip completely one way. But that's why the battle keeps going, and going. When evil stands, good rises to meet it. Perhaps that's the reason you brought your friends here, just as the Enemy made his move. They - and you - were an unexpected stumbling block he can't have foreseen. I believe, the next time Decymero stands, good will be there to meet him again.'

Willow looked sullen, but nodded. The glow around her faded. 'So what now?'

'Now?' Yulerin smiled sadly. 'Now we'll have war. The Factions will no doubt unite against the Doomgaard - or at least, they should - and meet them in the battlefield. When and where, I can't say. But the Druyad Brotherhood will help, where help is required and sought after.'

'And what about me?'

He looked at her then with both affection and pity.

'You? Why, you remain Willow of Nymm, the Woodsgirl warrior, defender of all that's good in Uland.' She grinned, and he added: 'And you remain as important as you have ever been, my lady.'

'If that's true, then I want to keep serving the Druyads,' she said.

'Perhaps it's time to - '

'No, not yet. I'd like to duty-bind myself to you in place of Everin.'

Yulerin raised his bushy grey eyebrows in surprise. 'Me? I can think of plenty of Druyads wiser and more powerful who - '

'I don't care,' said Willow, 'I choose you.'

He smiled and placed a hand on her shoulder. 'Then let it be so.' The golden hue flickered in her eyes.

'As your first act, humble servant, why don't you pay a visit to Birchfell and see if you can find me somewhere to stay for the night? These portals are too badly damaged for now and I wouldn't relish another trip with the Wee People. We can't all sleep comfortably in trees, you know.'

She laughed. 'I'll see what I can do.'

'And Willow,' he said as she turned to go, 'take care on the road.'

'I will.' Then she was gone.

With a tired sigh, Yulerin gave the Great Cavern a final sweep of his eye. It was in bad shape, but once the other members of the Brotherhood arrived and suitable protection was in place, it could be repaired fairly quickly. Then they'd be needed elsewhere.

As he turned to leave, he felt a weight in his pocket.

'Oh,' he said, only to himself.

Reaching in, he pulled out the last fragment of the Soulburn Talisman. The thing caught the light from the pyres above and glinted. How had something so small felt so heavy?

'What'll we do with you, then?' said the Druyad.

'*Yulerin.*'

He froze, still holding the talisman shard up to his face.

'*Yulerin, you old fool.*'

The hairs on the back of his neck stood on end.

'Who are you?'

'*You know who I am. And you know what I want.*'

'Get… get out of my head.'

But even as the voice continued to speak, he began to discern something within the shard itself. Some dark form, becoming more distinct.

A face, grinning.

'*You're a fool,*' it said. '*You've played your hand, and now I know. The* true *Empress, hidden away all this time. How clever of you Druyads to keep her close.*'

Yulerin felt nauseous, like he might faint. He still held up the shard - he couldn't put it down, much as he wanted to.

'*I'll have her soon,*' said Decymero. '*And then the others will return, and I'll have them too. They'll all be mine.*'

'No,' Yulerin stammered. 'You won't have them. You *can't.*'

'*It's too late. The Reckoning has already begun.*'

'NO!'

With everything he had, Yulerin heaved the talisman shard at the floor. It hit the stone and shattered further into hundreds of tiny pieces. Even as it smashed, he heard laughter, high and cold, echoing around the cavern.

It rang in his ears long after it died out.

Willow stood at the opening in the mountainside, watching as the sun went down over the Barrowlands. Across the continent, the people of Uland were settling in for the night, as they'd done every night previously. But the electric assuredness of war was already beginning to stir the air. She could feel it.

When evil stands, good rises to meet it.

She thought of her friends, now safely back in their own world. Maybe she'd never see them again. Maybe their time was done. But she didn't believe that, not really. Some part of her knew they'd be back. She knew their adventure was just beginning.

She breathed deep. The evening was warm and calm; the air carried the smell of trees and wildlife, and the unmistakable scent of magic.

Willow pulled up her hood and started down the mountain.

Epilogue

The key turned in the lock with a *clank* and the door swung open, spilling light from a flaming torch into the cell. A fat, hairy spider scuttled away from it, disappearing into the shadows.

In the far corner of the cell, Commander Hysst raised his head and blinked. Thick chains lashed his wrists and ankles to the floor; another, attached to a clamp around his neck, ran up to the ceiling. His eyes were still bright blue, but the whites were bloodshot and black bags hung below them, making him appear far older than he was. The purple scar on his jaw contorted as he grinned.

'Come to pay your respects?' he said softly.

Luno of Elementa met his gaze for a moment, then addressed the guard by her side. 'You can wait outside the door.'

'M'lady?' he said, glancing at the torch in his hand.

She snapped her fingers and a ball of flame materialised in the air. The guard nodded and left the cell, closing the door behind him. The key scraped in the lock again.

'Look at you,' said Luno contemptuously. '*Commander* Hysst of the Doomgaard. Did someone give you that title, or did you choose it for yourself?'

His grin became a sneer. 'I earned it, Lady Luno. I wrote my legend with the blood of lesser men. Some of them were yours.'

She took a step forward, her polished boots crunching on dead cockroaches. The ball of flame drifted after her.

'You're mad,' she hissed, 'do you know that? You've lost your mind. If you'd only kept your head for a little while longer - '

'Then what?' he spat. 'The city would've fallen? And I'd be Chief Commander by now? I suppose you'd have dropped right into line, too.'

'We'll never know, will we?' she replied, inches from his face. 'You let your pride get in the way of your once-good judgement. You were beaten by *children* in the end - children from an inferior world - all because you just *had* to get to them once you knew they were here. You were supposed to *besiege* the city, not take it by yourself. That's why we had to fight you, and that's why my people died. We played our part - why couldn't you play yours?'

'The warlock was the one who failed.'

Luno scowled, turning away. 'Zapharous was weak, he spent too long in that prison. He'd forgotten how to do the things he was once notorious for. I would've been better off turning him to ice on that beach instead of giving him not one, but *two*, Soulburn Talismans. As if one wouldn't have been enough. Speaking of which…'

She faced Hysst again, looking him up and down. His black armour was long gone - he was dressed in nothing but a shirt and trousers, still ripped and stained from the battle.

'Where is it?'

He glowered at her. 'It's always close to my heart.'

She moved close, putting a hand on his chest, searching. Then she reached down his shirt and pulled out the necklace. It was a silver chain with a clasp attached - fitted to the clasp was a glassy black stone.

Luno cupped the talisman in one hand, studying it in the flickering light. 'Zapharous gave it to you like this?'

'It was the safest place for it,' he said, watching her face. 'Better than carrying it around in a coin purse. Why, what are - '

The silver chain melted between her thumb and fingertip, and the necklace slipped off his neck. Instantly, Hysst lunged at her, straining against his shackles. The neck clamp dug into his throat.

'Give it back!' he snarled, veins bulging on his forehead. 'GIVE IT BACK NOW!'

Luno stepped away from him. She held the talisman up to the light.

'All that power,' she said, 'all that invincibility, and you wasted it running around the Barrowlands, killing peasants. Decymero was wrong about you after all. He'll choose his agents more wisely next time, I'm sure.'

Hysst thrashed in his chains, throwing himself from side to side, thumping off the cell walls. The bolts fixing them to the floor actually began to pull loose.

'GIVE IT TO ME!' he roared. His voice rose in pitch: 'Please give it to me! Please don't take it! I *need* it!'

She smiled. 'I'm not going to *take* it, Commander.' She held the talisman in her palm, extending it towards him. His eyes bulged, panicked and desperate. 'I'm going to destroy it.'

Flames erupted from her palm, consuming the stone.

'NOOOO!' Hysst screamed, flailing in his chains. The cell filled with heat and smoke and the stench of sweat.

The Soulburn Talisman turned red, then crumbled to ash in Luno's hand. The flames licked the last of it up and she dropped her arm. At the same time, Hysst slumped back to the floor, panting. Tears carved through the dirt on his face, dripping off his chin.

'And with that,' said Luno, 'you're nothing more than a man, once again.'

Splotches of red began appearing under Hysst's clothes, soaking into the fabric. Wounds from the battle - and one from a farm in the Barrowlands - opened up in his flesh, no longer sealed with the talisman's power. Blood pooled around his knees.

'Our secrets die with you, Commander,' said Luno. Her smile was cold and malicious. 'Decymero thanks you for your efforts - you helped us start the war. Farewell.'

She turned away and the ball of flame winked out. The guard opened the cell door, allowed her to pass, and closed it again without a glance inside.

Luno left the dungeons of Fort Hammerfall and returned to the entourage waiting for her on horseback by the city gates. They rode out across the plains as the sun set over Uland.

ACKNOWLEDGMENTS

This book wouldn't exist without the involvement of the following wonderful people: Christine, my Ideal Reader, who always gave me the freedom to write and patiently consumes every draft I put in her hands; my parents, who essentially bankrolled my entire education (and everything else, for that matter); my English teachers at school - especially Miss Taylor and Mr Cowan - who made books interesting; my publisher, Richard, for bringing *Soulburn* to life; my beta readers, Erin, Margaret, Becca and Megan, who actually finished the darn thing; all the fantasy writers who blazed the trail I merely followed; the Mourne Mountains, which served as the inspiration for Uland (I can thank mountains, right?); and of course, you, my reader, for coming this far.

ABOUT THE AUTHOR

David writes from his home in Northern Ireland,
where he lives with his beautiful wife Christine and
their two dogs, Lupin and Ghost. He loves books,
movies, football (he's better at watching than playing),
and getting his hiking boots dirty.

Subscribe to David McIlroy Fiction here:

SCAN ME

More books by Burton Mayers Books

When an enchanted garden is threatened with ecological disaster, an unlikely gang of fairy-tale friends must work together to save their home.

www.ingramcontent.com/pod-product-compliance
Lightning Source LLC
Chambersburg PA
CBHW031454260626
47154CB00017B/2888